Under Suspicion

Marlene Kurban

Under Suspicion

STAIRWAY PRESS—APACHE JUNCTION

Cover Design by Guy D. Corp
www.GrafixCorp.com

STAIRWAY≡PRESS

www.StairwayPress.com
1000 West Apache Trail #126
Apache Junction, AZ 88120 USA

Acknowledgements

I'd like to thank my husband Tom, whose love, support, and encouragement made finishing this novel possible. Better late than never!

Special thanks to my long-distance beta reader Charlene Dietz, my dear friends John and Linda Melody, who read each chapter hot off the printer, and Tom Matava, who filled me in on police procedures and investigations.

PROLOGUE

Virginia Beach, Virginia
Early June

THE MAN WHO called himself Francis Lake looked over his shoulder at the empty corridor and let himself into the hotel room with the keycard the woman had given him. The bathroom door was cracked open and from inside came the sound of the shower and a woman singing off-key. Steam fogged the mirror in the hallway.

He placed a box wrapped in shiny silver paper on the faded bedspread of the queen-sized bed. A bottle of red wine and two glasses waited on a round table near the sliding doors. The air conditioner wheezed and clattered like an old car, the musty smell reminding him of other second-rate hotel rooms he'd been in before.

"Jill, it's me," he called out, so as not to startle her. "But take your time, please. I'll sit outside."

The singing paused.

"Hello."

Did he detect a note of relief in her voice? For a second he was tempted to walk straight into the bathroom and take her right there. After all, she'd already shown him she didn't require the usual courtship rituals he'd learned as a youth. Women expected so little these days, especially those her age, single or divorced in their thirties or forties. Open the car door for them, pretend to be interested in their inane conversation and their boring lives, and everything else was easy as pie. Sometimes they were so lonely, so needy, he could practically read their little-girl minds when they sized him up and liked what they saw. A gentleman. The last of a vanishing breed.

He thought again about pulling the shower curtain aside and pressing her naked body against the wet wall tiles, his mouth on hers, smothering any protest. Women her age liked that too—a man who took charge.

The water stopped.

"I'll be right there."

He opened the sliding glass doors and stepped out onto the narrow balcony that barely fit two flimsy plastic chairs. The mild breeze offered no relief from the sticky wall of humid air. Her eighth-floor room faced the Virginia Beach boardwalk and afforded an expansive view of the Atlantic.

The fishing pier a few blocks to the left jutted out into the surf. The boardwalk was, as always, packed with people strolling, rollerblading, jogging and biking. He backed away from the rail, and watched the passersby below and the bobbing heads of swimmers in the rolling waves. He breathed in the salty air and waited.

She finally joined him outside, standing on the tips of her toes to kiss him lightly on the cheek.

"Hi, Francis."

She wore a short silky red robe tied at the waist. Her cropped brown hair was wet and glossy, and she smelled like lavender.

"I'm sorry I'm late getting ready. I had to finish some work first. Would you like a glass of wine?"

He nodded, his gaze lingering on her slender, tanned legs.

"You look lovely."

"You're sweet."

She blushed, and he followed her back into the room.

He opened the wine, an inexpensive California pinot noir with a screw top, and poured two glasses.

"So how were your seminars today?" she asked.

He'd met her in the lounge at the Marriott a few nights earlier when attendees from all of the large conferences there had converged in the hotel's several bars. This was fertile ground for trolling. He'd told her he was attending a large pharmaceutical tradeshow.

"Way too long." He didn't bother to embellish, although he could have spouted something convincing in an instant about the latest drug for arthritis or cutting-edge research on Alzheimer's. "What about yours?"

"I was bored at the last session and walked out," she said. "It was on care management, and the speaker was awful. Sometimes these seminars are a big disappointment."

She was a nurse supervisor, attending some conference on geriatrics. Forty-one, divorced. No kids.

He saw her glance at the package on the bed, her eyebrows raised in curiosity.

"What's this?"

"A little something I picked up for you today."

"Really?"

She touched the box and then drew back.

"Go ahead, open it."

He watched her carefully while she unwrapped his gift. Her dark eyes widened as she opened the box and pulled out a sleeveless black silk dress encased in white tissue.

"It's gorgeous." She ran her hand along the fabric and held the dress up against herself in front of the mirror. "You didn't have to buy me anything."

"I happened to come across it when I was walking by a shop in the resort, and I thought it would look great on you." He paused. "Why don't you try it on? Wear it tonight if you like it."

She was looking at the inside tag, head cocked to one side.

"How did you know my size?"

He shrugged.

"Took a guess."

Again she hesitated, but he gave her a reassuring smile.

"Go ahead. I'll wait for you to get ready. We're not in a rush, right? It's only seven o'clock."

"Okay."

He sat at the small, round table near the sliding doors and sipped his wine while she took the dress into the bathroom. Her laptop was open but not on. He moved brochures and newspapers aside on the table, but she had no personal papers out that he could see. He glanced at the nightstand. There was a TV remote and a can of Diet Coke.

She emerged from the bathroom.

"Ta da. What do you think?"

She pirouetted, her face pink and eager.

"You look like a young Demi Moore," he said. "A goddess."

She beamed.

"Thank you. You guessed the size well. You don't think it's too short though, do you?"

She pivoted around like a kid, flexing her calves.

"Not at all." In truth, it was. She looked more cheap than sexy in it. The realization annoyed him, and he set down his wine glass. "So tomorrow you're on the road for home. Are you leaving early?"

"My flight leaves at seven-twenty." She tilted her head, her lips pursed in a regretful pout. "I need to pick up my dog from the kennel in the afternoon. Max'll be so glad to see me. He hates it when I leave. He throws up for days. You have any pets?"

"Nope. I travel too much."

"Oh."

When he didn't reply, she added, "I hope we can see each other again. New York's not that far from Massachusetts."

Her voice trailed off, and she met his eyes, then looked away.

Right. That was about as likely as her turning into Cinderella.

He sighed, as though it were difficult for him to accept that their tryst was coming to an end. He looked down at his hands, flexed his fingers.

"I've really enjoyed spending time with you."

She smiled.

"I never expected to meet anyone so…interesting while I was here."

"Likewise." He moved closer to her, then cupped her chin in his right hand. "You have no idea how much these past few days have meant to me. With everything that's happened in the past year…."

He'd told her when they met that he was a pharmacist at Mass General and a widower, because his wife had recently died of lung cancer. He'd told similar stories so many times to so many women over the years that the details seemed almost real to him. The lies came naturally, effortlessly, and he knew she believed him. She was as trusting and stupid as a kitten.

"Well, I'm glad you felt comfortable with me," she said.

"Very much so. I felt I could finally talk to someone."

He watched her eyes fill with warmth. He drew her close and kissed her, softly at first, one hand stroking her hair, trailing down to her bare shoulder.

"I think dinner can wait, don't you?" she said.

She sighed and shivered as he kissed her lightly on her neck, lingering at her throat. Then he steered her toward the bed, pulling her close. His fingers slowly traced a path across the silky bodice of her dress, down to her thighs. Her flesh was warm and smooth, and she pressed her hand against his, murmuring her approval.

He froze.

This was all too easy. He wasn't even aroused, and he felt suddenly irritated at her complicity, her eager submission. She was probably like this with every man who paid her the slightest attention. These past few days he'd done nothing to earn such intimacy, other than buying her dinner and drinks and listening to her prattle. He couldn't stand another word about her stupid job, her stupid house, even her stupid *dog*.

She was nothing but an easy lay, a slut who gave a man she barely knew the key to her hotel room. For Christ's sake, she had slept with him the same night they'd met. He could have told her he was a brain surgeon from Timbuktu and she would have believed him. Nothing about her challenged him.

It was time.

He grabbed the hand she had placed on his and squeezed it hard, knowing he could snap the tender bones with ease. She gasped in surprise, and in one swift movement he grabbed her thin, bony shoulders and pushed her down on the bed. Her eyes widened in confusion.

"What are you doing?"

"Shut up."

"What are you doing?" she repeated, her voice rising in panic.

She made a move to get up, and his hand covered her mouth. Before she could react, he was on top of her, expertly pinning her arms and legs. Then his strong hands circled her throat, pressing deeply into her flesh. She could barely move under his weight, and she was no match for a man his size.

Still, her desperate hunger for air made her struggle violently, and he braced his body against her useless flailing, his pulse pounding. She broke one hand free and tried to claw at his eyes as his fingers dug deeper into her neck, compressing her airway. For a small woman, she put up a decent fight. For the first time that evening he felt his excitement grow.

"You dumb slut," he spat in her ear. "My wife didn't die."

Her eyes were bulging, and she tried desperately to dislodge him, her body writhing underneath him. Her efforts to scream were nothing more than breathy gasps as he squeezed harder and harder. She broke both hands free but they fluttered helplessly toward his face like two small birds. Her legs trembled beneath him, and she managed to free one knee, but all she could do was bang her shin against his left leg.

Sometimes he liked to choke them to unconsciousness and bring them back, but with this one he didn't want to stop. Her struggles subsided as he cut off the oxygen to her brain, and his excitement peaked. With one final squeeze, he shook her by the neck and heaved himself, still fully dressed, against her. The headboard thumped against the wall. He shuddered and groaned.

Her body grew limp beneath him and her wide-open glossy eyes stared straight into his, the whites red with a sunset of burst capillaries. A gurgle came from her throat when he finally relaxed his grip. Breathing heavily, he got off the bed and looked down at her with disgust. Her new dress was wrinkled and pushed up to her waist from her futile attempts to kick him away. She wore a red lace thong, stained now with her urine.

Whore.

All of it had been so easy, too fast and easy. She hadn't been worth his time or the risk.

He placed the bed pillow over her face and pulled latex gloves and a handkerchief from his pocket. He slipped on the gloves and retraced his every movement in the hotel room, wiping the wine glass and anything he'd touched. He lowered the setting on the air conditioner and dumped the wine down the sink in the kitchenette, ran the faucet, and put the glasses back on the countertop. With any luck she wouldn't be discovered by housekeeping staff until the next day.

He snapped the cover shut on her laptop and placed it in her computer bag. He crushed the silver wrapping paper and gift box and shoved those inside the bag as well. He paused at her open suitcase. The strap of a lacy blue nightie caught his eye, and he pulled it out and stuffed it into the computer bag too, along with her small black purse.

He made his way around the room again. There was nothing he could do about microscopic hairs or fibers, but those would be present from dozens of other guests too. When he was certain he'd cleaned up as much as he could, he quietly opened the door to the hallway. No one was around and he slipped out the door, her computer bag slung over his shoulder.

He looked again for any sign of cameras in the hallway, but this was an older hotel and when he'd done his reconnaissance earlier, the only cameras appeared to be in the reception area. Still, he shielded his face and made his way down the stairwell eight flights to the ground floor.

When he joined the crowd on the boardwalk, he breathed in the smells of the beach and the greasy fried food from the restaurants lining the boardwalk: French fries, hamburgers, fish sandwiches. His stomach grumbled, and he decided he'd get some take-out before he headed back home to Connecticut in the comfort of the Lincoln, parked several blocks away in a public lot.

The humid, sultry air made him sweat, and he felt his cotton shirt stick to his back. He felt curiously empty, restless, and dissatisfied, as though he'd finished a long, hard day at work and produced nothing.

He'd have plenty of time during the ten-hour drive to plan all the details of his next adventure. When he got home he'd need to start packing for his coming soiree, as he thought of it. The next one would be better, so much better, and it was happening soon.

His scheduled trip to St. Maarten would be a Caribbean dream.

PART ONE

It is better to travel hopefully than to arrive.
—Robert Louis Stevenson

CHAPTER ONE

West Hartford, Connecticut
Mid-June

ORDINARILY LOUIS D'MAIO would have been happy with a full day's schedule, particularly in the summer when his patients were more apt to cancel due to vacations. It wasn't easy running a solo practice. He should have been glad too for the distraction that work provided, but this afternoon he couldn't stop thinking about Paula and the pain he'd inadvertently caused her. And now she wouldn't even speak to him and she'd gone to St. Maarten alone.

He struggled to focus his attention on the anxious woman sitting in the worn leather chair across from him. She was his sixth patient today. She'd been seeing him for over a month.

"To get onto another topic I wanted to talk about now if I still have time left—I'm thirty-seven years old, Dr. D'Maio, but I don't understand men and after what happened on Saturday night, I'll never go out on a blind date again."

The well-dressed, well-heeled woman twirled a lock of her

dyed blonde hair and let loose a deep, melodramatic sigh.

"What happened?" Louis asked in a neutral tone.

He glanced at the clock on the oak mantel, discreetly positioned out of her range of vision. He should have stopped her. Her session was almost over.

"You won't believe it. He drove up in an old classic car—a convertible—a Cutlass I think? The *entire* car was painted like an aquarium. Pictures of fish, coral, mermaids, seaweed. And you know what the hood ornament was? A *blowfish*. An actual *blowfish*."

"Sounds eccentric, at the very least."

"Worse than that. Worse than that."

She crossed her legs and smoothed her black skirt over her thighs. He couldn't help but notice her thick ankles and heavy calves. He averted his eyes.

She sighed again. "After he parked this—this monstrosity in my driveway, where all the neighbors could see it—and you know West Hartford, who drives an aquarium car with a blowfish on the hood? He got out of the car and I wanted to die. It was mortifying."

She stared at Louis, wide-eyed.

"What was mortifying, Diane?"

She closed her eyes and titled her head, dark red lips pursed as if she were recalling some tragic memory.

"He was at least fifty years old. Maybe sixty. He said online he was only forty-five."

She blinked and stared at Louis.

"You were mortified that he lied about his age?"

"Plus he had on the ugliest. Suit. Ever." She emphasized each word, mouth twisting as though it tasted bitter on her tongue. "Looked like it was from the seventies. We were supposed to go out for dinner, can you imagine?"

Louis nodded.

"So what did you do?"

Diane looked up at the ceiling.

11

"I didn't answer the door. I pretended I wasn't home and eventually he left. I swear to God, I'm ready to join a convent. What's the matter with me, anyway? Why do I attract all these lunatics?"

Louis decided that now was not the time to remind her of the perfectly normal gentlemen she often mentioned whose advances she spurned because they were too short, too tall, too thin, too fat, too bald, too hairy, too smart, or too stupid. It was a jungle out there, for sure, but he suspected Diane had another agenda.

"I'm educated," she went on. "I have a good job. People say I'm fun to be around. So what's the problem? Why can't I find anyone? All my friends are already married with kids, but not me."

"Let's talk next week about what it is you're looking for, Diane. You said earlier that you're not sure any man can meet your expectations."

"Hmm." She looked at him, one eyebrow raised. Then she glanced at her watch. "We're done, aren't we? Same time, next week?"

"That's correct."

Louis stood up.

Diane picked up her enormous black purse and teetered out of his office on red spike heels, an invisible cloud of musky perfume in her wake. She stopped at the doorway.

"I hope you have a great day, Dr. D'Maio. And thanks for listening. I could never tell my friends about any of this stuff, you know?" She ran a hand through her perfectly coiffed hair and tilted her head. "I feel so much better after I talk with you. You're so understanding. Not like these men I meet."

She hesitated, her eyes wistful.

"I wish—"

He looked away, guessing at what she was thinking. It was transference: a patient falls in love with her doctor, attributing to him near god-like qualities. It was a common, even healthy phenomenon, especially with women like Diane. It was his task to guide her carefully and compassionately through this stage and resolve it while maintaining the strictest of professional boundaries. He picked up his appointment book.

"Yes?"

"Oh, nothing," she finally said.

He smiled and ushered her out the door.

"Have a good afternoon."

Once she was gone, Louis shut the door and sat at his cluttered desk. He had ten minutes before his next and last appointment of the day, and he checked his cell phone for voice mails, hoping for a message from Paula. There was nothing. No big surprise, but he was disappointed just the same.

She wasn't going to accept his explanations or apology anytime soon.

Maybe never.

He'd left her several voice mails over the past few days when she'd tersely informed him she was going to St. Maarten. He didn't even know where she was staying or when she planned to come back, and she wasn't returning his calls.

Goddamn it.

What a mistake he'd made, a stupid, stupid mistake. He should have been totally upfront with Paula. Apparently his white lie about Charlotte had been the final straw.

A motion-sensor chime sounded in the anteroom, signaling the arrival of his next patient, Mr. Rizzo. Louis snatched the chart off the desk, put on his reading glasses, and leafed through the case notes. John Rizzo was an old-school manager at a utilities company. He'd been sent to Louis for mandatory "coaching" by his employer. At their first session last week, the man had railed against the ADA, the ACA, the EEOC, and every law he could think of that prevented him from chastising or firing employees who were pregnant, sick, or slow. He had as much interest in coaching as Louis had in knitting. It was likely a matter of time before old Rizzo was collecting unemployment himself.

The session would be challenging and Louis took a few moments to gather his thoughts. Then he had a sudden inspiration and checked his Outlook contacts on his laptop. There was one person he could call who might know Paula's whereabouts. He looked at the clock, saw that he still had five minutes, and called Kristen Spencer, Paula's younger sister, at her work number.

Kristen's administrative assistant put him on hold for an interminably long time. He was about to hang up when Kristen finally came on the line.

"Hello, Dr. D'Maio. What a surprise to hear from you." Her voice was sarcastic. "Sorry to put you on hold for so long."

He didn't say what he was thinking, that he could have walked to her building in less time. Kristen's office on Farmington Avenue was a stone's throw from his building on Prospect. When Kristen had been his patient, she'd walked to her appointments on her lunch hour.

"Kristen, do you know that Paula went to St. Maarten yesterday?"

"Of course. I took her to the airport."

Kristen's voice had a hostile edge, and Louis paused.

What had Paula told her?

"Where is she staying?"

"Why do you want to know?"

Louis took a deep breath and looked at the clock. He was already two minutes late for his appointment. He heard Mr. Rizzo clear his throat loudly in the waiting room, likely to emphasize that point.

"Look, I just want to know if she's okay."

"This isn't a good time for me to chat," she said in a low voice. "But I'm actually glad you called. I wanted to talk with you anyway."

"Really? About what?"

"About Paula. But not now. I'm late for a meeting."

"When are you free?"

"I should be done by six," she said. "Do you want to stop over here? You know where I work, don't you?"

As if he didn't know. It was unusual she'd want to see him in person, but maybe that was better. He'd be done with Mr. Rizzo in fifty minutes.

"I'll be there."

She agreed and he hung up the phone. Sunlight created triangular shadows on his desk and on the few knickknacks he owned: a wooden zebra Paula had bought him at the Dallas Zoo, a large quartz crystal (another gift from her), and a small sandstone whale carving. Besides his scratched mahogany desk, two chairs and his leather recliner, a second-hand couch and a faded Georgia O'Keefe print on the scuffed ivory walls, his office was sparsely furnished. The shabby beige carpeting was worn in spots, which he tried to hide with strategic placement of the chairs.

If I renew his lease in a few months, I have to demand improvements.

New carpeting. Fresh paint.

Most of his patients were too wrapped up in their own inner turmoil to pay much attention to the décor anyway. With the exception of Kristen, he recalled. She was sharp, keenly observant of her surroundings. Not so aware of the problems he'd tried to help her resolve in her personal life, however.

He'd seen Kristen on a weekly basis for several months, a year before he'd met her sister Paula and before his career had been almost derailed by a wealthy Avon socialite, Victoria Rudemann. Ultimately he'd been exonerated of the ugly ethics charges the woman had filed against him, but his name and reputation had been marred. The press in particular had gleefully dragged his name through the mud. A year and a half later he was still recovering financially from the grim and protracted battle that almost cost him his license and his livelihood.

Louis stood up, straightened his tie, and opened the door to the waiting area. The thick-jowled, scowling businessman flung the magazine he was reading onto the coffee table and stomped into the office.

Louis finished the session with Mr. Rizzo—which was surprisingly more productive than he'd expected—before six o'clock and he spent a few minutes at his laptop catching up on paperwork. Then he locked up his office and headed out to Prospect Avenue. At this hour traffic was backed up in a long, snaking crawl and he decided it would be faster to walk the few blocks to Kristen's small nonprofit agency. His stomach growled and he rolled up his shirt sleeves in the sticky heat.

A cold beer would sure hit the spot right now, he thought. *That and a big ol' ribeye sizzling on the grill.*

Kristen's office was located in the basement level of a two-story beige brick building. He followed the signs for "CCRR - Central Community Recovery Resources" and rang the bell at the entrance. The threadbare carpeting in the hallway was old and stained. In a few seconds he heard the click of a deadbolt and Kristen opened the white wooden door.

"Come in," she said.

She was more petite than he remembered, a few inches shorter than Paula. Her wavy strawberry-blonde hair framed a delicate oval face with a lightly freckled nose and cheeks. She still looked like a kid, he thought, much younger than her thirty-plus years. She wore a short-sleeved crisp navy suit, white blouse, and high-heeled blue pumps.

"Still hot out there, huh?" she remarked as he stepped inside, welcoming the blast of air conditioning.

"Where is everyone?" Louis asked, looking around.

From what he could tell, there were at least a half-dozen real offices, not cubicles. Black and white Ansel Adams prints graced the light gray walls. He picked up an agency brochure from a table and scanned through it. CCRR. Substance abuse prevention programs for kids and teens.

"I'm not a slave driver. They all left at five," Kristen replied. "So how do you like my digs?"

The pride in her voice was unmistakable.

"Not bad," Louis said, taking in the modern, gleaming desks and ergonomic office chairs. "I expected to see junky hand-me-down Salvation Army furniture. Aren't nonprofits supposed to look poor?"

"We got a sizeable grant last year from the Jaycees and the Feds for our drug prevention programs in Hartford schools," she said. "Your tax dollars at work. Anyway I got rid of the hideous black and orange vinyl couches we used to have. Had to get them hauled away...not even Goodwill wanted them."

"Congratulations."

He followed her to her office, which was much bigger and tidier than his. Her oversized desk was another story. Stacks of folders, papers, and sticky notes covered every available inch.

Kristen gestured to a swivel chair facing her desk.

"Have a seat. Do you want coffee?"

"I'd rather have an ice-cold Sam Adams. I don't suppose you have one in the fridge."

"Sorry. We're a substance abuse prevention agency. There's coffee, tea, or bottled water."

Louis shrugged.

"I'll pass. Thanks anyway." He noticed a framed photo of a sagging farmhouse on the wall. "Is that near Keene? New Hampshire?"

She looked in the direction he pointed.

"Yes."

"I've driven by it. It's very distinctive. You take the photo?"

She nodded.

"I've been into photography lately."

"It's really good."

There was an awkward silence and Kristen cleared her throat.

"So I might as well get right to the point. Paula told me why she was going to St. Maarten without you." Her eyes narrowed. "In fact, I'm flying out there tomorrow to hang out with her."

"That's interesting."

He felt a curious sense of relief. At least Paula wouldn't be alone.

At least she wasn't there with another man, was the thought that had been beneath the surface all along.

"When's she coming back?"

Kristen frowned.

"What does it matter? If she didn't tell you, then she didn't want you to know."

Louis rubbed a hand along his chin, a nervous habit he'd tried hard to break.

"So what was it that you wanted to talk about then?"

Kristen glared at him.

"You know, she's been through a lot this past year."

"I'm aware," he said, studying her shifting gaze and her nervous foot-tapping beneath the desk.

She fidgeted in her chair and it gave a faint squeak.

"I'm not so sure you are aware, *doctor*. Did you know she's so stressed out she's been on medication? It's not because of Bill or the divorce, or anything about her job. I think it's because she found out you were sleeping with your old girlfriend—"

"Oh, for Christ's sake," Louis interrupted. "Don't play armchair psychologist with me."

"Then don't fuck around with her head," Kristen shot back, eyes blazing. "Don't you think that poor girl's been through enough? First you wreck up her marriage, then when she finally leaves her husband and gets divorced—*to be with you*—you go and screw around behind her back. How the hell can you live with yourself?"

Louis felt the heat rising up in his face.

"It's not true and it's none of your business—"

"Oh yes it is, she's my sister. I care about her."

"And we will work this through."

"Oh no, you won't." She shook her head. "She's done with you. And I wanted to tell you myself—in person—that you should leave her alone and let her get on with her life. Go mess up someone else's life. Go back to whatever-her-name is. But leave my sister alone."

"You don't know what you're talking about. I'm not involved with anyone else." He stood up, a sudden pain like hot pins jabbing his lower back. "That's all I'm going to say. I don't have to defend myself with you."

"You know what?" Kristen said, making no move to rise. "I'm happy Paula blew you off and went to St. Maarten by herself. I hope she's having a blast."

"Yeah, okay." Louis turned to leave, resisting the impulse to slam the door on his way out. "Thanks a lot."

He thought he heard her mutter something under her breath as he left. He should have known. He walked back to his office, hungrier, hotter, tired, and irritated. As far as Paula's family was concerned, he was a home wrecker, an older man looking for a trophy wife. They didn't know the whole story and probably never would. Louis was especially irked that Bill, Paula's Neanderthal ex, came out of the ugly mess smelling like a rose.

Back in his office, Louis noticed the message light blinking on the land line and he checked his voice mail one last time. All he wanted to do now was head home. Watch SportsCenter. Read the newspaper, and his case notes for tomorrow. Clear his head.

There were three messages. The first voice mail was from his nineteen-year-old daughter, Heather. Her voice was panicky and indignant.

Dad, UConn didn't get my tuition payment and my room deposit yet. What if they don't give me the classes I want? Can you PLEASE send the check out? Or you could pay them online. That would be faster.

He sighed. That bill was on top of his stack at home, waiting to get paid along with many others. It was his turn to pony up since his ex-wife had covered Heather's spring semester. He was never late but his patients' insurance companies often took their time sending payments. Thank God Heather had chosen a state university but even so, it was a sizeable nut.

"Don't worry, I'll take care of it," he said out loud. "I always do, don't I?"

The second message was from his golfing buddy Frank, reminding him of their tee-off time at eight AM the next day. The third message started out with so much static, he had to raise the volume button on the phone.

Louis. It's me. I got your voice mails. I won't be back for a while. But that's okay, I'm sure you'll amuse yourself with Charlotte. Stop calling me.

The message ended abruptly. Louis listened to Paula's clipped sentences again, his heart sinking.

He tried her cell phone, but there was no answer. Feeling numb, he sat at his desk and stared out the small window at the cars passing by on Prospect Avenue. His stomach rumbled but he no longer felt hungry. He wondered for the umpteenth time how things had gotten to this point. Granted their relationship had been on shaky ground for a while. Paula's divorce had been long and bitter, and she often lashed out at him as she dealt with her ex-husband Bill and struggled to get her fledging consulting business off the ground. They stopped going out when Louis's finances got tight. He couldn't remember when they last did something fun.

And then he'd made his big mistake with Charlotte, his former live-in girlfriend. Charlotte was a smart, angular woman in her fifties who'd always intrigued him more with her wit than her looks. She'd called him out of the blue and said she urgently needed to talk about an issue with her daughter. He'd met her for lunch and offered his help. Out of respect for Charlotte's wish to keep their discussion confidential, Louis hadn't told Paula anything about it. He let her believe he'd been golfing that afternoon. She'd discovered his lie of omission a few days later when she used his computer and came across an email from Charlotte thanking him for lunch and for all he'd done for her.

He would never forget the way Paula's face fell—how she seemed to *dissolve*—when she saw that message.

So this is why things have been so tense, she'd said. *This is why you're distant and we never go out. You've been seeing Charlotte. You've been having an affair.*

And then she'd simply walked out.

Kristen's words ran through his mind when he finally got into his car to drive home.

I'm happy Paula blew you off and went to St. Maarten by herself. I hope she's having a blast.

CHAPTER TWO

Cupecoy Beach, St. Maarten

PAULA WONDERED HOW it would feel to shed her Yankee inhibitions and red bikini and swim naked in the roiling surf. Jagged rocks and scrub framed this sugary white, isolated stretch of sand called Cupecoy, where a couple dozen people, young and old, fat and trim, white and black, sprawled on their beach blankets like chess pieces and worshipped the sun *au naturel*. No worries on St. Maarten, mon, the One Friendly Island.

She had a few days to herself before her sister, Kristen, arrived. God knew she needed a break. A break from Louis, from work, from everything. She'd even forced herself to leave her laptop at home.

The sun was uncomfortably hot, the foaming turquoise waves seductive. Paula wiped the sweat from her brow, lay on her side, and unfastened her bikini top. She glanced at her fellow skinny-dippers, but no one paid her the slightest attention. She lay flat on her thick terrycloth beach towel, closed her eyes, and savored the novel sensation of warm air on her bare chest, white as cream. She guessed that the last time she'd been topless in public was when she was two years old in her wading pool.

Finally she vaulted over the last Puritan hurdle and pulled down her bikini bottom. She stuffed it in her beach bag and smiled to herself. If Louis could see her now...stark naked on the sand. He'd be shocked. She had shocked herself.

A cool breeze slid in over the water, smelling of salt and seaweed, and suddenly she sensed goose bumps covering her body, from her ankles to the nape of her neck. She shivered and the wind blew across her thighs, her belly, her breasts. It was exquisite, this contrast of warmth from the sun and the sudden cool sweep of air.

I'm being caressed by the wind god.

She smiled and stretched out her legs, tightening and relaxing the muscles. Eyes still closed, she felt for her tube of sunscreen. She squeezed a dollop of warm coconut-scented lotion in her palm and smoothed it onto her belly.

"Beautiful lady."

The hoarse voice startled her. Her eyes fluttered open and instinctively she covered her breasts with her left arm. The black man who squatted before her in the hot sand had chocolate brown eyes, and his amused gaze focused about eight inches south of her face. Despite the heat, he wore khaki pants and a long-sleeved navy tunic.

"What do you want?"

She felt the heat rising in her cheeks as he stared at her body. Her bathing suit was wadded up in the beach bag, and she grabbed the ends of her towel and tried to cover herself.

The man shifted a worn vinyl bag hanging from his shoulder and proceeded to remove item after item from the satchel, like a magician pulling scarves from a hat.

"Beautiful necklace for beautiful lady," he said in a singsong voice, offering her shell necklaces strung on long black cord.

"No, no," she stammered, acutely aware that now he was

studying her legs and crotch while he dangled the jewelry in one hand. "I'm not interested."

He was close enough for her to smell his stale body odor.

"You here alone, miss?" the man asked and edged forward. There were deep wrinkles at the corners of his eyes and flecks of gray in his short, cropped hair. His ebony forehead was beaded with sweat.

"My husband is coming," she lied. "He'll be here in a minute."

"Lucky man." His smile grew wider and he continued gawking at her as if she were the Playmate of the Month. "Where you from, sugar?"

Paula sat up and crossed her arms over her breasts.

"I don't have any money."

"That's okay, you pay me later," he said. "Tell me your name and your hotel."

"No. I'm not interested," she said, louder this time.

She looked around but no one was paying attention.

"Come on, pretty lady, try them on."

He leaned forward with a shell necklace as though he intended to drape it around her neck. Paula recoiled. Anger even stronger than her fear surfaced like a shark.

"Leave me alone, goddamn it."

She blocked him with her forearms.

They locked eyes. She read cool contempt in his narrowed gaze, but his gap-toothed smile never wavered. Humming to himself, he gathered his necklaces and bracelets, inspecting each one before he stuffed them back into the satchel. Then he rose to his feet and shaded his eyes, the smile gone.

"Bitch," he murmured, so low she could barely hear him.

He spat close to her feet and sauntered off down the beach.

Paula took a deep breath, watching him go. She knew what Louis would say.

What were you thinking? What do you expect, lying naked in public by yourself? Is this a surprise?

She pulled on her suit and sat hugging her knees, her heart pounding. A sun-bronzed naked young man strolled by her to the water's edge and dove into the waves. He swam with firm, smooth strokes away from shore and was soon joined by an equally buff nude young woman, who giggled when he swam close to her and grabbed her arm. She struggled to free herself and the two of them collapsed with a splash in the waves.

Paula sighed, watching the couple frolic like dolphins. Maybe she should have accepted the olive branch Louis extended and returned his phone calls. Instead, she'd left him a snarky message telling him to stop calling her and amuse himself with Charlotte. He'd lied to her about seeing his old flame. Maybe he'd slept with her too.

Things hadn't been great between the two of them for months. Time away in a romantic setting might have been good for them both, a new start for their languishing relationship. She'd struggled in the past year, in the midst of her divorce, to launch her own training and consulting firm. After working countless twelve-hour days, she'd landed a juicy plum of a contract with a large insurance company in Hartford.

It was a sweet, sweet success with a sweet, sweet profit margin. She was back on her feet financially, her divorce from Bill was final, and more importantly, she was gaining back her emotional health. No more Prozac, no more nights spent crying on the phone to her sister and her friends.

The sun disappeared behind a rolling bank of gray clouds, and seconds later raindrops pelted the sand. Paula stood up and made her way to the water. A year ago she would have chosen a root canal over a day at the beach. The stress of the divorce and work had taken a toll, and she'd dealt with her angst by overeating. Before she crossed to the world of plus sizes, she'd joined a gym with her younger sister, Kristen. For months she toiled and sweated on treadmills and weight machines, and it showed. At thirty-five, she looked better now than she had in her twenties.

Raindrops hit her face and she walked into the waves and dropped into a floating position in the warm, heavenly saltwater, luxuriating in the primeval sensation. The palm trees swayed in the wind and the rain stopped as quickly as it had begun. She let the gentle current tug her along the edge of the shore and pretended she was a mermaid gliding through the sea. I can start over, she thought.

My life is starting over, and this time I'll do it right. With Louis or without him.

Paula left Cupecoy Beach in the late afternoon. Her rental Hyundai barely made it up Cole Bay Hill Road leading back to the resort, and an impatient driver in a van tailgated her until she pulled over near the top of the winding road to let him pass. The view from the overlook was extraordinary. She stepped out of the car and admired the volcanic shapes of Saba, Statia, and St. Bart's in the distance. Down below the cliffs, the waves lapped at the shore of Great Bay where the cruise ships laid anchor.

The traffic was miserable near the one main intersection close to town. While she waited at the one stoplight, she watched a skinny brown goat chomp on the weeds at the side of the road. A small brown rooster ran across the street and a young child chased the bird back to a cluttered yard.

She reached her hotel, located less than a mile from the Dutch capital, Philipsburg. Her room facing the bay was pleasant, even luxurious by Caribbean standards. After showering and changing into a cool white linen sundress, she made her way past the open-air lobby with its gleaming marble floors.

The air was fragrant with the scent of blooming jasmine. Pink anthurium, heliconia, and ginger lilies spilled over large ceramic urns in a cheerful burst of color. She descended the spiral staircase to the pool terrace, where couples lounged with drinks in hand.

The bartender smiled as she approached. She smiled back and made her way to a vacant stool at the end of the bar. She'd flirted with the young man yesterday when she'd arrived. He was tall and lean and wore the uniform of the hotel wait staff, a turquoise Hawaiian shirt and tight black pants.

"Hey, Michael," she said.

"How you doing, *cher*. Wine for you tonight?" he asked in a thick, French-Creole accent.

He was in his late twenties, a native of St. Lucia, she'd learned, and the eldest of seven siblings. Tonight he wore a gold chain and his shirt was open a few buttons, exposing his smooth, dark skin.

"Chardonnay."

"You got it."

He turned away to pour the wine and she stole a long look at his broad shoulders and narrow waist.

He set the full glass before her.

"Did you take the boat to Anguilla today?"

"No. My sister's coming soon and maybe she'll want to do that with me. I drove to Cupecoy instead."

His smile widened.

"I waited for you last night."

"You did?"

"Thought we'd take a walk on the beach. In the moonlight." His voice was a low, silky baritone. "The moon was full and the stars were out. Beautiful."

She exhaled, recalling their conversation the night before. Her flirty comments about moonlit strolls and warm Caribbean nights. She felt her cheeks flush and she sipped the cold oaky wine. She looked away from his earnest dark eyes.

"I went to the casino. Lost fifty bucks in the slots."

A red-faced American man wearing a stained St. Maarten t-shirt stretched tight over his beach ball of a stomach appeared next to Paula. His hair was a tufted gray nest and he reeked of booze. He plopped two empty plastic cups on the bar and held onto the counter to steady himself.

"Sir, can I get a refill of these? Whatever the hell they are—Painkillers. And how about making 'em stronger?" To Paula, he commented, "What a rip-off, huh?" he snorted when he caught her eye. "You pay ten bucks for nuthin' but ice."

Paula said nothing. Michael was all business and made a show of mixing two frothy drinks. He was generous with the rum.

"That's more like it."

The man slapped a twenty on the bar and stalked off.

"Thank you, sir," Michael called out and turned back to Paula.

"Does it get to you sometimes?" she asked. "The tourists, I mean. The rude and nasty ones like him."

Michael shrugged.

"Is no problem. Most people aren't rude. They're here to have a good time."

"Come on, Michael," she said. "Some of these people act like they own the place. Tell me the truth. What do you really think of the tourists? I swear I won't tell. You can break the code of silence."

The young man shook his head.

"I think you need another glass of wine, *cher*."

"I think I need more than that."

When Paula dared to meet his gaze again, his eyebrows rose in mock surprise.

"I'm off work at nine. Come meet me in the lounge upstairs. There's a band tonight. We'll dance. Will you come?"

His eyes met hers, full of promises and desire.

She hesitated.

I'm ten years older than he is. But why not? Why not?

"Maybe I'll see you then."

That would show Louis.

He grinned.

"Nine o'clock."

He lightly touched her hand and moved away. Customers were waiting at the bar.

Paula swiveled in the bar stool to face the pool terrace and watched the diverse mix of couples come and go: French, German, Dutch, Hispanic, American. She felt a sudden pang as the memory resurfaced of her and Bill on their honeymoon in St. Croix. She and Bill had danced to the rhythm of reggae and steel drums and toasted the start of their life together with strawberries and champagne. Later, Bill had held her on the terrace of their beachfront bungalow and tilted her face to capture the silver glow of the moon before he kissed her.

She would have been astonished had someone told her then—*in ten short years you'll be strangers to each other, you'll be divorced. You'll be sitting on a pool terrace by yourself in St. Maarten wondering what the hell happened. You'll be drinking alone and flirting with a stranger.*

Her heart felt like a stone in her chest, weighted by her reverie. She finished the glass and set it on the bar. Moments later Michael reappeared with a refill.

"On the house," he said.

"You'll get me too drunk to dance tonight," Paula said before he turned away, but she took the glass anyway.

Why was starting over so difficult? Kristen had warned her not to anesthetize herself too much during this time, but picking up and sorting through the pieces of her life was a painful and bewildering task. One minute she felt optimistic, full of hope, and the next minute she wanted to drive off a cliff. On top of it all, things had crumbled with Louis.

"Tonight," Michael whispered when she settled her check.

She did not reply. She watched him move away to the other end of the bar and pushed the thoughts of Bill and Louis to another corner in her mind. Thinking and remembering too much would ruin this little vacation.

Yeah, tonight. Why not. It would serve Louis right.

The sun dropped low in the sky and twilight was a fleeting lavender blur before darkness settled. Clutching a paperback novel in one hand, Paula made her way from Front Street to the center of Philipsburg, her sandals padding softly on the road. She felt warm and mellow but a bit unsteady from the wine. The walk to town was less than ten minutes from her hotel, but the first quarter-mile brought her past a cemetery and concrete shacks where idle men watched her pass and thin yellow dogs sniffed at the sidewalk. She could have driven her rental Hyundai but it was such a short walk, after all, and parking spaces downtown were scarce.

Tonight there were few people about the poorly-lit, no-man's land of empty storefronts and ramshackle homes not yet taken over by hotels. A group of men playing cards on a crumbling porch halted their conversation, but she hurried past and in a few moments reached the heart of town and the stores selling jewelry and crystal, Dutch linens, discounted liquor, cheap souvenirs, and scores of products hawked to the cruise ship set. The French restaurant Petite Pier was her destination tonight.

She was amused by the maitre'd's puzzled look when she made her entrance and requested a table for one. He ushered her to the corner of a large dining room and seated her at a small square table covered with a white linen tablecloth, adorned with a single pink rose and a candle.

After she ordered an appetizer, she picked up her novel. Her eyes scanned the pages but registered nothing. Instead, she looked out at the lights of the boats anchored in the bay and the pale strip of moonlight reflected on the calm, dark water. She heard the murmuring voices of the couples surrounding her and felt a sudden, intense regret that Louis wasn't sitting across the table from her. He'd be sipping a martini straight up with a twist, and he'd probably order the most exotic dish on the menu. He'd joke with the waiter and make her laugh with his dry, caustic wit.

He could always pull her out of her blackest moods and bolster her shaky self-confidence. She would never have summoned the courage to start her own business without his unwavering support and continual reassurance. She would never have had the guts to leave Bill without him.

Louis was her friend, her mentor, her lover...and the grenade that she'd tossed into her troubled union. Would her marriage have ended anyway? She'd pondered that question a thousand times but the answer was always the same.

Bill and I grew apart. We had nothing in common but I didn't want to admit it.

That bastard.

Bill had screamed in her face when he'd learned the truth. He'd pushed her hard against the wall of their tiny kitchen. It was the first and last time he'd ever laid a hand on her.

Why are you doing this to us? Can't you see what he's after?

Paula opened the book to her bookmarked page but the words were blurred. She blinked away the unexpected tears and looked at her watch. In an hour or so she was supposed to meet Michael, whose world was as far removed from hers as the summit of Denali. It meant nothing, and she knew she meant nothing to him.

Sometimes alcohol had a paradoxical effect. Sometimes instead of numbing pain, it brought it into sharper focus. When her appetizer arrived, Paula picked at the crabmeat with her fork, but there was a lump in her throat that felt like a tennis ball and her stomach felt unsettled.

I should have stayed at the hotel.

Her pulse raced and she suddenly broke out into a sweat. She labored to breathe normally, her clammy hands clenched in her lap.

Breathe deeply. Louis said to breathe deeply when this happens.

She practiced long, deep breaths and the waiter came back to take her dinner order. He was a short, squat, red-faced man in a black tuxedo. He paused and leaned forward.

"Would madam care for a glass of wine? Compliments of the manager."

"The manager?"

The man motioned to his left, and Paula saw a tall, gray-haired man in an identical black tux leaning against the railing. He waved at her and smiled. He looked to be in his fifties.

Paula nodded.

"Tell him I said thank you."

When she was finished with dinner, she paid her bill with a credit card and left the restaurant, concentrating all her efforts on placing one foot after the other. Walking a straight line was damn near impossible.

Why did I drink all that fucking wine? I have to stop this.

"I hope everything was all right. Do you need a taxi?"

The manager of Petite Pier stood at the door, hands crossed behind his back. He smiled, eyebrows raised.

"I shall call for a taxi if you wish?"

He had a very British accent.

Even if she wanted a cab, she didn't know if she'd brought enough cash to pay the fare and she was too embarrassed to fumble in her purse. Her head throbbed.

"No thanks. Everything was fine."

"Enjoy your evening."

Paula met his kindly eyes. They were a startling blue, even in the dim light. She looked away.

"Thank you."

She stepped out into the street. A light rain filled the road with puddles, and soaked her feet in her open-toed sandals.

No matter. I'm not a bar of soap, I won't melt in the rain.

Front Street was deserted.

I'll be back at the hotel in ten minutes. Ten minutes, that's all.

Then she remembered that Michael was waiting for her in the lounge. What time was it anyway? Surely long past nine o'clock? She couldn't see the numbers on her watch. By now he'd probably given up on her and gone home. She felt a mix of regret and relief. They were just flirting. He probably hadn't taken her seriously anyway.

She passed by the last store on the strip, feeling the rain soak through her linen dress, probably ruining the goddamn thing. She flinched when a car barreled down the narrow, empty street, splashing dirty water on her bare legs. No one was outside the shacks she'd passed by earlier; the card game had ended or moved indoors. She hurried past the cemetery.

"Miss! Excuse me, miss."

Footsteps behind her, splashing in the puddles. Paula turned her head and a tall figure holding a black umbrella beckoned to her. She could barely see him under the streetlight's dim illumination.

"You forgot your credit card in the restaurant."

He waved something in his hand and quickly closed the gap between them on the sidewalk.

Paula stopped and he hurried over to her. He was slim, nicely dressed in black pants and jacket. She guessed he was in his late thirties, early forties.

He peered at the card in his hand.

"Paula Spencer, right?"

"I must have forgotten it," she said. "Thanks."

"I noticed it on the table when you left," he said, but made no move to give her the card. "Here, take my umbrella, you're getting wet."

He handed her the umbrella before she could refuse. Paula looked up and down the deserted street, holding the umbrella at an angle, and shifted from one foot to the other.

"Can I have my card back?"

He smiled.

"Sure. By the way, I'm Francis Lake."

"I'm Paula," she said, then remembered he had already addressed her by her first name.

"Where are you from?"

"Connecticut." She stared at his clean-cut features and even, white teeth. She squinted. Didn't remember seeing him in the restaurant. "Can I have my card back now?"

His smile faded a bit and he handed her a gold MasterCard. She was about to stick the card in her purse, but something made her stop and she held it up to the streetlight, struggling to make out the name.

Francis Lake.

"What is this? This isn't my card," she said.

"Paula, did I make a mistake?"

Even in her less than sober state, she felt the hairs on the back of her neck rise.

"How'd you know my name?"

He snatched it out of her hand.

"Oh, I know who you are, love, and you know me too."

"No, I don't," she said, dropping the umbrella.

He grabbed her arm.

"Not so fast." His fingers gripped her wrist and his other hand slid under his jacket. "I've got a gun. You'll walk with me nice and easy. Not a word. Understand?" His voice was low and deliberate, the phony friendliness gone. "Don't scream or I'll put a bullet in your spine. Got it?"

He drew her close to him, and she felt the muzzle of the revolver jab into the small of her back.

She nodded, unable to react other than to do what he said.

He quickly propelled her off the sidewalk and into the darkness of the graveyard, one hand holding the gun, the other gripping her wrist, forcing it behind her back. As soon as they were out of sight of the road he stopped, seized her other wrist, yanked it behind her back, and handcuffed her.

"What are you doing?"

Her mouth was dry and her heart pounded.

"Keep moving."

Oh Jesus, Oh God. This can't be happening.

Her entire body trembled and she feared her knees would

buckle beneath her. Her thoughts were jumbled, panicked, and she opened her mouth to scream. Just as in her nightmares, nothing but a croak escaped her lips.

"I said no noise," the voice ordered, and he punctuated the command with a nudge of the gun, this time at the nape of her neck. "Do you want your fucking head blown off? Because I'll do it. Don't make me do it."

"I won't."

Oh God, help me. Help me!

He steered her past the tombstones, through mud and prickly wet grass. Too much rich food, too much wine, and the terror of what was happening made her stomach lurch. She bent over and vomited even as he kept pushing her forward.

"Oh, Christ," he said as the stinking mess splattered her dress and legs.

Her stomach contracted painfully, a warm sour taste filled her mouth, and she dropped to her knees on the damp earth and retched again, delivering the remains of her expensive dinner on a mound of dirt.

He grabbed a fistful of her hair and yanked her up hard.

"Get up."

Paula yelped and stumbled forward, her limbs shaking uncontrollably.

Was he going to rape her? Would he shoot her if she tried to run?

She didn't have time to think. They were already out of the cemetery and on another side street. He forced her to a gray van parked at the end of a narrow, dead-end road.

He slid open the rear door, one hand still gripping her arm hard.

"Get in."

Whatever you do, never get in the car. You're dead if you get into the car.

It was all Paula remembered from a class she'd taken on self-defense years ago. Her mouth dropped and this time it was a real scream that emerged, loud and clear, and she jerked away from him, loosening his grip.

"Shut up."

He grabbed her arms, helplessly pinned behind her back, and shoved her inside the rear of the van. Paula screamed again at his contorted face above her, his teeth bared like an animal's. He smacked her hard across the face and shoved the muzzle of the revolver in her mouth, smashing against her teeth. She fell on her back and without thinking, writhed and kicked in a burst of adrenaline. Her knee caught him under the chin in her frenzy and she drove it up and into the soft flesh of his neck.

He cursed and pulled away, and she scrambled for the door. She almost had a leg out before he backhanded her. She cried out and fell again on her side, scraping against jagged, rough edges of exposed rivets on the sheet metal floor of the van. He lunged on top of her, pinning her with his knees, and she twisted beneath him, almost dislodging him before he yanked her up by her hair again. He slid something metal around her head to her neck—*a chain,* she realized—and pulled hard. Her head snapped up and then he released her, letting her fall.

"Bitch."

Stunned, Paula lay on the floor of the van and gasped for breath, the metal chain biting into her throat. She felt him scramble over her and slam the door shut.

She struggled to lift her head. She found her breath and her voice, shrill and shaky.

"You bastard. Let me go!" She tried to move but the choke chain tightened, cutting into her neck. "Let me go! Let me go!" Panic and hysteria overcame her and she screamed and thrashed.

He started the engine and the radio blared a Bob Marley tune. The van lurched forward.

She heard him singing along and grew quiet. He turned the volume down.

"Are you done screaming, love?"

The handcuffs hurt her wrists and she tried to stretch her neck and loosen the chain. Her breath came in ragged gasps.

"It's time to relax," he said cheerfully. "Our vacation has just begun."

CHAPTER THREE

West Hartford, Connecticut

LOUIS AND HIS two-times-a-week golf partner and buddy, Frank, breezed into the Nineteenth Hole restaurant, packed with a horde of hungry, thirsty golfers. They made their way past the crowded bar and tossed their brimmed hats on the last vacant oak table. Frank Roth's long legs splayed out before him like a giraffe when he sat down, and he motioned to the short, chubby waitress at the other side of the bar.

"Usual?" Belinda hollered over the din of the golfers and the television.

Frank nodded and she hurried off.

Frank watched her retreat behind the bar.

"She wants me."

"Yeah, I can tell by the way she can't keep her eyes off you," Louis deadpanned, keeping the Nineteenth Hole ritual alive. "By the way, I kicked your sorry ass."

He stretched out his sore legs, feeling an unpleasant pull in his lower back. He winced.

"Add 'em up," Frank said. "I bet I missed at least five putts on the back nine."

"Every one short."

"Don't say it," Frank warned as Belinda returned with their drinks.

"Never up, never in," Louis taunted. "Like Yogi says, ninety percent of the putts that are short never go in."

"You lost again, huh, Frank?" Belinda smiled, as much a part of the ritual as the four and a half hours of actual golf.

She plunked three drinks on the table, a Sam Adams, ice water, and a glass of red wine.

"Yep. Still putting Louis's daughter through college." He batted his eyes at her. "Does that mean you won't marry me? Trust me, my 401K is still riding the wave."

"She wants a real man, not a sissy wine drinker who's allergic to hops," Louis snorted. He picked up his glass and took a long swallow. "Notice how you're the only one in the clubhouse drinking mary-low?"

"What are you talking about?" Frank held up his glass, swirled the ruby liquid, and inhaled. He took a quick swallow and paused for dramatic effect. "This wine has a stunning nose of currants, cedar, leather, and spice. It's full-bodied with magnificent extract, outstanding purity, excellent delineation, and layers of complex—"

"Pretty damn good for wine-in-a-box," Belinda interrupted. "You guys want anything else?"

"A cheeseburger with fries," Louis said, his stomach growling. The hell with watching the cholesterol. "Make that extra fries and two pickles."

"I'll have the same diet plate he's having," Frank said. "So when are you gonna marry me, Belinda?"

"I couldn't break up the two of you after all these years," she said, wagging her finger at them. "You make the perfect couple."

She winked at Louis and turned her back on both of them.

"Let's get down to business." Louis slid the score card across the table. "You took the front total, I took the back and total, plus your three putts at fifty cents a clip, minus my three, three putts." He grinned at Frank, blew him a kiss, and said, "We were even in specials. I had two greenies and you had two sandies. You owe me a buck fifty, you chumpmeister."

"Wait," Frank said. He peered at the score card. "I don't trust your math. Let me add this up." He chewed on the end of the pencil and made his way across two sets of nine squares, mumbling, "Uh, five, seven, ten to you—jeez, I looked like Watson with the yips, didn't I?"

Louis extended his hand, palm up.

"You wish you looked like Watson. So hand over my winnings before I go public about your sorry-ass game."

Frank groaned.

"I don't know how you do it, buddy. I get close, so goddamn close, but I just can't getcha."

"Visualizing." Louis took a long sip of his beer. "That's the key. I visualize my shot. I visualize the ball going straight into the hole."

"Gimme a break."

"It's a psychology thing," Louis said. "That's what I went to school for."

Frank shook his head.

"Come next Saturday when you're standing eighty yards from the flag on the fourteenth, lying four already, you'll wish you never visualized that 60-degree wedge of yours." He took a swallow of his wine and made a face. "So what's up with you and uh, what's her name?"

"You know what her name is."

Frank rubbed his eyes.

"I forgot. Must be a psychology thing."

Louis looked away.

"She went to St. Maarten by herself a few days ago," he said, all trace of humor gone. "She won't talk to me. She thinks I fooled around with Charlotte."

"Did you?"

"No."

Frank propped his elbows on the table.

"So why does she think so?"

"Because Charlotte asked me for a favor and I met up with her one afternoon. Paula found out about it afterwards. I lied to her—well, not directly, but by omission—about where I was going. She assumed the worst, and now she won't let me explain."

"What was the favor?"

"I really can't say."

Louis sighed, thinking of Charlotte's daughter Annie, arrested for drug possession and hanging out with thugs. She was only fifteen and Charlotte hadn't known who else to call. He'd pulled some strings and gotten Annie evaluated at record speed and enrolled in a drug treatment program. He hoped she was doing okay.

"Point is, Paula won't speak to me now. I've tried calling but she won't answer her phone."

"Text her. Email her. Heck, send her a letter. That would get anyone's attention these days."

"I wish she hadn't left like that," Louis said.

"So go to St. Maarten and surprise her."

"I thought about it. But her sister's flying out there today."

"Too bad. Three's a crowd."

"Especially since Kristen's not my biggest fan." Louis shifted in his chair, trying to find a comfortable position. His backache was getting worse. "She thinks I broke up Paula's marriage and messed up her life. She ripped me a new one the other day when I asked her when Paula was coming back."

"That's special," Frank said. "She sounds like a real sweetheart."

Louis said nothing. Frank had no idea Kristen had once been his patient. Louis would never voice his suspicions that Kristen's prickliness had as much to do with that awkward fact as with anything else.

"You ever been to St. Maarten?" Frank asked.

"Nope. Bet it's nice though."

"I wonder if they have any good golf courses there," Frank remarked. "Hey, did you see that shot Rory McIlroy hit on eighteen the other day?"

At six that evening, Louis called his ex-wife Carol from his condo in West Hartford, hoping his daughter might be home to pick up the phone. He kept a wary eye on his cat, Bogie, the stray who'd adopted him a few months earlier. The skinny black and white cat had just wolfed down a can of tuna and was hunched on top of the refrigerator, staring at him like the Sphinx.

Carol's voice barked in the receiver.

"Yeah?"

"It's me. Lou."

"What do you want?"

"Yeah, nice to talk to you too," he said. "Is Heather there?"

"No. She's out with David."

"Well, I wanted to let her know she doesn't have to worry, I made the payment to UConn."

"About time."

Why do the women in my life have to be so damn difficult?

"I took care of it. Let her know, all right? And tell her to call me sometime. She hasn't stopped over in a while."

Heather was nineteen years old, a college sophomore, and apparently too involved with her friends, parties, and concerts this summer to call or drop by more than a few times a month, if he was lucky. Pretty much par for the course, he supposed.

"Yeah, I'll tell her."

Louis was about to ask who David was, but heard the definitive click of the line disconnecting. He and Carol hadn't had many civilized conversations since their divorce when

Heather was a toddler. Then again, they hadn't had many civilized conversations during their eight-year marriage either. If it weren't for Heather, they'd have nothing to do with each other.

Next he called his work number to check voice mails, as he did several times a day. The robotic female voice informed him there was one new message and recited the number—he recognized it as Paula's cell—and the time, 2:05 PM. He'd still been on the golf course then. He pressed the hash sign, his pulse racing.

"Louis, just wanted to let you know I met someone here. I'm having fun. Maybe we'll talk when I get back next week. Beady nine—"

There was static and then nothing.

End of new messages.

He listened to it again. The reception wasn't great, but even so there was something odd. Something flat about her voice. Who the hell did she meet? And what was…beady nine? He replayed it again and turned up the volume. Interesting she hadn't called his personal cell phone. She'd left the message on his work number, which almost always went directly into voice mail. He punched the redial key to call her back, but was instantly connected to her voice mail. He hung up.

"Shit," he said out loud, startling the cat, who hissed, leaped off the refrigerator in a huff and stalked off down the hallway. He tried Paula's cell again and this time left a message. "Hey Paula, please call me back. I got your message. Call me at home or on my cell, not my work phone, okay?"

He paced around the kitchen, found a clean glass in the dish drainer, added three ice cubes, and a splash of Stolichnaya. He sat at the small kitchen table, an IKEA bargain, and flipped through his stack of bills. With Heather's tuition payment and the town property taxes, it'd be a lean month. Pretty much every month was a lean month, although he was in better shape than last year at this time, when Victoria Rudemann had sued him and referrals dried up.

He did some calculations and sipped the Stoli, but his mind wandered back to Paula's cryptic message. In a few minutes he decided he wasn't in the mood to work on finances, and he shoved the bills into a pile and straightened in his chair, cursing at the sudden, sharp spasms in his lower back. The ibuprofen he'd taken at the golf course wasn't working.

He hobbled over to the kitchen counter to top off his glass of vodka and thought of the last massage Paula had given him. She used to knead his back with her long, strong fingers, taking away the pain with silky scented oils, hot stones, and heated towels. He was more than happy to be the recipient of her patient, sensual ministrations.

Paula. If she heard him out, let him explain and apologize, maybe they'd get back on track and put the past behind them. He was beginning to realize that life without her would be no life at all.

Louis, just wanted to let you know I met someone here...

He made his way slowly to the bathroom, peeling off his sweaty blue polo shirt. He glanced in the mirror as he ran a hot shower—granted he could stand to lose a couple pounds—but for a man of forty-five, he wasn't in terrible shape in spite of his french fry habit. He ran a hand through his thick graying hair, stripped off the rest of his clothes, and stepped into the steaming shower.

He heard the phone ring just as he'd soaped up, and he hesitated for only a second before jumping out of the shower stall to answer the phone in the bedroom. He grabbed the receiver with one slippery hand.

"Hello?"

"Louis, it's Kristen. I'm calling you from St. Maarten."

He stood naked and dripping on the soft, plush beige carpeting.

"Okay."

"There's something wrong," she said, and he heard the

worry in her voice. "Paula's not here and I can't reach her on her cell. I've been trying to call her all day."

"What do you mean, she's not there?"

"Like I said. She's not here. She knew I was coming and we're sharing a room but her luggage isn't here either."

Louis, just wanted you to know I met someone…

He took a deep breath, shivering in the air-conditioned bedroom.

"She didn't leave you a message or anything?"

"Only a text I got on my phone saying she was hanging out with some guy she met, and she'd see me soon. Hanging out with *some guy*? She knew I was coming this afternoon. I don't understand why she won't answer her phone and I sure don't get why she took off with her bags."

Alarm bells were going off in his head. This wasn't like Paula. She might blow him off, but Kristen?

"Did you talk to anyone at the front desk?"

"No. I got my key when I arrived. That was it. What would they know?"

"Where are you staying?" Louis asked.

"The Sun Bay Resort. It's on the Dutch side."

He hesitated. He had clients scheduled all week and his bank balance wasn't exactly robust. Taking off on the spur of the moment wasn't usually his thing, but…. *Paula.*

"I think I should fly out there."

"Who knows, maybe she'll call me later," Kristen said, but there was no mistaking her doubt and anxiety.

Why else would she contact him, especially after their last interaction?

He wondered if she was telling him everything.

"I'll catch the next flight out of Bradley," he said more firmly. "How long does it take to get there?"

"There's no direct flight from Bradley. My flight had a stop in Miami, and from there it took about two and a half hours." She told him which airline had the best deal when she'd booked her ticket.

"Maybe I'm overreacting," she said. "Maybe Paula will show up later tonight. This could be a big waste of your time and money."

"I'm coming," Louis said. "I want to speak to Paula in person anyway. It might as well be in St. Maarten."

Kristen offered no protest.

"I'll call you after I make my plans," Louis said, and they hung up.

He hopped back in the shower, rinsed off, wrapped a towel around his waist, and fired up his laptop on the kitchen table. In minutes he found morning flights departing to Miami and from there to Prince Juliana Airport. He'd land in Philipsburg by early afternoon. There were no bargains to be had, and he winced when he saw the ticket prices. Not only would he be losing revenue from clients he'd have to reschedule, but now his credit card balance would be higher than ever.

He stared at the computer screen for a long moment and then booked the flight.

CHAPTER FOUR

Cupecoy Beach, St. Maarten

LOUIS'S FLIGHT LEFT Bradley International Airport at seven o'clock in the morning and landed in Miami before eleven. He had an hour to kill before the connecting flight to St. Maarten, and he paced through the terminal with his carry-on. He was hungry and made his way to the food court, finally settling on a Coke and a slice of cheese pizza. He devoured it and checked his cell phone again but there were no new messages from Kristen. As far as he knew, Paula was still AWOL and had not communicated any further with her sister.

He had the nagging feeling that Kristen hadn't shared everything. She was a good one for keeping secrets. When she'd been his patient long before he'd met her sister, his toughest job had been helping her break through her thick emotional walls. He hadn't really succeeded. As soon as she allowed one brick to fall, exposing any weakness, she replaced it with two or three others for extra reinforcement.

She'd had problems with men, love, and intimacy—the

usual grab bag of emotional angst. The one she wanted to marry treated her like crap. Chris—that was his name. Chris, the alpha man outdoor adventure type who climbed Mount Kilimanjaro for fun, swam the English Channel, and ran with the bulls in Pamplona. The Wonder Man, as she described him, fearlessly competed in Ironman triathlons but intimate relationships were too formidable a challenge.

Over time Kristen had made some strides toward recognizing that Chris did not love her and never had, and that their relationship was conducted only at his whim and convenience. Louis suspected that this humiliating realization, perhaps more than anything else, had led her to angrily terminate therapy after a couple of months. Another example of killing the messenger. Except he hadn't really been the messenger of bad news, just the conduit for her to recognize it herself.

If he had to guess, Kristen was probably involved now with yet another Stone Man whose masonry, like hers, was impenetrable. Sometimes the brightest people seemed compelled to repeat their mistakes over and over. He'd seen it a thousand times in his practice.

Hell, he was guilty of some major flubs himself. Marrying Carol, for instance. And then hooking up with Charlotte after his divorce. He'd lived with her and her daughter, Annie, before meeting Paula. He'd never felt a torch-carrying passion for Charlotte, but they got along fine. Until they didn't. Until she'd wanted to get married and tired of his lame reasons to maintain the status quo.

He chewed the tough pizza crust and thought about Annie's descent into teenage hell. Hopefully she was making progress in the treatment program. The uncomfortable truth was, he hadn't done Charlotte or Annie any favors by playing house, by acting as surrogate husband and father. It really hadn't been fair to any of them.

Since Charlotte had called him, he'd wondered more than

once if he bore some responsibility. Were Annie's problems partly due to his leaving when she was on the cusp of adolescence? He was, after all, a father figure she'd bonded with and who'd abandoned her, just as her biological father had. He worked with enough families to understand the dynamics.

Louis boarded the connecting flight to St. Maarten before noon. His seat-mate was a dignified-looking black woman in her late twenties, he guessed, who stared straight ahead, chin up, not acknowledging his presence. She wore a short, bright turquoise silk dress, and she sat upright with her hands folded in her lap. She had rings on every finger: gold, silver, some with stones and some without. No wedding ring. During the two-hour flight, he inhaled her musky perfume.

His longing for Paula was like a heavy sigh in his chest. It'd been a dog's age since he'd seen her. Since he'd held her. He closed his eyes and imagined finding her on a deserted beach somewhere on the island. Then the image of her with another man made him open his eyes, unwilling to pursue that train of thought.

He caught his first glimpse of St. Maarten's green volcanic peaks through the small, dirty window of the plane. He stretched forward, feeling a warning twinge in his lower back. The young woman next to him turned to look out the window too.

"Excuse me," Louis said. "Are you from the island?"

The woman slowly turned her head and there was no mistaking the message he read in her frosty brown eyes.

Back off, Jack.

"Yes."

"I'm meeting my wife in Philipsburg and I want to take her out to dinner tonight. Someplace special. Any recommendations?"

Her expression softened the tiniest bit.

She tapped her fingers together and said in a lilting accent,

"Go to Front Street. Try Le Bec Fin or Antoine. Or even Petite Pier. It's pretty by the water there."

She looked away.

Louis nodded.

"Thank you."

That was one thing he knew for sure about Paula. She liked to eat at nice restaurants. No Whoppers or pizza for this kid. He'd have to get into her head and figure out where she'd been.

As the plane began its descent to Princess Juliana Airport, he wondered if he would ever have the opportunity to take Paula out to dinner if he found her.

If I find her…and she's not with some other guy.

After they landed, Louis called Kristen on his cell phone but got her voice mail. He left her a message that he was in the airport and after waiting his turn in the long line for Immigration, he hailed a taxi to the Sun Bay Resort. Kristen had told him it was cheaper to rent a car at the hotel. He slid inside the back, shoving his one travel bag on the torn black vinyl seat. The cab was clean but smelled faintly of cigarette smoke and vanilla air freshener. The driver, a chatty young black man, launched into a history lesson as they drove up the steep and winding road to Philipsburg.

"And so the Spanish left in 1648 and then came the French and the Dutch," the man grinned into the rear view mirror. "The border separating the two parts was settled by a walking race between a Dutchman and a Frenchman. Frenchman musta walked faster 'cuz the French side is bigger. They divided the island and no problems since. Where you from, mon?"

"United States. Connecticut." Louis stared out the window at the shoreline below. The sapphire water sparkled in the early afternoon sunlight. Paula was there…somewhere. "Tell me where all the tourists go."

The young man laughed.

"Depends what you want, mon, depends what you want.

Beaches? Fishing? Diving?"

He paused and glanced at Louis again in the rear view mirror, as though waiting for him to suggest something else less benign.

"Beaches," Louis said, thinking of Paula's love of sun and sand.

"Oh, you try Dawn Beach…or Mullet Bay or Cupecoy…lots of places, you know? I can take you on a tour of the island. You want a tour now?"

"Thanks, not now," Louis said. He settled back and reviewed his mental checklist: beaches, restaurants, stores. At some point he would also call the Dutch medical center and the French hospital in Marigot to make sure Paula hadn't been in some sort of accident. He hoped they didn't have U.S.-style privacy laws to prevent them from providing information.

He was too deep in thought to pay further attention to the scenery or the driver, and soon the taxi lurched onto a narrow side street and came to a stop at the entrance of the Sun Bay Resort. Louis fumbled in his wallet and pulled out cash and a photo of Paula. It was a close-up he'd taken in the springtime when they'd gone hiking at a state forest. Paula was smiling shyly, her blonde hair pulled back from her face in a tight ponytail.

"You didn't happen to give a ride to this young lady, did you?" he asked, handing the man the cab fare and a generous tip.

The driver examined the photo for a few seconds and shrugged.

"Don't think so." He looked curiously at Louis. "You the police?"

Louis shook his head.

"No. Thanks for the ride." He turned away and picked up his bag.

Louis checked in at the hotel's front desk. The tall black man who stood behind the counter handed him his card key and Louis pulled out Paula's photo from his wallet.

"You have a guest here named Paula Spencer," he said, holding out the photo. "By any chance have you seen her around the past couple days?"

The man looked at the photo and nodded. "I see her around the hotel, yes."

"Did you happen to see her yesterday or the day before?"

He scratched the side of his head, looking away and squinting at his computer screen.

"I don't know. I was off yesterday."

"Was she—did you ever notice her—with anyone? A gentleman?" Louis drew in a long breath and watched the man's face closely.

"I don't think so."

"Her sister and I are worried about her. We haven't heard from her in a couple days." Louis tapped his fingers on the counter. "Would you mind printing out a copy of her room charges? I'd really appreciate it."

The clerk's large brown eyes widened.

"Oh no, sir. Can't do that. The manager has to approve."

"And he'll be in when?"

"Tonight. He come in at six."

"Thanks."

He picked up a guidebook of St. Maarten from a display rack on the counter, and made his way across the gleaming marble floors of the open-air lobby. The scent of the ocean and tropical flowers filled his nostrils, and he slowed for a second to take in the view. Palm fronds swaying in the breeze, rolling turquoise waves, guests lounging on the beach...it was pleasant. Very pleasant. Like a postcard. He turned away and walked toward the elevator, his sense of dread and anxiety growing worse by the moment.

His room on the third floor faced the bay. Louis threw his carry-on bag on one of the double beds and went into the bathroom to splash cold water on his face and run a comb through his hair. He stared into the mirror at the reflection of a middle-aged, bearded, gray-haired man with narrowed blue eyes who looked like he was ready to jump out of his skin. Jesus, he was tense.

And the room was too goddamned hot. Oppressive. He cranked up the air conditioner, which sputtered a weak protest and finally blasted tepid air through dusty vents. He opened the sliding glass door to the balcony. The ledge was narrow and barely fit a white oval resin table and two plastic chairs that had seen better days. Directly beneath him were palm trees and vinyl beach chairs stacked in small towers.

A warm breeze stirred his hair as he leaned over the railing and peered at the sailboats and catamarans in the bay. Under different circumstances he would have enjoyed a vacation here, although he didn't care much for the beach. Why hadn't he offered long ago to take Paula someplace like this? They could have spent uninterrupted time together away from work and nasty ex-spouses, and rejuvenated their love affair. Clearly their relationship needed a lift. It'd been ages since they'd gone away, and maybe that was another reason things had fallen apart.

The last time had been a weekend at Cape Cod over a year ago. They'd driven to Provincetown in a snowstorm. Maybe he'd been too much of a tightwad, what with his daughter's tuition bills and other financial hits.

Shoulda, woulda, coulda.

His cell phone rang, jolting him out of his reverie. He stepped back into the room to answer it.

"You can meet me in the hotel lounge," Kristen announced. "I was just about to order lunch."

She hung up before he had a chance to respond.

Kristen sat at a wrought-iron table in the outdoor terrace restaurant. She wore a light blue tank top and denim shorts, and her arms and slender legs were dotted with freckles. She sipped a frozen drink the color of plums and acknowledged his presence with a nod.

"How was your flight?" she asked.

"Uneventful, just the way I like it."

"Yesterday I sat next to this creepy old guy on the plane who said he was a Welsh architect from the Bahamas. He wouldn't leave me alone. By the time we got to Miami, he was inviting me to his beach house in Nassau." She made a face. "The perils of the single woman traveler."

"A lot of things can happen to a woman traveling by herself. That's what I'm afraid of," Louis said. "You still haven't heard anything from Paula? All I got was a voice mail yesterday saying she met somebody."

Kristen hesitated.

"Nothing. Her phone still goes right to voice mail."

"And you said all her luggage is gone."

"There's nothing in the room except for toiletries in the bathroom...her toothbrush and things like that. Makeup. Which seems odd if she was planning to spend some time with anyone," she said. "Women need that stuff. Hard to believe she could be in that much of a hurry."

"Or that she would run off with some stranger in the first place. She was supposed to spend time with you, right?"

"Well, sure," Kristen swirled her straw in the odd purple drink. "She didn't exactly invite me here though. I offered to come when I heard...you know, when I heard about what happened with the two of you." She frowned. "It's not like this is the first time Paula's ever gone on a vacation by herself. She likes her freedom. She's always been that way. When we were kids, she'd take off by herself on these long bike rides or she'd go fishing the entire day.

"She didn't care if she was alone. Last year she wanted to drive by herself from Miami to Key West—go to the Everglades and snorkel at Bahia Honda—but Bill gave her too much grief.

He gave her such a hard time, she finally decided not to go. In retrospect I don't blame him."

"Bill didn't want her to leave the house by herself," Louis said. "Wanting that much control over a person is sick."

"Yeah, well maybe he loved her so much he didn't want to let go of her," Kristen said, looking directly into Louis's eyes, her lips pressed tightly together. "He didn't want a divorce."

Louis sighed. He thought of several responses before verbalizing the simplest one.

"I know."

They sat quietly, each looking out at the water and the dozen sailboats that drifted by in procession. Louis was sweating and he adjusted the umbrella over their table to shield himself from the sun. Unlike Kristen, he hadn't been smart enough to wear shorts. He couldn't remember the last time he had subjected anyone but Paula to the sight of his pale legs. Come to think of it, he hadn't worn a bathing suit or gone swimming in years.

A waitress finally ambled to their table. She was a short, plump woman in her twenties whose name tag read "Lucy." Kristen ordered a roast beef sandwich and another guava berry colada, and Louis ordered a beer. While Lucy scribbled on her pad, Louis pulled Paula's photo from his pocket.

"Excuse me, miss," he said before she moved away. "This is my friend Paula who's staying at this hotel. Did you see her around here by any chance?"

The woman bent forward and her eyes crinkled at the edges as she studied the photo. She smirked.

"Oh yes, I saw her. She liked talking to Michael."

"Who's Michael?" Louis asked.

The young woman's expression changed, as if she worried she said something out of line.

"Oh, he's a bartender."

"Is he here now?" Kristen asked.

Louis glanced toward the bar.

Lucy looked at her wristwatch.

"He comes in at five o'clock."

She gave them another anxious glance before turning away.

"You better chill out," Kristen said. "You're making me nervous, and you'll make everyone else nervous. They won't want to talk to us."

Louis stared out at the lovely white sand and the gentle blue waves a hundred feet away. He felt queasy and the beginnings of a headache shot through his temples.

"I have a very bad feeling about this."

"Me too. But—"

"But what? What are you not telling me?"

She said nothing. Louis wanted to shake her.

"Did you find out who she's with? Is that what you don't want to say?"

Kristen looked at him with narrowed eyes.

"I don't know who she's with, okay?"

"But was she seeing anyone?" he persisted. "Before she came here?"

"What difference would that make?"

He couldn't help himself.

"So she was, then. Is it possible the guy met up with her here? Who is it?"

Kristen shrugged.

"Look, all I know is that she was trying some online dating thing. I don't know if she actually met anyone in person or not."

Louis studied her poker face, unable to tell if she was lying.

"Whether or not she was seeing anyone, taking off like this isn't like her. Do you agree?"

The message Paula had left on his voice mail popped into his head again.

Louis, just wanted to let you know I met someone here. I'm having fun...

"Yes."

"Then we should be reporting her as a missing person to the

police," he said. "I want to talk to the people in this hotel and the police in Philipsburg."

He pushed his chair back as if he planned to leap up and start that very second.

Kristen touched his hand.

"Hold on, hold on. Let me get my sandwich and I'll go with you. I haven't eaten all day."

Their waitress eventually returned to the table with a beer and Kristen's roast beef sandwich, a huge deli roll stuffed with meat, lettuce, and ripe, red tomato spilling out the sides. She picked up the sandwich and mayonnaise dripped onto her right hand and onto a gold ring with a large purple stone on her middle finger. She took a bite, put the sandwich back on the plate and wiped her hand, taking special care with the ring.

"My boyfriend gave this to me," she said. "It's an unusual stone. Lavender jade."

He glanced at her hand.

"Oh."

"I dumped Chris a long time ago." She smiled. "You remember Chris? The first man who roller-bladed up Mount Everest? Backwards?"

Her derisive laughter was more like a cough.

"Yes."

He didn't know what else to say. This was why talking to her was so difficult. This was why she disliked him—it wasn't entirely because of Bill or Paula, he was sure. It was because she'd spilled her guts to him in a dozen therapy sessions and revealed her vulnerabilities, her weaknesses, and her shame.

Kristen had terminated therapy a year before Louis met and started dating her sister, and in fact, he hadn't known right away that Paula was her sister. He hadn't violated ethical standards, but even so.

"His name is Eric," she went on, turning her hand this way and that, admiring her ring. "He's almost too good to be true. Smart, successful, gorgeous…and best of all, he adores me."

Louis had the impression it was important to her that she tell him this. That she finally had a man in her life who cared about her, who was good to her.

"I'm glad for you. You deserve it." He decided to confront the issue head-on. He leaned forward and said in a low voice, "Kristen, I'm sorry if it's awkward for you being my former patient. It feels strange to me too. I don't usually associate with any former patients."

She snorted.

"You think *that* bothers me? That was a long time ago. Besides, Paula knows I saw you professionally. I told her so myself."

"I suspect I'm an unpleasant reminder of a bad time in your life."

"Oh, please," Kristen said, rolling her eyes. "Skip the psychobabble. So what if you knew all about my dysfunctional relationships or my crummy sex life. I don't care about that anymore. It's all ancient history."

They both knew she was lying. Her face turned red. It was entirely possible, Louis thought, that despite her emotional rigidity in their sessions, she had shared more of her feelings with him than any other man in her life.

"Besides that," Kristen continued, "You didn't help me that much. You were the first and last shrink I'd ever see."

"Sorry you feel that way," Louis said, and he meant it.

She looked away.

"I don't want to talk about this anymore."

"All right."

Louis finished his beer while she ate the rest of her lunch. When she was finished, she wiped her lips with the white linen napkin on the table and reached for her purse.

"So where do we go first?"

CHAPTER FIVE

THE BEAUTIFULLY COIFFED young black woman at the oversized concierge desk looked up from her computer and smiled sweetly at Kristen and Louis.

Her dark lipstick, the color of ripe plums, perfectly matched her long polished nails and low-cut dress. Her light floral perfume reminded Louis of the rose gardens in West Hartford's Elizabeth Park.

"May I help you?"

"Yes, please," Kristen said.

She sat down in the brown wicker chair facing the desk and moved it closer, scraping along the tile floor. Louis followed suit in the second chair, which creaked under his weight.

"We have a few questions about the island, and we'd also like to rent a car," Louis said. "What do you have available?"

"Let me check." The woman's nails clicked on her keyboard. "We have Jeeps, larger sedans, and economy cars. Hyundais."

"An economy car would be fine," he said. "I'll need it for a couple of days."

"Is this your first time in St. Maarten?" the woman asked,

her full lips pursed.

Kristen nodded.

"Yes. This is such a lovely island. Are you from St. Maarten originally?"

The woman nodded. "I was born here...but I lived in London for ten years. Came back here a year ago."

Louis feigned interest as Kristen and Ms. Concierge made friendly small talk about London. While the woman printed out the necessary forms for the car rental, Kristen leaned forward.

"My sister is staying at this hotel too. Paula Spencer. She rented a car a few days ago when she checked in, right?"

The young woman tapped at her keyboard.

"Spencer? Yes, I see. Paula Spencer."

"Can you tell us what kind of car it was?" Louis asked, and felt Kristen nudge his foot.

He remembered what she'd said about making people nervous.

The woman was still looking at her screen.

"A Hyundai. Yes—she returned it on Friday? I see here...yes, she left the keys in the night slot Friday night."

Louis and Kristen looked at each other. Then as if on cue, Louis pulled out Paula's photo from his wallet.

"By any chance have you seen her around? She's about five-nine, hard to miss."

The young woman looked from Louis to the photograph and her smile faded.

"Is something wrong?"

"Yes," he said. "We're trying to find her. She was supposed to meet up with us yesterday but isn't answering her cell phone. We don't know where she is."

"I recognize her," the woman said. "But I don't remember seeing her lately."

"Was she alone? I mean, when you last saw her," Louis said.

Perhaps it was his tone of voice, or the fact that now he was tapping his fingers against her desk like he was sending Morse code. The woman hesitated.

"She was alone," she finally answered. "I hope she is all right."

"Me too," Kristen said. "Is there anything else you remember about her? Did she book any other trips through you?"

"No other trips." She glanced at Louis. "I don't know how else I can help you. She was alone but she seemed okay."

He didn't know whether to feel reassured or more worried. He signed the forms for the rental car and the woman spent a few hurried moments explaining the rental policies. She handed him the keys and a map of the island.

"The car is parked in the lot across the street."

"Do you remember if Paula asked you for directions to any specific places?" Louis asked the concierge, who seemed eager to finish up with them.

The woman paused.

"I don't think so. Just the closest beaches. I showed her where Maho Bay and Cupecoy are." She pointed to different locations on the map spread across her desk, tapping her long nails on the landmarks.

"By the way, where's the police station?"

"Downtown. Across from the government administration building. You go left on Peterson Street. It's a few minutes from here."

"Thanks for your help," Louis told the woman. "If you think of anything else, please call me. I'm in Room 391."

He stood up stiffly. His back ached.

Kristen nudged him as they walked out of the lobby.

"You sound like a cop, and I'm not sure that's a good thing. Do you watch a lot of police shows or something?"

"No. I read a lot," Louis replied. "The true crime stuff—like Ann Rule. By the way, how many times have you been to London? You talked to that girl like you'd been there a hundred times."

Kristen smiled.

"Never. I read a lot too."

They were outside now, and he squinted in the sunlight. Once again he wished he'd had the sense to wear shorts.

"You know what Paula told me once?" Louis said.

"What?"

"She told me that ever since she was little, she had dreams she would be murdered some day. She was absolutely convinced that that was how she was going to die."

Kristen stopped. She stared at him, her mouth twisted as though she'd just swallowed a jalapeno.

"That's a horrible thing to say. Why are you telling me that?"

"I don't know. Maybe because I'm afraid she's taking too many chances. This online dating crap for example," he said, waving his hand in the air. "Or if she met someone here that she doesn't know from Adam and then went off with him."

"But she did text me," Kristen said. "And she's an adult, not a teenager who ran away from home or something."

"That was yesterday and you haven't heard from her since. Right? By the way, I want to see that text."

Kristen pulled out her cell phone and scrolled through several screens.

"Here."

He read the message.

K—Met someone interesting I'm hanging out with, see u soon. Don't wait up, LOL.

There was a smiley face emoticon after the message.

Louis took a deep breath and handed the phone back to her.

"When's the last time the two of you spoke?"

"Thursday morning sometime. When I told her I could fly out on Saturday so we could spend some time together. I thought she could use the company."

"And she never said anything then that she met some guy?"

"No," Kristen snapped. "I told you this already. And why

were you asking where the police station is? Aren't we going to give it a little more time before we actually file a missing persons report?"

"Nope. As far as I'm concerned, she is a missing person. The sooner we let the police know, the better. What's your problem, anyway?"

So much for using his professional skills to draw her out. So much for being calm and patient.

"*My* problem? Really? *My* problem?" She looked at him as if he had just confessed he was a pedophile. "Seems like you're the one with the problem. Can't keep your pants zipped..."

She turned on her heel and crossed the street to the car rental parking lot. She didn't look back.

Louis stared at her, furious beyond words. He watched her stand by the rental cars, her hands on her hips as though she were waiting for a recalcitrant child. He didn't need her. All he had to do was leave without her. Ignore her, get in the car and go. And that would be the end of their unlikely, fragile alliance.

It was tempting. He watched her pause at the row of small, silver dented Hyundais past their prime. From a sideways angle she looked no older than a kid and as vulnerable. A petulant teenager with wispy strawberry hair. Physically, she and Paula were nothing alike.

He sighed. It didn't seem right to let her fend for herself, no matter if she was being a royal pain in the neck. She was Paula's sister after all. Paula wouldn't want him to abandon her. He crossed the street to the parking lot and found his rental car, which rivaled the others for Wreck of the Month. When he opened the dented passenger door, she finally turned and looked his way.

"I'm going to the police station first. You can come along for the ride," he said, and gestured at the open door. "Or go back to the beach and drink your damn guava berry coladas or whatever the hell they are. I don't care."

Just like a freakin' teenager, he noted, she rolled her eyes and got into the car without a word.

The police station in downtown Philipsburg was easy to find. They explained to an officer at the front desk why they were there, and were promptly escorted to a sparsely-furnished, air-conditioned conference room.

"Sergeant Durand will be with you in a moment," the officer said.

He left the room and they barely had time to get settled in the high-backed plastic chairs before a uniformed man carrying a notepad entered the doorway. He was trim and powerful-looking, and his white, short-sleeved shirt revealed arms as wide around as Louis's thighs. Louis and Kristen stood up and made their introductions.

"I understand you're here to report a missing person," the sergeant said, motioning them to sit. He was soft-spoken, but Louis guessed that very little escaped his thoughtful gaze. He began writing in his notebook as soon as Louis explained their concerns.

"So you're saying Ms. Spencer is possibly a missing person because neither of you has heard from her since yesterday?" the sergeant asked, studying the photo Louis handed to him. "And what is her age?" He glanced up.

"Thirty-five," Louis said.

"She's my sister. Her luggage is gone from the room we're sharing," Kristen said. "We've both tried calling her many times on her cell phone, but all we get is voice mail."

"Can you describe your last communication with her?" the officer asked, looking first at Louis.

"She left me a voice mail on Friday," Louis said. "Since then she hasn't called me or returned my calls."

"I was expecting her to pick me up at the airport when I got here yesterday," Kristen said. "But she didn't show up, and since then I've only gotten one text from her on my cell phone saying that she was hanging out with some guy. The point is, this isn't like her."

"And do you know who this guy might be, this person she said she was 'hanging out with'?"

"A waitress at the hotel said Paula was talking with a bartender there. Someone named Michael," Louis said. "He's supposedly working tonight."

Sergeant Durand wrote something on his notepad.

"And what is your relationship with Ms. Spencer?"

He looked away from the officer's stare. The walls of the conference room were off-white, clean but bare.

"I'm her—I'm a friend."

"Why was she traveling alone?"

"She needed a vacation," Kristen said. "And we planned for me to join her yesterday, as I said."

"And you too?" Sergeant Durand asked Louis. "Ms. Spencer knew you were coming?"

"Not exactly," Louis said.

He'd deliberately left out much of the back story. No need to get into that level of detail, at least not yet.

Kristen explained that she'd been worried enough to call Louis, and he'd been concerned enough to fly out the next day. Louis could practically read the cop's mind.

He thinks I'm a jealous boyfriend.

Sergeant Durand asked a few more questions related to Paula's possible state of mind, but Louis had the distinct impression that little or nothing would be done. There simply wasn't evidence of foul play or abduction. Paula was an adult, free to talk to a bartender or come and go as she pleased, whenever and with whomever.

"Can you check her credit card charges?" Louis asked as the sergeant closed his notepad. "At least we'd know if she's still on the island somewhere."

"Usually the credit card companies won't provide that information without a subpoena. Unless the person's at risk." He looked at Kristen. "You're a relative—you can give permission and sometimes they'll do it. Not likely in this case, but you can try."

"I don't even know what cards she has," Kristen said.

"We'll find out," Louis said and looked at the officer. "Are you basically saying you can't conduct an official investigation?"

"We'll file your report," the sergeant replied. "We'll notify Customs and police on the French side of the island as well. But at this point, there's no reason to believe Ms. Spencer is in danger. Or a missing person per se." His tone was not unsympathetic, but Louis saw a cool detachment in the man's brown eyes. He'd bet his plane ticket that Sergeant Durand thought Paula was off screwing around with someone she'd met on the island, and would turn up eventually. After the lovin'.

The interview was clearly over.

"Thank you for your time, Sergeant Durand," Kristen said as they got up to leave. "Hopefully my sister's all right."

"What happens if we find some proof that Paula was abducted?" Louis asked. "Or let's say we still don't hear from her tomorrow or the day after. What do you do then? When exactly would you consider her a missing person?"

"It depends." Sergeant Durand's tone was calm, professional. "But when crimes occur in this jurisdiction, I'm one of the investigating officers." He led them down the narrow hallway to the exit. "If it helps, we've had very few incidents, very few crimes against tourists on St. Maarten. Very few. Petty theft, mostly. Almost always, when someone is reported missing, they turn up safe and sound. Especially an adult."

Louis and Kristen left the police station and walked past the pastel-colored clapboard buildings and storefronts back to the rental car.

"We still have a couple hours of daylight left," Louis said. "Let's take a ride to one of the beaches Paula might have gone to."

"Okay, but what do we do when we get there?" Kristen

asked. "Ask people sitting on their beach towels if they ever saw her? And then what?"

Louis had asked himself the same question. What did he hope to accomplish next? He'd been disappointed, but not surprised, by the police interview. "It seems important to check out the places she might have been."

"The police aren't going to do much," Kristen said. "Isn't there an American embassy or consulate we could contact?"

"I already checked on that. The United States doesn't have a consulate in St. Maarten—the closest one is in Curacao for the Dutch side and Barbados for the French side. I don't think we'd get any further with the officials there. At least, not right now."

"You're probably right," she said. "Well, if you want to drive to a beach, I'm game. Which one?" She pointed to different locations on the map. "There's Maho Beach near the airport, Little Bay Beach, Simpson Bay, Mullet Bay, Pelican Key, and Cupecoy…and that's just the Dutch side of the island."

"I don't know," Louis said. His head hurt, his back hurt, and the Hyundai was like a toaster oven. The sweat dripped down his face as he started the car.

"The concierge woman said she gave Paula directions to what—Maho Bay and Cupecoy? Let's start there."

"Maho is closer. I'll navigate," she said.

Maho Beach, located at the end of the Juliana Airport runway, was a narrow, sandy stretch with perfect turquoise-clear water. Still, Louis doubted that this beach was one that Paula would have liked much—it was too close to the airport and the frequent roar of incoming jets was anything but relaxing. He parked the car nearby and they stood on an outcropping in the shade of palm trees and surveyed the lay of the land. There were a few sunbathing couples and a family or two, but this beach was certainly uncrowded.

"I don't get the feeling Paula would have liked it here," he said.

67

"I was thinking the same thing," Kristen said, shading her eyes. "Makes me want to go swimming though. It's hot."

"No kidding."

Kristen walked towards the frothy waves and waded in up to her knees. She bent down and splashed water on her arms and face. Louis stood silently and scanned the shore. It would be intrusive and probably fruitless to approach and question the few people on the beach.

He went over his mental checklist: he needed to talk to the night manager at Sun Bay, the bartender Michael, contact the credit card company, maybe talk to some storeowners and restaurant managers downtown. There was a lot to do.

Kristen was still standing in the water. The waves had soaked her shorts.

"Let's get going," he said, looking at his watch. "I want to talk to the night manager at the hotel."

"Okay." She waded ashore, her light blue tank top clinging to her slim torso.

She brushed the sand off her feet and pulled her sandals on.

"Why don't we take a quick ride to Cupecoy before we head back to the hotel?" Kristen suggested when they were in the car.

Louis fiddled with the air conditioning, trying to coax a little cold air out of the uncooperative Hyundai.

"It's not far. Maybe there's a snack bar or a souvenir stand and someone working there saw Paula," she added.

"All right."

Louis gave up on the air conditioning and rolled down the window. Goddamn "economy" car.

"Kristen, I want to ask you a question without starting an argument," he said in his calmest professional voice. "Do you think it's possible that Paula did, in fact, meet someone she's so enamored with, she doesn't care if she's left you alone? Like maybe she never wanted you here anyway? You said you invited yourself."

Kristen looked out the window intently, as though a spacecraft had landed in the road in front of them.

He waited. She finally turned her head, and her long sigh sounded like a tire going flat.

"The longer she's gone, the more I think something bad happened," Kristen finally answered. He could practically hear her guard going up like a shade. "And that, Dr. D'Maio, is all I have to say."

The first thing Louis noticed when they arrived at Cupecoy were the naked people sprawled out on the beach as if they hadn't a care in the world.

"Jesus Christ," he muttered. They had just rounded a sandstone cliff adjacent to the parking lot. "I'm really overdressed."

Kristen stopped. "I don't see any snack stands, do you?"

"Nope."

She snorted.

"Guess we can cross this beach off our list."

"Guess so."

Louis couldn't help but cast a final glance at the scenery before they turned away. A slender, twenty-something woman with luxurious red hair strolled by holding the hand of a short, balding man at least fifty pounds overweight and twice her age. Both were buck naked.

Kristen looked too. "He's got money."

Louis smiled.

And Viagra.

Kristen fiddled with the large jade ring on her finger, twisting it on and off during the ride back to the Sun Bay Resort. Louis noticed her uneasiness but said nothing.

"So I guess it's easy for you to take time off from work, being in a private practice," she commented, when she couldn't find anything interesting to listen to on the car radio.

"I rescheduled my patients," Louis said. "What about you? You're able to take off when you want to?"

"My assistant director is in charge while I'm gone," Kristen said. "We finished our quarterly reports for the state, so it was a good time to get away for a few days."

"So what does your new boyfriend do?" Louis asked after another long silence.

She shifted in her seat.

"Eric's a sales engineer. He sells metal alloys to manufacturing companies on the east coast and in Canada."

"So he travels a lot?"

"He's usually gone a few days at a time. Some days he only works from home." She looked at her watch. "In fact, I need to call him pretty soon. He's supposed to come back from Miami today."

"How did you meet him?" Louis asked, just to make conversation.

"Online. Isn't that how everyone meets these days?"

He didn't respond. Kristen was quiet until they pulled into the parking lot of the Sun Bay Resort.

"So what are you going to do next?"

"Talk with the bartender and the night manager first."

"Do you want me to come?" she asked.

"If you want to."

"First I'm going to make a phone call from my room and change my clothes," she said.

They walked toward the entrance of the hotel.

They had just stepped into the lobby when Kristen uttered a startled "Oh."

Louis turned and saw a tall, brown-haired man approach them from the elevators.

"Eric." Kristen rushed toward the man and embraced him. "What on earth are you doing here?"

"I wanted to surprise you. I got a direct flight out of Miami this afternoon." He looked past her to Louis. "This must be your sister's friend?"

Louis extended his hand.

"Louis D'Maio."

So this was Mr. Too-Good-To-Be-True. He looked to be about Kristen's age, mid-thirties or so.

"Eric Welch." He drew Kristen close to him, draping his arm around her shoulders and nuzzled her hair. "I tried calling your cell when I got here."

"We were on the road. Maybe I didn't have service." She pulled out her cell phone from her purse, glanced at it and put it back. "I never heard it ring, I guess. Anyway, we went to the police station and then checked out a couple beaches we thought Paula might have gone to. If I'd known you were here…"

"So what did you find out?" the man asked, his voice growing deeper.

He stepped closer, drawing up to his full height. He was slim but athletic-looking, his short sleeves revealing biceps tanned and cut. For a beat Louis felt the man's eyes on him, sizing him up.

"Nothing helpful," Kristen said. "The police said they couldn't start an official investigation." She squeezed Eric's arm. "I can't believe you came here. That's so sweet of you."

"I have to get going," Louis interrupted. "I have things to do."

"We'll catch up with you later, Louis," Kristen said.

Louis waited for the elevator while the two of them walked down the hallway, arm in arm.

CHAPTER SIX

ERIC LED KRISTEN to the stairwell.

"I have a room on the second floor," he said.

As soon as they reached his room and the door closed behind them, he pressed her back against the wall and kissed her as though he hadn't seen her in weeks. After a second's hesitation she responded in kind, flattered that he seemed to find her so irresistible.

"I missed you," he said in a low voice, his lips tracing a path down her neck, pausing at the gold hoop earring in her right ear. "I couldn't stop thinking about you when I was gone."

Kristen shivered as his hands slid down her sides, resting at her waist as though he meant to pick her up. He easily could have if he wanted to; he was a foot taller than she was and strong, the type of man who could protect her.

She looked up into his narrowed brown eyes and felt a rush of excitement that he was actually here, that he had flown to St. Maarten to surprise her. Their relationship was still new and blossoming, filled with uncertainties and things to discover. She'd been trying to take it slow, let things unfold without rushing and enjoy the attention. God knew the last thing she needed was to get involved again with a man like Chris, who'd been incapable of demonstrating affection or sustaining a real relationship.

She hadn't even slept with Eric yet, letting the anticipation build over the past few weeks. From what she'd seen so far he was a gentleman, a man who believed in old-fashioned courtesies. He was patient and didn't push her for sex, a rarity among the men she'd dated since the break-up with Chris.

Best of all, he seemed to be falling for her more and more, and he wasn't afraid to show it. He'd even told her before he left for Miami that he wanted to take her to Montreal with him on his next business trip.

"I missed you too," she said, and touched his cheek.

They looked at each other for a long moment, and she inhaled his cologne, feeling her heart pound. He reached forward and gently eased one strap of her tank top down over her shoulder, never taking his eyes off hers. His fingers barely grazed the curve of her breast and slowly, ever so slowly, he touched her warm flesh, his thumb circling her nipple.

She sighed and closed her eyes, barely able to breathe, as he undressed her.

Louis spent the next half hour in his room checking his home and work messages, and then contacted the two hospitals on the French and Dutch sides of the island. There was no patient matching Paula's description at either facility.

Promptly at five o'clock, he made his way to the pool terrace. A low beat of reggae music filled the still, humid air. Many of the lounge chairs circling the sparkling pool were vacant, and he sat at the bar and ordered vodka straight up from the good-looking young black man whose name tag read "Michael." Louis guessed that he was in his mid to late twenties.

Way too young for Paula.

"Would you like anything else, sir?" the man asked in a

thick, lilting accent.

Louis forced a casual smile.

"No, I don't think so. So how's business? Seems a little slow here tonight."

"It's still early," the man replied. "We have a barbecue later. There will be more people here for dinner. Would you like to make a reservation for tonight?"

"No, thank you," Louis said.

The man turned away to pour his drink and Louis took out his wallet and fished out his photo of Paula. He laid it on the bar and when Michael returned with his glass of vodka, he held the picture up.

"Do you remember this woman?" he asked, watching the man's face closely.

There was an instant flash of recognition in the young man's chocolate brown eyes.

He was polite, but there was no doubt the question caught him by surprise.

"Why do you ask, sir?"

Louis took advantage of the fact there was no one else sitting nearby to overhear their conversation.

"This woman—her name is Paula—is my girlfriend. She was supposed to meet her sister here yesterday but no one's heard from her and we don't know where she is. Someone in the hotel said she liked talking with you."

The young man licked his lips and cleared his throat.

"She came to the bar, yes."

"And talked with you? About anything in particular?"

He shrugged.

"Small talk. I talk to all the customers."

"Did you ever see her with anyone?"

"No, sir," the man said again, and his eyes darted toward the few people in the pool area, as though he hoped someone would summon him and provide him with a graceful exit.

Louis watched his body language, noting how uncomfortable

he seemed. He wouldn't look Louis in the eye, and he batted at the side of his face at some invisible bug.

"I'm just trying to find out if she's okay," Louis said, not unkindly. "I've spoken to a lot of people in the hotel." He paused, thinking about how to word his next question. "Did she spend time with you—hang out with you—when you weren't working?"

Again the young man avoided his gaze.

"No, no, no. She never did."

Louis had learned long ago to trust his instincts, no matter how disturbing. He threw out a curve ball.

"She never did—but you asked her to, didn't you? She's an attractive woman."

The young man rocked on the soles of his feet, turning his head away from Louis completely.

Bingo.

He didn't respond, and Louis nodded.

"You didn't know much about her, I'll bet. She was here by herself. You didn't know she had someone back home."

"I ask her to go out dancing one night after work," he fumbled. "She never say she have a boyfriend. I didn't know."

"And what happened?"

"She never show up," Michael said, finally looking at Louis. "I never saw her again."

"Do you remember what day that was?"

The man considered. "Couple days ago. Thursday, when I was working. Yes, Thursday."

Louis wasn't sure if he should feel relieved or not. He believed the young man. Of course Paula had rejected his advances. What would she see in this bartender ten years her junior? But it still didn't answer the question of where she was.

"Do you have any idea of where she might have gone?"

Michael shook his head.

"She said she wanted to go to Anguilla or St. Bart to snorkel sometime. But I don't know. We only talk a couple times, when she came to have her wine."

"And you're sure you never saw her with anyone?"

"No. I never saw her with anyone," he said. "I need to go back to work now, sir."

"If you think of anything else, will you contact me? I'm staying here at the hotel." Louis took out a business card and wrote his cell phone and room number on the back. "Will you do that? I'm really worried about her."

"Sure," Michael put the card in his pocket. He hesitated. "I hope she's okay. She's a nice lady."

Louis took a long swallow of his drink. "Yes, she is."

After he left the bar, Louis walked to the front desk and asked to speak to the manager. The same clerk he had questioned earlier that afternoon disappeared into an office and in a moment, a thin man dressed in black pants and a crisp white shirt came to the desk. He had no name tag.

"How can I help you, sir?"

The young clerk hovered nearby while Louis repeated his story to the manager and showed him Paula's photo. The man listened without interruption, frowning when Louis emphasized that Paula was a missing person. Still, it took some convincing before he printed out her room charges. Only when Louis assured him he would look at the print-out right then and return it immediately did the man finally agree.

Louis reviewed Paula's bill. Other than breakfast and lunch, she hadn't charged anything to her room. He noticed the hefty bar tab and inwardly winced at the image of the young bartender asking her out. Did she find it amusing? Flattering? Did she really flirt with him? If she did, was it because she was lonely? There were no bar or food charges to her room after Thursday.

"What did she use, her MasterCard?" Louis asked, taking a guess. Only the last four digits were listed on the bill.

The manager, a wide-faced man with worried eyes, glanced at his computer screen.

"Visa," he finally said.

"Can I please have the full number of the card?" Louis asked. "It's so I can check with the credit card company about any charges she may have incurred elsewhere on the island."

The man shook his head.

"I cannot do that, I'm sorry. You will have to work with the police. I cannot give out more information."

Louis hadn't expected he would, but it was worth a shot. He could tell the manager's patience was wearing thin.

"Is there anything else you can tell me that might help me find her?"

"I don't know, sir."

"Thanks," Louis said. There was nothing else he could learn from this exchange. "I appreciate your time."

The man nodded.

"You're welcome. I hope you find her soon."

Louis hit nothing but more dead ends later on in downtown Philipsburg, buzzing with activity. After a dozen fruitless inquiries at various jewelry stores and gift shops hawking Dutch linens and Delftware, he realized that Paula probably made no more of an impression than the other hundreds of tourists and cruise ship passengers who strolled down these narrow streets and mobbed the stores. He crossed a side street and spotted a woman walking several blocks away who looked like Paula. Heart thudding, he rushed across the road and nearly caught up with her as she entered an ice cream shop.

Immediately he realized his mistake. Up close, the blonde woman had a similar build and hair style, but that was all. He turned and left the store, his mood sinking like a stone tossed into the ocean.

This was all his fault. He should have told Charlotte from the get-go that he didn't—couldn't—keep secrets from Paula. He'd felt guilty about the whole thing and paradoxically, the more upset he was with himself, the more distant he'd become with Paula. She hadn't failed to notice. He would never forget the hurt and pain he saw in her eyes when she'd learned he'd seen Charlotte. Trust was like deposits one made at a bank...no matter how many deposits, one big fat withdrawal like this had depleted almost everything. Given how shaky things had become and with both of them dealing with other stresses, it was no wonder she thought he was having an affair.

Just one more chance.

All he wanted was another chance to show Paula he loved her. That he wouldn't take her for granted. The terrible possibility was dawning on him that maybe she really didn't want to see him again, that she was moving on with her life. If that were the case, he wanted to hear it from her directly, no matter how difficult it would be to accept.

His thoughts meandered back and forth between the possible explanations of where she was right now. For all he knew, she could be snorkeling on another island while he wandered the streets of Philipsburg. If she'd gone off to St. Bart's or Anguilla, as the bartender Michael had mentioned, where would he even begin to look for her? He knew nothing about those islands. What if her voice mail message stating she had met someone else was true?

There was still the possibility that she'd been abducted by someone, like the young girl who'd gone missing in Aruba years ago. If so, was the bartender involved or did he know more than he'd let on? Maybe one night he'd convinced Paula to see him after his shift. Maybe they'd gone out for a walk on the beach at night and he'd attacked her in some remote area. Louis wondered if he could persuade Sergeant Durand to question the man. Unlikely.

He gave up on the gift shops and with the help of a guide book, eventually found the fancy restaurants that the woman on the plane had mentioned, Le Bec Fine, Antoine's, and Petite Pier. The manager at Le Bec Fine studied Paula's photo and shook his head. Ditto for Antoine's. The manager at Petite Pier, a tall, silver-haired man with piercing blue eyes, gave the photo a cursory glance and said in a clipped British accent he thought he'd seen Paula come in a few days earlier. Yes, she was by herself, and no, there was nothing unusual he'd noted, although it wasn't often that a single woman sat down to an expensive dinner in his restaurant.

"I remember she was reading a book," he told Louis, and then said he was sorry, there was nothing else he could think of that might be of assistance.

Louis left Petite Pier. The delicious smells wafting from the kitchen had reminded him he hadn't eaten since the slice of pizza in the airport, and his stomach was growling. He found a food stand that sold sandwiches, and he ate a cold turkey club at a small table outdoors as dusk fell. He watched the tourists stroll by, tanned young couples holding hands, seniors laden with shopping bags, families speaking languages he couldn't easily identify. He felt suddenly weary, spent, physically tired from getting up before dawn, and mentally tired from the events of the day.

When he finished his sandwich, he made his way back to Front Street. The steady hum of crickets filled the air. He found where he'd parked his dented rental Hyundai, got in, and started up the car. There was nothing more he could accomplish today. Nor did he expect he would get any help from Kristen, now that her boyfriend had suddenly appeared on the scene. He wouldn't be surprised if the guy was more concerned with getting laid than with searching for Paula.

There was nothing to do but go back to the hotel, get a good night's sleep, and come up with a new plan in the morning.

Eric had called room service to order dinner after they'd finished making love a second time. And now a tray filled with dirty dishes, an empty bottle of champagne, and two wine glasses stood on the dresser. He and Kristen lay in bed watching American television and she lazily draped her arm across his chest. She felt sated, and warm and mellow from the champagne.

"It's not late...do you want to get dressed and go take a walk on the beach or something?" she asked.

They hadn't left the room all evening. Much as she enjoyed making love with Eric for the first time, it would have been fun to go out to dinner and watch the sunset. But Eric had had other ideas.

"We can do that tomorrow," he said, grasping her hand in his own. "You don't have any plans with what's-his-name, do you?"

He seemed distracted, maybe tired, she thought.

"Louis? No. He'll probably keep looking for my sister."

"Why do you think he came here, anyway?" Eric asked. "He must know she's with someone else."

"I'm not a hundred percent sure of that," Kristen said. "I'm worried, but I don't know what to think."

"I know what I think," Eric nuzzled against her cheek. "It's a good thing I came here. Otherwise you'd have to chase the men away with a stick. A beautiful woman like you shouldn't be going off to an island by herself. It isn't safe."

His tone was light, but she detected a note of—jealousy, perhaps? She was amused. She couldn't remember when any man had cared enough about her to demonstrate the slightest hint of possessiveness.

"You're silly," she said, and kissed his forehead.

He smiled, but his eyes were somber.

"I looked Louis D'Maio up on the Internet," he said. "Did you know that he was accused of making advances toward one of his clients a couple years ago? Some rich woman named Victoria Rudemann. The story was in the newspaper."

"I remember reading about that. I thought he was cleared of any charges." She squirmed in the soft bed. That was something she decided Eric would never need to know...that for a brief time Louis had been her therapist.

"He's still bad news. Your sister's better off without him."
Eric lightly stroked her hair, shifting his position to face her. "I
don't know Paula—not yet, that is—but from what you've said
about her, I think the most logical thing to assume is that she
met someone exciting and she'll be back any time. You didn't
have cell phone service when you were out today, and maybe
she doesn't either, so that's why you didn't hear from her." He
pulled Kristen close to him. "But if you want to spend time
tomorrow looking for her, that's fine. I'll help you in any way I
can. You can rely on me."

His voice was calm and reassuring.

Kristen snuggled against him, feeling the warmth of his skin.

"I hope you're right. I have a feeling she'll turn up
tomorrow."

"And I'll finally get to meet her," Eric said.

"You don't think anything bad has happened to her, do you?"

"Of course not."

"I should go back to our room in case she turns up tonight,"
Kristen yawned. "Otherwise she'll think I'm the one who
disappeared."

Eric held her close.

"Stay with me. Text her and tell her you're with me and
you're safe and sound. Go ahead…call your room too and leave
her a message."

She did. After she hung up the phone, she closed her eyes
and sighed.

"I'm going to take a shower and settle in then. You really
wore me out, mister."

"You ain't seen nothing yet," he teased. "I've always wanted
to spend a romantic vacation on a Caribbean island."

"Me too."

"With someone special," he added. "Someone who really
means a lot to me."

Kristen felt her face flush. She didn't know what to say.

"You don't have to say anything," he said, as if he'd read her mind. "Now go take a shower, will ya?"

She smiled and got out of bed, suddenly self-conscious about being naked. She looked at the pile of their clothes on the floor. "I'll need to get something to wear for tomorrow."

He got up and offered her a light cotton robe from his suitcase.

"Here you go, you're all set for now." He pulled on his pants. "While you're busy I'll go get some soda and ice. Do you want anything?"

"No thanks."

He kissed her.

"Maybe I'll see you in the shower? Help you wash your hair or something?"

She swatted him with the long tie of his robe.

"In your dreams."

Kristen took a long, hot shower and emerged in Eric's robe from the steamy bathroom. She towel-dried her hair in front of the bedroom mirror, watching him. He was stretched out under the sheets, the TV remote in one hand and eyes half-closed.

"I think your phone was beeping," he said.

Kristen took her cell phone out of her purse.

"Oh thank God. It's a text from my sister. I was starting to wonder."

Eric opened his eyes.

"So?"

"She says she's very sorry she didn't get in touch with me sooner." Kristen scanned the message. "She didn't have cell service. She's been on her new friend's private yacht all day and they decided to sail to St. Bart's. She won't be back until tomorrow night."

"Well, well," Eric said. "What did I tell you? And a private yacht to St. Bart's no less."

"Oh, and she says she got my message and she's glad you're with me. She looks forward to meeting you." Kristen shook her head. "I guess she really didn't need me here, huh? I should tell her to take her time coming back." She looked at Eric and frowned. "What should I say to Louis? I feel stupid now that I called him in the first place."

"The truth is always best. If I were in his position, I would want to know."

"This sucks," she said, looking down at her phone. "I mean, I'm glad that Paula's having fun and all. But Louis came all the way over here because of me. I know he deserves it, but I feel kind of bad for him."

"What do you mean, he deserves it?"

"It's a long story," Kristen said. "I don't want to bore you."

"You won't bore me. What happened?"

She sighed and moved toward the bathroom to hang up the towel.

"My sister broke up with him because she thought he was unfaithful."

"Good enough reason."

"When should I let him know? Should I call him right now?"

She thought about Louis' anxiety and his insistence that Paula was a missing person.

"Go ahead. Might as well get it over with."

Kristen picked up her cell phone.

"He's going to be very disappointed."

She punched in Louis' cell phone number. He picked up on the first ring and she told him about Paula's text. There was a long silence and Louis asked if she knew who the guy was.

"I don't know," she said. "I'm guessing I'll be meeting him tomorrow. But I have to go, Louis. I'm sorry you flew out here for nothing."

She put the phone back in her purse and looked at Eric.

"He didn't sound too happy. I knew he wouldn't take it well."

Eric turned off the television.

"Come here," he said.

She moved toward the bed and let the robe drop from her shoulders and fall at her feet.

Alone in his hotel room, Louis sat on the bed and stared at his cell phone. The lack of information was maddening. Kristen had just told him that Paula was sailing to St. Bart's on some guy's private yacht, but their brief conversation had left him with more questions than answers.

Or maybe I don't want the answers, he thought.

He was tempted to call Kristen back and ask her to read him Paula's text word for word. He wanted to hear something—anything—that would indicate this was an elaborate ruse Paula had concocted to make him suffer, make him sorry he'd seen Charlotte. Goddamn it. He knew his thoughts were irrational and sprang from jealousy.

Would he really *prefer* that she'd been kidnapped?

Of course not, of course not.

But now he wouldn't have the chance to clear things up and make a new start with her.

Sailing to St. Bart's on a private yacht.

Who the hell was this guy and how could he compete with that?

He felt like a fool. He'd gone to the police station, made a fuss with the hotel manager and the bartender, called hospitals, searched for Paula on the streets of Philipsburg, and for what? His last-minute trip here had been a huge financial strain, another credit card bill that would take months to pay off.

There was no point staying. The last thing he wanted was for Paula to see him at the hotel when she showed up with Lover Boy in tow.

Talk about humiliating.

He thought for a moment about how satisfying it would be to deck the guy though. Take out his anger and frustration.

Like being a caveman would get her back.

He pictured her in the arms of another man and there was a

part of him that wanted to weep, another part that wanted to put his fist through the wall.

He put on his glasses and picked up his phone to search for the next flight home.

CHAPTER SEVEN

Two DaysLlater, Wednesday

KRISTEN WAS NEAR tears. She picked at her plate of scrambled eggs and finally put her fork back on the table. Eric had already finished his breakfast and was looking at his tablet. They sat in the outdoor restaurant of the hotel yards from the beach. Gentle waves lapped at the shore.

They hadn't heard from Paula at all, not Monday night when she was supposed to return from her sailing trip, and not yesterday. Kristen didn't know how many times she'd tried to call and text her sister to no avail. She had no idea who the man was Paula had met up with, and who knew where he'd taken her?

On top of that, Eric had gotten a call last night from the nursing home where his elderly father lived. The poor man, who suffered from dementia, had fallen and broken his hip. He was hospitalized and not doing well. Eric was his only son and there were no other family members who could help. The spotty cell phone service made communicating with the doctors difficult.

"They've put it up on their Facebook page already," Eric said, and he handed the tablet over to her so she could see it.

The photo of Paula on the Police Force Facebook timeline was not a recent one, but it was the only photo Kristen could find in her iPhone to give to Sergeant Durand. She scanned the brief copy:

Police Ask for Information on Missing Person

The Police Department is asking for the public's help to locate a 35-year-old American woman by the name of Paula Spencer, who has been reported missing by a family member. According to her sister, Paula Spencer arrived on St. Maarten on Tuesday, June 24 and was last heard from on Monday, July 1 in which she said she was sailing on a private yacht to St. Bart with a male companion whose identity is unknown. Repeated attempts to get in contact with Paula Spencer have been unsuccessful. Anyone with information concerning her whereabouts or who have seen her can get in contact with the Police Department at...

"They said they would alert the media too, right?" Kristen asked and handed the tablet back to him.

"Yes, the local paper and probably the news stations," Eric said. "Maybe today or tomorrow."

"I don't want to leave," she said, staring out at the water. "Maybe I should cancel my flight and check with the marinas again. Or take a boat to St. Bart's and start looking there."

Eric took her hand.

"Hon, we've talked about this already. Let the police do their job." His voice was gentle but firm. "I know this waiting is terrible. But I have to go home and I simply won't let you stay here by yourself. If we need to come back later, we will. But we have to leave today."

Kristen understood Eric had to go home and he was right: they weren't equipped to conduct a full-scale search for Paula. But it didn't make leaving any easier. They had spent a tense and fruitless day yesterday asking around at various marinas about yachts sailing to St. Bart's and if anyone had seen Paula. At least the St. Maarten police seemed to take her disappearance more seriously. Kristen could thank Eric for that. He'd persuaded Sergeant Durand to do more than file a report.

"When do we have to call a cab to the airport?" she asked.

She was having a hard time focusing on mundane details.

Eric looked at his watch.

"Soon. I'll go down to the front desk and check us both out. I'll have them call the cab too."

She nodded. He'd arranged their flights, had done everything that needed doing.

He got up and she watched him walk past the pool, its clear water sparkling in the sunlight. It was still too early for the usual pool crowd, she guessed. Most people were still sleeping or making morning love. The lucky ones, she thought and licked her chapped lips. Her throat felt dry and tight and she finished her cup of coffee. She picked up her phone and composed a brief message to Louis that Paula was still AWOL. Although he'd flown home yesterday morning, he'd asked her to keep him posted. He wanted to know Paula was safe, even if she was with another man.

Kristen sighed. She clicked "send" and sat back and waited for Eric.

Frank Roth had stopped in at Louis's condo on Wednesday night. The two of them sat at Louis's small kitchen table.

"It's not sounding good, buddy," Frank said. "You're saying you never got hold of Paula even once in St. Maarten?"

Louis shook his head.

"I can't tell you how many times I called her cell phone. She never picked up, and then Kristen told me on Sunday that Paula sent her a text saying she was off sailing on a private yacht to St. Bart's. That was the last time she heard anything. Paula's still missing but at least the police are taking it more seriously. But not the police here. I went down to the station when I got back and filed a missing person report, but they didn't seem too concerned."

"So what's your theory on what happened?"

Louis put his phone onto speaker and punched in the codes to access his voice mail.

"Listen to this."

Louis, just wanted to let you know I met someone here. I'm having fun. Maybe we'll talk when I get back next week. Beady nine.

Frank shrugged.

"You don't think it's legit?"

"That was the last message I got from Paula before I left."

"What's beady nine?"

"I don't know," Louis said. "The thing is, did she leave this message for me at work because she knew it would go right into my voice mail? I wonder if someone made her call. Her voice sounds strange to me, like she's reading from a script."

"So...hate to say it, but it sounds to me like she took off with this dude," Frank said. "You know, maybe to stick it to you because she thought you were fooling around with Charlotte."

He always got straight to the point.

Louis winced, thinking of Michael at the hotel bar.

"It occurred to me when I was flying home that Kristen didn't say she ever actually *spoke* to Paula the entire time she was in St. Maarten. Doesn't that seem odd? All she got were texts."

"I guess." Frank said, putting both hands on the table. He sported a small bandage on his left thumb, which he displayed to Louis. "By the way, your stupid cat bit me when I stopped over yesterday."

As if on cue, Bogie appeared at the end of the hallway. He arched his back and hissed.

"I'm sure you provoked him," Louis said. "But thanks for feeding the little bastard."

"He's lucky I didn't drown him in the sink," Frank said. "How come he drinks from the faucet, anyway?"

"He doesn't like my glassware," Louis said. "So anyway, what I know right now is that Paula still isn't back from her so-called sailing trip."

"Where's her sister?"

"Kristen's coming home today. By the way, did I tell you that while I was in St. Maarten her boyfriend showed up to surprise her? Never saw her after that."

"Some help."

Louis looked at his friend.

"I'm thinking I'll go to Paula's house and look around. Maybe she left her laptop home. I can't help but think she got mixed up with some creep she met online."

Frank's eyebrows rose.

"You still have a key? Or are we talking breaking and entering?"

"She took her key back," Louis said. "But I think I can get in through the garage."

"You really think that's a good idea?"

Louis shifted in his chair.

"Sounds a little stalker-ish, I know."

"More than a little. You better be careful," Frank warned. "Paula gets wind of you snooping in her house and you're in deep shit."

"There's a chance she was abducted, Frank. I think that justifies me checking things out. I don't know what the hell else to do, and I can't just sit around wondering."

"There's also the possibility she took off with this guy willingly and they got carried away. Just saying. Besides, do you really want to find out the gory details?" Frank asked, frowning. "It's like somebody hiring a private dick to spy on his wife if he thinks she's cheating. Even if he knows she's up to no good, getting the hard evidence is no fun, not much of a relief. I shouldn't have to tell you any of this, you're a therapist."

"I need to know the truth."

Frank sighed.

"Watch yourself." He fumbled in his pocket. "If I were you, I wouldn't do it. By the way, you want your house keys back or do you want me to keep them for the next time you go off gallivanting?"

"Nah, keep them."

Frank looked at his watch.

"I gotta run. Things to do, places to see. When's the next tee time?"

"Maybe Friday. I have a lot of work to catch up on."

Frank stood up and stretched.

"Work, schmerk. Make time for the important things in life."

"Plus Heather said she'd stop by to see me this week. Haven't seen her since she went back to UConn a couple weeks ago for a summer course."

"Kids. They only call ya when they want something, huh?" Frank said. "My daughter visits when her car needs gas or she runs out of beer money. Never stops in to see the old man otherwise." Frank's eldest was a student at Quinnipiac University. "I could drop dead and she wouldn't know it until the tuition bill was due."

"I hear ya. I think I saw Heather four times her entire freshman year. I don't expect this year to be any different," Louis said. "By the way, I have a present for you. I almost forgot." He got up and went to the foyer where his suitcase stood against the wall. He unzipped the outside compartment and fumbled through a pair of rolled up socks, extracting a plastic bag with two cigars. "Genuine Cubans. You'll like these bad boys. It's the one good thing I found on St. Maarten when I was waiting in the airport."

"Huh." Frank took the two cigars out of the bag to inspect them more closely. "Montecristo. You're wasting these on me, you know. I hardly ever smoke a cigar anymore. Only when somebody has a baby or gets married or something." He looked suspiciously at Louis's open suitcase. "These were wrapped in your socks? No thanks."

"Your loss," Louis said. "I'll see you later. Thanks for feeding the cat."

Frank ambled toward the door, holding out his bandaged thumb again.

"When this gets infected and falls off from gangrene, you'll be hearing from my attorney."

Louis waved his arm around the small, cluttered kitchen.

"All this will soon be yours."

"Yeah, I'll see you in court," Frank quipped, and made his way gingerly past Bogie, who sat like a sentry near the doorway. "Stupid cat."

After Frank left, Louis drove the seven miles from his condo to Paula's house in Farmington. A year ago she'd bought a small gray Cape Cod-style home near the end of a wooded cul-de-sac. He pulled into the empty driveway, and immediately the motion sensor light on her garage illuminated his car, the driveway, and part of the front yard. Other than the one light in the living room that he knew was set on a timer, the rest of the house was dark.

He got out of his Mazda, an old faithful car with almost as many miles racked up on it as the distance from the earth to the moon. The night was warm and sticky, and a humid breeze stirred the leaves of the oak tree in the front yard and carried the delicious smell of someone's barbecue. Louis entered the numbers on the garage door keypad, but the door didn't budge. Paula had indeed changed the combination. Another bad sign, he thought. Apparently her asking him to return the house key was not just a symbolic gesture. She still had the key to his condo though, he realized.

He'd come prepared for the possibility that the garage keypad wouldn't work, and after a glance at the next door neighbors' homes—no one seemed to be around—he quickly walked to the back yard, filled with maple trees and humming with the sound of crickets. He reached up and unscrewed the spotlight in the motion sensor attached to the gray vinyl siding. The near-full moon provided enough light for him to find the window in her sunroom that had a broken lock, which they'd discovered by accident a few weeks earlier. He doubted she'd had time to fix it yet. He had planned to take care of it for her.

The screen was easy enough to pop out, and once he'd removed that, he used the screwdriver he'd brought to pry open the window. In seconds he was able to push it open. It was wide enough and tall enough for him to squeeze through, although he needed something to stand on to boost himself up high enough. An overturned, empty pail on the deck did the trick.

With some effort and no finesse—he was more accustomed to entering homes through doors—he got himself through the window, knocking into a white wicker chair beneath. It scraped across the tile floor.

Some cat burglar I am.

The door from the sunroom to the house was locked, but the spare key was still in the usual place under the large Madagascar palm tree in the corner of the room. Louis retrieved the key, taking care not to get too close to the razor-sharp spikes of the tall plant. He unlocked the door, returned the key to its hiding place before he forgot, and let himself into the house. The air was oppressively hot and thick. The windows were shut and Paula obviously hadn't had the air conditioning on for over a week during this heat wave.

There was no point in wandering around in the dark, so he turned on the dim kitchen light over the sink. As was typical of Paula, she had left everything neat and tidy, no dirty dishes in the sink, no empty glasses on the countertops. The faint smell of apples emanated from a small bottle with reeds sticking out of it, some sort of air freshener that seemed popular these days. He felt a sharp pang of regret once again. If only things could go back to normal. If only she'd just come home and let him talk to her, give him the chance to start over.

He flipped through the mail she'd left on her kitchen table. Nothing out of the ordinary: a cable television bill, store circulars, and a few magazines. He made his way from the kitchen to the living room and then to her home office. The hallway seemed unusually bare and when he saw a visible nail hole he realized that a photo of the two of them was gone.

The one thing he wanted, her laptop, was not set up as it usually was on her solid cherry desk. Had she taken it with her? He'd assumed she would leave it at home, take a break from work and disconnect from everything. But maybe not?

He opened the closet door in her office and heard a loud clang come from the basement.

He stopped in his tracks, head cocked, and listened. Slowly he left Paula's office and stood in the shadows at the top of the basement stairs. It was pitch black down below and he strained to see any movement. He waited a long moment, hearing nothing but the faint drone of crickets outdoors and his own ragged breathing.

He hesitated for another few seconds and then flipped on the light switch, illuminating the cellar stairs. Something could have fallen. She had a lot of crap down there. He slowly descended the dark wooden steps, smelling the musty odor of old books and cardboard boxes.

When he reached the bottom of the steps, he flipped the light switch to the room on his right. This was Paula's work-out area, complete with treadmill, a yoga mat, and exercise balls. From what he could tell, everything looked normal. He paused, turned to the left and made his way to the laundry room, past two overstuffed bookshelves, several cardboard boxes, and plastic bins.

She hadn't gotten around to unpacking all of her things, even though she'd lived in the house for a year. He could understand that. He still had boxes in his condo that he hadn't unpacked for nearly a decade.

He turned on another light when he reached the washer and

dryer. To his left were the oil furnace, a folded Ping-Pong table, plastic bins marked 'Christmas decorations,' and numerous paint cans. He stepped past the furnace, pulled the cord to the last bare bulb hanging from the ceiling, and froze.

The door to the hatchway entrance was ajar.

He knew instantly what the clanging sound had been. Was there someone lurking behind the solid wooden door? In five steps he crossed the room and swung the door open. The old wooden steps leading to the hatch cover were dark, dirty and littered with cobwebs and dead bugs. In seconds he was up the stairs, hands pressing against the steel hatchway cover. It creaked and opened to the outdoors with nothing more than a shove. It too had been unlocked.

He clambered up the remaining steps and into the backyard, heart thudding. There was no one in the yard and he ran to the side of the house, looked behind the thick bushes and shrubs, and down the empty street. Nothing. Whatever—whoever—had been in the basement was long gone.

He returned to the back yard and walked the perimeter, bordered on all sides by towering maple trees that littered Paula's yard with mounds of leaves in the fall. Without a flashlight or the motion detector spotlight he had unscrewed, he couldn't see much. The irony of an intruder searching for an intruder was not lost on him. Calling the police was hardly an option.

Finally he went back down the hatchway stairs. He latched the ancient steel doors of the hatch cover and locked the door to the stairway as well. He tried to remember the last time he or Paula had had any reason to use the hatchway—maybe when she'd gotten the treadmill six months ago? He could swear it had been locked ever since, not that he ever spent much time in the cellar himself.

He turned off the lights in the basement and went upstairs to the second floor. Nothing in Paula's bedroom appeared to be disturbed. Her king-sized bed was neatly made, a light summer blanket pulled over down-filled pillows. He saw that his alarm clock was absent from the nightstand on his side of the bed. So was another photo of the two of them that he remembered had been next to the clock.

More bad signs, he thought. She didn't want reminders of him, and sadly, he realized how few there really were. Besides the photos and a few odds and ends, he had kept very few possessions in her house. He checked the drawer where he kept a change of clothes and an extra pair of jeans. The drawer was empty.

He opened a few drawers in her bureau, revealing nothing but her folded shirts and pants. What was he expecting to find?

He was less certain now that the noise he'd heard had definitely been the sound of the hatch door clanging shut. Maybe he'd been mistaken.

Maybe something else had fallen somewhere in the house. As far as the unlocked doors went, it was certainly possible that Paula had used the hatch at some point. She could have forgotten to lock the cover and the door to the stairway, careless as that was.

And if there had been someone in the cellar—how would the person have gotten in? He supposed anyone could have entered the same way he had, although the door from the sunroom to the kitchen had still been secured. He went downstairs and checked the windows in every room on the first floor. All were closed and locked.

He was puzzled and more than a little unnerved as he returned to Paula's office. He resumed snooping in her closet and found her black computer bag in the corner, behind a black dress that had fallen off a hanger. He grabbed the bag and unzipped it. The laptop was inside.

Bingo.

He left her house through the back door, locking it as he went.

Louis had driven halfway down the street when something smashed into the side of his door.

What the hell?

He pulled over to the side of the road, tires crunching on soft gravel, and jumped out of the Mazda. There was a shallow dent near the door handle and a large stone in the middle of the pavement. He turned and looked toward the dark woods. Had some kid thrown a rock at his car? He stared into the blackness of the trees and listened to a chorus of peepers. Nothing moved. No rustling of branches or crackling of leaves.

He waited for a few moments and got back into his car, Paula's laptop next to him on the cracked leather seat.

CHAPTER EIGHT

Thursday

VICTORIA RUDEMANN WAS trying on her new yoga outfit in her upstairs bedroom when the doorbell rang. She examined herself in the full-length mirror—damn, she looked good, the skinny black pants made her ass look smaller—and then she glanced out the screen. One floor below a young bearded man holding a brown satchel stood on her wide front porch and rocked back and forth on the balls of his feet. His eyes scanned the windows and he smiled when he spotted her face.

"Hey, you the lady put the ad in?" he called out.

He tapped the bag he was holding.

"What ad?" she said, frowning. "What do you want?"

"You know," he said. He set the satchel down, partially unzipped it, and pulled out what looked to her like a black leather whip. "I got what you need, baby. Let me in and I'll show you."

He cracked the whip in the air and grinned up at her, showing a mouthful of yellow teeth.

Victoria stared at the stranger, her mouth going dry. First there'd been the phone call that morning from a number she couldn't identify. She thought it might be the mobile vet service finally calling her back about an appointment to see her sick cat, but when she picked up, the deep male voice had immediately launched into a vile description of what he wanted to do with her.

You wanna be raped, you slut? I'll show you a real man. I'll be over there tonight and I'll tie you up good...

She'd hung up the phone, heart pounding, and a few minutes later, it rang again. This time she didn't answer it.

"Get out of here. I'll call the police," she said, hearing the quaver in her voice.

Oh God, had she locked the front door?

As if he'd read her mind, the man laughed and jiggled the door handle. His long dark hair fell about his face.

"Come on, baby, open up for daddy. You know you want it."

"Get out!" she shrieked and ran from the window to her cordless phone near the bed.

She punched in 911 and raced back to the window, phone to her ear. The man saw her talking to the dispatcher and shrugged.

"Okay, baby, I'll come back later with my friends," he chortled. "We'll gang-bang you to the moon and back."

He mumbled something else she couldn't hear and sauntered down her winding driveway to the street, swinging the satchel. The tall oaks obscured her view although it looked like some sort of blue sedan was parked at the bottom of the hill.

She couldn't tell what kind of car it was, nor did she see the license plate, she later told the Avon police officer who came by in his cruiser. By then the man with the satchel was long gone, but her phone had begun to ring incessantly.

At home at his kitchen table, Louis held the phone to his ear and reluctantly tore his eyes away from the screen of Paula's laptop.

To his amazement, he was able to access it using the same password she'd given him when he'd borrowed her laptop once to look up a restaurant review.

"Dad," Heather said. "You're not listening to me. You're doing something else, aren't you?"

"Sorry, kiddo. I was looking at something."

He absently took a long sip from a lukewarm cup of coffee.

"I could tell." Heather's voice was petulant. "I don't have class and I'm planning to come home tomorrow afternoon. I'll stop by and see you if you'll be around?"

"Sure," he said. An instant message flashed on the screen and again he was riveted.

Hey Paula. How's everything?

"Okay. I'll call you when I'm in town," she said. "We can go somewhere for dinner?"

"Dinner?" He could barely speak. "Sure."

His fingers fluttered on the keyboard.

Fine. What about yourself?

"Dad, I can tell you're busy."

He looked away from the screen.

"Yes, I want you to stop over. How about if we go out for sushi?"

"Okay. See ya tomorrow, Dad. You okay?"

"Yeah. Sorry. I was a little distracted."

He felt bad about that, given how few conversations he had with his daughter these days. She had called him just when he'd opened Paula's online email account, and no sooner had he done that when instant messaging had started from someone named "Willibear." He had no idea who Willibear was or where he lived, but he'd make it his business to find out.

I got accepted into the MBA program last minute. I'm starting next week. Can you believe it?

Louis typed: *Congratulations. We should celebrate.* He paused, and decided to go for it. *Want to meet for a glass of wine?*

He waited. The response came back in a few seconds.

That would sure be nice, darlin'—are you coming to Vancouver or am I flying out to Connecticut? I always wanted to see New England.

Vancouver?

Let me get back to you. Gotta go—talk to you later.

The instant messaging dialogue box disappeared, and Louis skimmed through the other messages in her folders. Her email password had been entered automatically, saving him the trouble of trying to guess what it was. Ditto for the emails she'd stored on the hard drive from an online dating site.

He scrolled through the inbox. There were several innocuous emails from "Tique," "Zipzas," (*what the hell was that?*) and "DrLes," Two offered their phone numbers and one suggested meeting for a cup of coffee, so "they could determine if any chemistry existed." He checked the dates of the emails. It seemed that her correspondence with these people had started almost immediately after their break-up. She sure hadn't wasted any time, he thought, although knowing Paula, her motivation may have been less a desire to start a new relationship than to prove something to herself. Still, he felt a pang of hurt as he continued to read.

Dear Danny—(aka "Yachtman") *Thanks for inviting me to the boat show in Essex. I'll be on vacation that week but I'll email you when I get back.*

Who the hell was Danny?

Louis got up and refilled his mug. She'd written that email two days before she'd left for St. Maarten. For a moment he wanted to shut the laptop down, feeling the hurt expanding like ever-widening circles in his heart. She really was moving on. Still, he couldn't imagine that she would actually—see someone else. Be with someone else. His fingers paused on the keyboard. There were more; many more. He'd started reading them last night and had only gotten through the first folder. He clicked on the most recent email she'd sent to a "BD9908."

Hi BD—I'm confused. You say you're an internist at a hospital I'd recognize—you say you're recently divorced, good-looking, intelligent and funny—so why are you looking for someone online? I would think you'd have your pick.

Louis clicked back to the inbox and BD9908's response.

Same reason you're online—it's hard to meet quality people when you work full time and then some. I would think you'd have your pick too, given the right time and opportunity. And speaking of the right time and opportunity—I know I haven't sent you my photo yet, but how do you feel about meeting in person? Perhaps over a cup of tea—or a grande soy mocha latte, if you prefer?

☺

Her response: *How about when I get back from St. Maarten?*

His: *I've been there before, several times. Are you staying on the French side or the Dutch?*

The Dutch.

His: *Check out the brunch at the Marriott.*

Louis scrolled down and couldn't believe his eyes. The stranger asked several innocuous questions, so innocent on the surface, until she told him where she was staying.

Ah yes, the Sun Bay. I believe it's close to downtown Philipsburg? Anyway, enjoy yourself. You deserve a rest.

It was getting late and he had to get to his office soon for his afternoon clients, but he kept reading. At least one weirdo knew where she was going. There could be others. God, how could she be so naïve? He clicked on an earlier email she had sent to BD9908 and felt his throat constrict.

Dear BD: It's late, and I'm sitting here at my kitchen table with a glass of Chardonnay listening to the peepers out somewhere in the wetlands—you know, the little frogs that make such a racket. I'm sitting here and thinking about what you wrote last night—about wanting nothing more than to find a woman who is loyal, who would devote herself to you as much as you would to her...and I thought about what you wrote about the exquisite tenderness of making love to that special person. How it would feel, that very first touch...that very first kiss....

Louis looked away from the screen, feeling sick. He felt worse when he skimmed the rest of her note, not wanting to fully absorb the words or the emotion behind them. She actually believed this guy's complete and utter bullshit. Louis knew exactly what this was leading to, and sure enough, BD9908's response was charming and encouraging, even as he became more and more explicit.

It was woman porn, Louis thought. Veiled sex and romance. BD9908 wrote about taking control, and she wanted, *needed*, someone strong and assertive to finally take control, didn't she? To make her feel like the sexy, feminine, desirable woman she was.

It's all too rare these days, isn't it, for a woman to be treated the way she deserves to be treated, by a gentleman who adores her.

Oh, please. Louis smacked the table. That bastard. He imagined Paula sitting at her kitchen table in the middle of the night, writing this crap, reading this crap, imagining Prince Charming out there in cyberspace eager to make love to her with "exquisite tenderness" and make her life complete.

The way he hadn't? He couldn't stomach any more of it. He was about to log off when an instant message appeared on the screen—from BD9908.

Hey Paula—I was wondering. Did you have fun?

Louis stared. Couldn't be the same guy Paula met up with on the island. Or was it? If it was, why hadn't Kristen heard from her? What was going on? When he didn't answer, a second message appeared.

You still there?

Louis typed. *I had a great time.*

The response was swift.

Meet tomorrow night? Starbucks?

What the hell? Was this the guy? If they'd spent a few days on his yacht, why would he want to meet with her now at a coffee shop?

He typed. *Sure.*

He squinted at the screen, unsure of himself. Heather was

coming but he'd take her out to dinner first, and find out who this BD character was afterwards.

He wrote: *How about 8 PM in Farmington?*

In seconds BD9908 replied.

Great. See you then.

CHAPTER NINE

Friday

WITH THE EXCEPTION of a brown pelican soaring overhead and plump sandpipers turning over shells and stones looking for food at the water's edge, Dawn Beach was deserted. Mike and Nicole Peska, who had risen early to snorkel one last time before their flight home to Dallas, strolled on the powdery white sand to their favorite spot. They each carried their masks, fins, and snorkel in black mesh bags. The calm water sparkled in the sunlight.

"Babe, we need to come to St. Maarten to celebrate our anniversary like this every year," Mike said to his young wife, who wore a neon orange bikini that set off her tanned olive skin.

"I'm in," she replied and leaned sideways to plant a big fat kiss on his cheek.

With a teasing smile he pushed her away and they made their way to a string of large boulders that jutted into the sea. A coral reef ran parallel to the shore.

"I hope I see another octopus," Nicole said. "That was so

cool."

They reached the first boulder and sat down to don their fins. As usual, Nicole was ready first and she lumbered over awkwardly like a giant duck to the gentle waves that curled on the shore with barely a whisper. Mike soon followed her and they adjusted their masks and snorkels while they stood in the warm, waist-deep water.

"Maybe we'll spot some sea turtles," Mike said as she kicked off.

She was soon several yards ahead of him, and he dove beneath the water. He swam in long strokes toward the reef and spotted the silvery flash of a reef squid. He detoured to follow it and as he came close to a pile of submerged rocks, crusted with barnacles, he saw what first looked like a white shark lying about ten feet below on the sand, covered with dozens of greenish-blue crabs. Except it wasn't a shark, and when he swam closer, he could clearly see a swirl of dark hair and an exposed shoulder blade. Then legs. Arms. Crabs clustering on the unclothed areas. The body was lying face-down on the sand, half-wedged between two large boulders, barely stirring in the current. A parrot fish swam right by his mask, and Mike broke the surface of the water, gasping.

"Oh, shit," he said, treading water, looking for Nicole.

He saw the orange tip of her snorkel sticking up several yards away as she swam slowly on the surface. He called to her and without telling her what was wrong, gestured wildly for her to follow him back to shore.

Louis had three appointments on Friday afternoon: a young man suffering panic attacks, a middle-aged single woman exhausted and stressed from taking care of her elderly parents and her own kids, and a new client, a woman in her early twenties complaining of depression. In between clients he checked his phone for messages. There were none. He hoped Kristen would let him know if she heard anything concerning Paula. Maybe he would call her later in the evening.

When his last client left at four o'clock, Louis called Heather and made plans to meet her for sushi at six. He worked on paperwork in his office for an hour and then spent some time trying to coax his fax machine to work. Damn cheap fax machines. Damn insurance companies that wanted all this paperwork. He finally gave up and went home to change into jeans and a polo shirt.

He arrived at the restaurant ten minutes early and ordered a beer while he waited for Heather. He hadn't seen his daughter much that summer. Seemed she was always busy or had better things to do. Not that he could blame her. When he was her age and in college, he'd been far too busy chasing girls and partying and rarely went home.

She breezed in at five minutes past six and spotted him at his booth. Louis stood up to give her a hug.

"Hey, kiddo, haven't seen you in a dog's age," he said.

"In a cow's eye," she said, the nonsense banter they always used.

She hugged him back. She was lean and long-legged, her hair the color of dark maple syrup, the shade his used to be. She wore frayed denim shorts, a pink tank top, and was perfectly tanned, looking like she belonged on a California beach.

"So what've you been up to?" Louis asked when she settled into the booth. "Your classes going okay?"

"Meh. I might change my major from marketing to accounting. That's where the jobs are." Her cell phone rang. "Sorry, I should take this. It's Mom."

He waited while she chatted briefly, assuring her mother that yes, she was fine, she was going to eat dinner and then head back to school. No, she didn't have time to stop at home again. When she hung up the phone, she rolled her eyes.

"You know Mom. Always worried about something. Can't

stop being a helicopter parent. So how was St. Maarten? How come you're back so early?"

Louis hadn't said much to his daughter about his brief trip. She might be a mini-adult, but he saw no need to disclose the awkward details.

"It was okay," he finally said.

She studied him.

"Did you go with Paula?"

"No. I was actually looking for her," he admitted. "Long story. She went to the island by herself."

Heather shot him a look of disbelief.

"Why didn't you go with her? Did you guys break up or something?"

"Something like that."

"So did you find her?" she asked.

"No. She was busy somewhere else."

"That's pretty weird, Dad," Heather said with characteristic bluntness. "I can't believe you went all the way to St. Maarten to look for her if you guys broke up." She shook her head. "I never liked her anyway."

"You've only seen her a few times," Louis said, remembering the first occasion he'd introduced Paula to his daughter.

Heather had been aloof and unimpressed, and that hadn't changed.

"Yeah, well, she's too young for you," she continued. "Plus she's immature. I can tell."

He suppressed a laugh.

"And how can you tell that?"

"Something about the way she acts. You're better off without her. Mom doesn't date anyone," she said, as if that clinched it. "She says she's too old to start over again and go through all that aggravation."

Louis thought of his ex and her perpetual negative attitude.

"That's her choice."

"I would never get married," Heather added.

"Why not?"

"Because I'd probably end up getting divorced like you and Mom," she said matter-of-factly. "I read somewhere that kids from divorced families usually get divorced too."

Louis winced.

"Not necessarily true. You can have a happy relationship." He looked at her and grinned. "But don't rush it. Wait until you're thirty-five or so. By the way, how's your boyfriend? What's his name —Duane?"

"Dave," she corrected, with a trace of annoyance. "He's okay."

"When am I going to meet him?"

"Oh, sometime," she said.

Her cell phone buzzed and she glanced at it and started texting.

"Can't you turn that thing off at the table?"

She looked up.

"Sorry, there's a party tonight. I have to get back to school soon."

He could tell she was tapping her leg impatiently beneath the table. She'd always been a hyper kid.

She glanced at the menu, then at him.

"Oh, I was going to ask you for gas money. To tide me over? I got a job at the fitness center but I don't get paid until next week."

"Sure," he said, mentally calculating how little he had left in his checking account. "Remind me when we leave."

"Trust me, I will."

Louis smiled, realizing with a pang how much he missed spending time with her. Here she was, already a sophomore in college. The years were going by, speeding up, as a matter of fact. All the old clichés about the older you get, the faster it goes, and blah, blah, blah. Pretty soon she'd be graduating from college, going off on her own, getting married. His little girl.

"Dad?"

"What?"

She laughed and gestured to his right.

"Talk about me texting and not paying attention…hello, the waitress is ready to take our order."

Kristen sat at her dining room table in front of her laptop. She had decided to work from home, although in the hours that had passed, she'd barely managed to get through all of her emails. There was always a price to pay for taking days off and this time was no exception. Her assistant director had held down the fort for the most part, but it was always a strain when someone was gone. The agency was small and they all had to wear many hats.

She found herself checking the St. Maarten Police Force Facebook page several times during the course of the day.

Would anyone comment on the posting about Paula?

So far there was no response. Her cell phone was silent too. No word from her sister and here it was, four days since Paula's last text. She hadn't heard from Eric either since they'd gone their separate ways from Bradley Airport on Wednesday. She wondered if his father was doing okay. She'd volunteered to go with him to the hospital but he'd politely declined her offer. He'd said he'd call her soon, and to keep him posted if she heard any news.

What was the next step? Were there other people that should be notified about the situation? She'd already informed Bill, Paula's ex, and he'd offered to help in any way, but what could he do? She wished there were other family members she could contact, but their parents were deceased and she was not close to any of their cousins, who lived out of state. Besides an elderly aunt in Oregon, there was no one she communicated with on a regular basis.

At a loss, she Googled "missing persons in St. Maarten" and read through a hodge-podge of old cases of people gone missing, some never found. If only she knew someone in law enforcement, preferably the FBI, she thought.

The name popped into her head.

Les Sellack.

Les was her former boyfriend Chris's older brother, a retired FBI legal attaché. She'd met him once, years ago when she and Chris had first started dating. She didn't know where he lived and doubted he would remember her. There was no way, no way in hell, she could contact Chris and ask.

She got up and paced around her living room. There were times she wondered what Chris was up to these days. Swimming with sharks in the Bahamas? Biking in the Aran Islands? Images of his sheepish grin, his unruly gray-blonde curls, and narrow blue eyes engulfed her suddenly, along with a flood of memories. There was the time they'd flown spontaneously (he always did spontaneous) to Niagara-on-the-Lake one weekend before Christmas. He was six-feet four and he'd worn a full-length mink coat, torn jeans, and alligator boots, oblivious to people's stares.

He'd smoked a cigar as they'd strolled hand in hand on the festive snowy streets, Christmas lights everywhere. They'd stopped in lovely little shops along the boulevard to warm up and talk to the friendly shop owners. She'd wanted to burst with happiness, pretending all the while it could always be this way. Pretending he was as madly in love with her as she was with him.

It was a whirlwind blissful weekend, complete with a visit to a butterfly farm that was like a Caribbean haven in the midst of winter, the tacky Ripley museum, the Imax version of Niagara history, and of course, the Canadian side of the Falls, nearly empty of tourists in the winter's chill. In spite of herself, she smiled at the memory.

Eric would never in a million, billion years wear a mink coat and cowboy boots. She'd never even seen him unshaven or dressed in an old pair of jeans and a t-shirt. Comparing Chris to Eric was like, well, comparing Ronald McDonald to Clint

Eastwood. They couldn't be further apart on the continuum.

Her cell phone rang and she almost jumped, surprised at how much on edge she was. The Caller ID said Unknown Number, and she picked it up.

The voice was deep and unfamiliar.

"Is this Kristen Spencer?"

She listened as the man identified himself. Her throat went dry and she looked at her hands, which began trembling uncontrollably.

Louis and Heather finished dinner at seven-thirty.

"So don't be a stranger, okay?" Louis said as they walked out to her car, an old Kia.

He peeled out a wad of twenties from his wallet and counted out five.

"Thanks, Dad. Maybe I'll be home next weekend."

She gave him a hug. He watched her leave the parking lot and then he got into his car and headed to Starbucks for his eight PM rendezvous with BD9908.

He was ready to get an up-close-and-personal look at the creep who'd been emailing and manipulating Paula, though he still wasn't sure exactly what he hoped to accomplish. His response to the man's instant message hadn't been well thought out, he realized. Paula was bound to be furious about this invasion of her privacy but now it was too late. Well, if nothing else, he'd make sure the guy would look elsewhere for someone to target.

He got to the coffee shop ten minutes before eight. He ordered a regular coffee and sat at a small wooden table in the corner with a view of the store and the window to the parking lot. The store was busy this evening and he glanced at the other customers: an overweight woman in her thirties stood in line, college-age kids with laptops occupied other tables, and an older man with a silver beard sat in the opposite corner reading something on a tablet. Too old to be BD, Louis thought.

Although how many people accurately described themselves on an online dating site?

Louis waited and watched. In a few moments a man came in who looked fortyish, decked out in black spandex bike shorts and neon yellow short-sleeved shirt. Louis concluded this couldn't be BD either. No one would show up for a first date looking like Chris Froome on a break from the Tour de France.

He sipped his coffee; it was exactly eight o'clock now. Then a man entered the shop who hesitated at the entrance, scanning the patrons. Was this BD9908? He was a little over six feet tall, slim, maybe mid-forties. A large nose, dark hair. Average-looking. He wore a dark blue polo shirt and khaki pants. He didn't wait in line to place an order, but laid claim to a table a few feet away from Louis. He was definitely waiting for someone, Louis decided. The man kept glancing at the entrance and then once at his watch. Louis continued sipping his coffee. So was this Paula's cyber knight in shining armor? The guy who wanted to make love to her with "exquisite tenderness?"

Louis waited another minute and then stood up, his chair squeaking across the floor. The man shot a glance at him and Louis made eye contact.

Before he could think about it any longer, he blurted, "Are you BD?"

The man's eyes narrowed and his forehead creased in irritation.

"Excuse me?"

Louis repeated, louder now.

"Are you BD9908? Are you waiting for Paula?"

"I don't know what you're talking about," the man said, his expression puzzled.

Nervous even, Louis thought.

He turned away and Louis hesitated.

What was he supposed to do now? Was this BD9908 or not?

Suddenly the man rose from his seat and without looking at Louis, stalked out of the shop in three strides. Louis stepped outdoors in time to see him quickly cross the parking lot. He didn't look back.

Now that was odd. If this man had been BD, he'd sure been spooked. But what if it wasn't?

By now it was almost quarter past the hour. Louis returned to his seat and waited another fifteen minutes, but no other single men arrived.

He gave up at 8:35 PM.

Either he'd just scared off Mr. Cyber-wonder, or Paula had been stood up.

The phone was ringing when Louis returned home, but by the time he'd unlocked the door, it had stopped. He turned on the hallway light and went back out his car to bring in the new fax machine he'd bought on the way home from Starbucks. The phone rang again and he picked up the cordless handset.

Kristen sounded like she was having trouble breathing.

"Louis."

"What's the matter?"

"I got a call...from the St. Maarten police. They think they've found Paula."

"What?" he said. She'd been talking so fast he wasn't sure he heard her right. "Is she okay?"

"No, no, she's not okay," Kristen's voice broke into a sob. "They found her body in the water. They think it's her. They said they're not sure if she drowned—or what happened. They think it's her because she has a starfish tattoo on her ankle. They think it's her."

Louis swayed. He stared at the phone in his hand and flexed his fingers, feeling a strange tightness in his chest. They found her body in the water? He barely heard Kristen say something about dental records and positive identification. He vaguely heard her say that the police would be calling with more information soon.

"Sorry we had to tell you this on the phone."

Louis dimly recognized the deep voice as Eric's.

The boyfriend, his mind registered.

"We'll get back to you when we have more information," the voice continued. "I'm really sorry. Kristen was trying to reach you earlier."

Louis heard Kristen's muffled sob, and the call ended. He stood frozen. Thinking straight was nearly impossible. As if in a dream, as if in slow motion, he wondered if he should go to the airport, buy a ticket, get on a plane to St. Maarten right now. He needed to find Paula. Bring her home.

Instead he sat down on the couch. In his mind, in his memory, she was smiling. She was angry. She was lonely. Maybe she was with some other man, but for goddamn sure she wasn't dead. How the hell could they think that? She was alive somewhere on that fucking island.

He couldn't grasp it. He couldn't wrap his mind around it. They had to be mistaken. Surely it was someone else, some other woman with a starfish tattoo.

Hours later during that night from hell, as he paced from room to room unable to sleep, waiting for more news, he paused at his kitchen table and stared at the mess of papers. It didn't register at first. Then he realized what was missing.

Paula's laptop was gone.

PART TWO

Think'st thou there are no serpents in the world
But those who glide along the grassy sod,
And sting the luckless foot that presses them?
There are who in the path of social life
Do bask their spotted skins in Fortune's sun
And sting the soul.
—Joanne Baillie

CHAPTER TEN

Friday, Two Weeks Later

KRISTEN STOOD AT the pulpit and surveyed the rows of family, friends, and colleagues. The church that normally had an attendance of fifty or so during regular Sunday services was packed. The faces that stared back at her were sad, kind, and concerned.

Paula's ex-husband Bill sat in the front row with Kristen's elderly uncle and looked at her with a vacant gaze, his thin shoulders slumped. Two distant aunts with silvery white hair and wrinkled faces clutched their purses in their laps as though they were life preservers. Cousins she hadn't seen in years murmured to each other as she took several deep, ragged breaths.

In the second row, Eric sat rigidly upright in a tailored black suit and maroon tie. His eyes locked onto hers, and she felt as if he were throwing her a psychic lifeline. His lips moved and she strained to make out the words.

Are you okay?

Someone coughed. Someone else cleared his throat. Kristen saw Eric's brows knit in concern, and he began to rise. He was going to help her back to her seat. He didn't think she could collect herself enough to do this, to read the eulogy for her sister. No one would blame her. Eyes on his, she shook her head ever so slightly. Then she looked down at her piece of white paper and found her voice.

Louis sat next to Frank Roth in a pew at the back of the church. Even now, a week since Paula's body had been recovered, he still had trouble believing any of this was happening. He felt numb and had lost his appetite, as if the shock and grief were wound into a tight little ball in the center of his gut. There hadn't been a wake or a viewing.

Never had a chance to say goodbye.

A medical examiner flown in from the Netherlands had conducted an autopsy and Paula's remains had been cremated.

The details were sketchy. Days earlier Kristen told him the M.E. in St. Maarten had determined the cause of death to be drowning. Toxicology reports showed there'd been tranquilizers found in her system. The most important questions of all went unanswered: who was her male companion and what role did he play, if any, in her death? Had she actually gone to St. Bart's? No one had come forward. Her luggage was still missing, and even the time of death was uncertain.

Was it possible she was still alive when he'd been on the island looking for her? The thought that he could have found her in time—if he'd only known where to look—was torture. He was sure he didn't know all of the details Paula's family might be privy to, since he'd been cut out of any discussions between Kristen and the authorities in St. Maarten and Connecticut.

Louis was all too aware that he was persona non grata when it came to Paula's family. No doubt one reason was Paula's ex, Bill, who had swooped in like a giant vampire bat as though he were the widower. Bill's unpredictable personality and unfettered hostility had not changed at all. He seemed barely able to contain his expression of contempt when he spotted Louis coming into the church, but at least he hadn't made a scene.

The Episcopalian minister took over the pulpit after Kristen delivered her eulogy. Louis watched her return to her pew and slide next to her boyfriend, who whispered something in her ear. He recognized a few of Paula's friends, the few he had met when they were together, although they had seldom socialized.

He had never met her relatives, most of whom lived out of state. Overall, he reflected, it was a sad commentary that he had occupied so little space in the sphere of Paula's life. Sitting like a pariah in the back row of the church emphasized that point. How much of that was her doing, or his, he wasn't sure.

They all stood up to sing "Amazing Grace," and that was when the tight ball in his gut migrated to his throat, making it hard to breathe. Tears welled up in his eyes and he blinked them away, struggling to hold onto his composure. He looked at his hymnal silently, the words and music a blurry film.

When the service was finally over, Louis and Frank were among the first to exit the church. There would be no mingling with Paula's family and friends at the reception to express their sympathies. Louis knew his presence would be tolerated but not welcomed, particularly with Bill and Paula's former in-laws around. There was no point in making everyone uncomfortable.

"I'm not going back to work today," Frank asked, once they were out in the parking lot. They both blinked in the bright sunlight, shading their eyes. Frank looked at his watch and then loosened his tie, wincing as though it had been strangling him. "Want to go get a drink?"

"Yeah," Louis said.

He was glad Frank had asked. Truth be told, he hadn't worked much in the past week or so after he'd gotten the news about Paula. He'd cancelled and rescheduled many of his appointments. He had nothing to do the rest of the day, and he didn't look forward to going home.

"Any place in particular?"

Louis considered. "Let's go to the clubhouse. I'll meet you there."

When he pulled into the driveway, Louis was glad to see that the parking lot of the Nineteenth Hole was nearly empty. Only a few golfers were out on the course today taking advantage of the pleasant midweek weather. He parked next to Frank's vintage white Corvette, took off his tie and suit jacket, and made his way to the entrance. Frank was already seated at a table next to a window overlooking the course.

Louis eased into the wooden seat, which was as uncomfortable as the church pew.

"Hey, thanks for going to the funeral."

Frank shrugged and sighed.

"Jesus, what a shame. I'm so sorry. Let me get you a beer."

He went up to the bar and returned with two drinks.

Louis picked up his glass and took a long gulp.

"Who the fuck would have thought this would happen?"

Frank asked, "I know you don't know too many details yet—but any chance you'll find out more? From the sister?"

"Kristen hasn't called me in a week. Not since she and Bill made the funeral arrangements. She said it was a big hassle dealing with the funeral home in St. Maarten and getting the paperwork done." Louis sighed. "She had to have Paula cremated or else it would have taken another week to get her body transported home."

"The whole thing sucks," Frank said.

"I have to tell you something."

Frank cleared his throat. He sat back in his chair and folded his arms, as though he were expecting a confession he didn't necessarily want to hear.

"What?"

"I took Paula's laptop the night I went to her house. When I got back from St. Maarten. I wanted to see what she was up to, and I got an eyeful." Louis paused, his thoughts drifting. He told Frank about the messages from the dating site, and the blind date he'd set up with BD9908. He finished his story with the night he'd gotten the phone call from Kristen about Paula. "I didn't notice right away, but later on I realized Paula's laptop was missing. Gone. Someone took it from my condo."

Frank's thick eyebrows raised.

"What the hell? Did you call the police?"

"How could I call the police when I was the one who stole it first?"

"You've been sitting on this the past two weeks? What were you thinking? Was anything else taken from your place?"

"Nope," Louis said. "Not as far as I could tell."

"How'd the person break in?"

"I don't know. The windows were closed. The doors were locked."

Frank picked up his wine glass, swirled the ruby-colored liquid, and took a long sip.

"So somebody really wanted her laptop. What for?"

"I've been wondering that myself. Why would someone break in and only take that? Not that I have a lot of valuables, but still. Is there some connection between that and Paula's death? No one knows who she was with in St. Maarten."

"Anyone else have a key to your place?" Frank asked and then frowned. "Besides me?"

"Nope. Paula was the only other person with a key. Oh, and I forgot to mention that there may have been someone in her house the night I went there."

"What? Who?"

Louis told him about the noises in the cellar and the unlocked hatchway door.

"But I never saw anyone," he concluded. "I know I heard something and the hatch door was open, but I can't say for sure there was someone in her basement that night. Believe me, I've gone over this time and time again. Tried to make sense of it, especially now. I've wondered if someone here stalked her, followed her to St. Maarten, and killed her. Maybe some whack job she met on the Internet or through a dating service."

Frank leaned forward.

"You got a lawyer? And I'm not talking about that moron who represented you in the Rudemann case."

"You think I'll need one? For what?"

"You might. Depends on how diligent the St. Maarten police get with an investigation. If there is one."

Louis frowned.

"I'm not following you. Why would they want to investigate me?"

Frank gazed out the window, propping his chin on one big hand.

"Paula breaks up with you and goes to St. Maarten. She claims she met some guy there but you go looking for her, and come home empty-handed. A few days later she ends up dead. In the meantime, you've gone to her house, stolen her laptop, then someone steals it from you. If I'm a cop and I hear that story, I'd think something was pretty fishy."

"Yeah, it's always the boyfriend or husband, isn't it."

"It usually is," Frank said. "No kidding."

Louis took a deep breath. He heard the frustration in his voice, the ball of grief unraveling again.

"All I know is that she wrote to at least one guy online who knew where she was going. Some character who called himself BD9908. That was the guy I set up the meeting with, although I don't think he showed up. Never emailed her account again either. I tried to get him to respond but he fell off the face of the earth. I still don't know who he is."

"Maybe that has nothing to do with any of this," Frank said. "Could be Paula did drown accidentally. The stolen laptop though—I can't explain that."

They were both quiet.

The bartender came by and asked if they wanted another round. Louis declined. Light-headed, he hadn't eaten a full meal in days and his ears buzzed from the alcohol and lack of food. Frank insisted on paying the check, and they left the clubhouse.

"Thanks for the beer." Louis said. "Stop by whenever you want."

Frank clapped him on the back.

"Take care of yourself."

Louis got into his car. His hands trembled as he put the key into the ignition. He felt fuzzy, as though he'd had a six pack. He'd expected to feel better once he'd told someone about breaking into Paula's house and the events that followed. Instead he felt more confused.

As soon as he reached his condo, he had the feeling something was wrong as soon as he pulled into the long driveway leading to his unit. When he turned the corner, he saw a police cruiser parked in front of his garage. He parked his Mazda in a visitor's spot and walked up to his doorway. The driver's side door of the cruiser swung open.

The officer stepped outside the car and stretched.

"Dr. D'Maio?"

He was at least a foot shorter than Louis and thirty pounds heavier. He was clean-shaven, squat and compact, and carried himself as though he were a prizefighter. Louis turned his head in the man's direction and fumbled with his key.

"Dr. D'Maio," the man repeated, and in three quick strides he was at the door in front of Louis, invading his personal space. He pulled out an ID badge from his breast pocket. "I'm Officer Millson. I'd like to speak with you, please."

His voice was raspy, and Louis guessed he was, or had been, a heavy smoker. His black hair was cut short, and his eyes were deep brown.

Louis took the badge and inspected it closely.

"What's this about?"

He glanced up and saw that one of his neighbors was staring

out of his window at them. He had the unreal sense he was in a movie, a screenplay with some corny plot soon to be interrupted with an equally bad commercial.

"May I come in, please?" the man asked, still standing too close to Louis. He motioned at the neighbor's window. "Don't want an audience, do we?"

"All right," Louis said, and unlocked his door.

For a second he wondered if he should call Frank and get the name of a good lawyer right that moment. Then he wondered why he was letting this guy in. Did he have to? Could he refuse? As if reading his mind, Officer Millson hurried in behind him.

Instantly there was a loud clang and a hiss. Bogie had leaped from the kitchen table, knocking a plate to the floor. The black and white cat backed into a corner, ears flattened, fur bristling. His tail was three times its normal size.

"Jesus," the man said, startled, and then laughed. "What the hell is that?"

"Don't mind him," Louis said. The brief interruption gave him a few seconds to collect his thoughts. "Watch your ankles."

He motioned for the man to sit at the cluttered kitchen table. He pulled up a chair himself, waving a hand in Bogie's direction to shoo away the cat. He saw the cop take in the half-empty Stoli bottle on the kitchen counter and the general disarray.

Shit, it wasn't as if he'd been expecting company.

"So what is it I can do for you?" Louis asked, trying to keep his voice calm and even.

Had someone seen him break into Paula's house?

The cop took out a small notepad.

"Do you know Victoria Rudemann?" the cop asked, watching him closely.

Surprised, Louis nodded.

Rudemann? What the hell was going on?

"Yeah, I know who she is."

"When's the last time you saw her?"

"In court about a year and a half ago," he said. When she'd made up the bald-faced lie that he'd come on to her, complained to the Department of Public Health and the American Psychological Association, and sued him for malpractice. All because he'd recommended that she not get custody of her kids. "What's this about, anyway?"

The officer looked him straight in the eye.

"When did you list the sex and bondage ad on the Internet with her name and phone number?"

CHAPTER ELEVEN

Three Days Later

MUCH AS KRISTEN would have liked it to, the world didn't stop during a crisis.

There were reports due to the state and her board of directors, emails that had to be answered, programs and staff requiring her attention. She had to juggle many balls and make sure that none of them fell, no matter what was happening in her personal life. On Friday evening, three days after Paula's funeral, she sat at her desk feeling completely overwhelmed and stared at her pile of work. All of her staff except for her administrative assistant had already gone home.

"Roshana, you can leave," Kristen said when she passed by the young woman's desk to refill her coffee mug.

Roshana looked up from her computer screen. She was a petite black woman with a wide, infectious smile.

"I still have data to enter. Aren't these reports due on Monday?"

"I got an extension until Wednesday," Kristen said, inwardly chiding herself for forgetting to let her assistant know this earlier. Roshana was a dedicated employee who never missed a deadline, but she was also a single mother and Kristen knew she had to pick up her little girl from daycare by six. "You don't have to finish this tonight," she added. "Go pick up your daughter and start your weekend."

"Thanks." Roshana straightened out the paperwork on her desk. "Are you leaving now too?"

"Pretty soon."

Kristen returned to her office and set her full coffee mug on top of a grant proposal draft. It too was due next week but she was having a difficult time starting it. Ever since her sister's death, she'd had trouble concentrating at work. Her cell phone rang, interrupting her gloomy thoughts, and she hurried to fish the phone out of her purse. She knew from the ring tone that it was Eric.

"Am I still picking you up at six?" he asked.

She loved the sound of his deep voice.

"You still want to go? Is your father doing okay?"

"He's stable," Eric said. "I saw him this afternoon. He won't be discharged to rehab until next week."

She hesitated.

"Okay, I'll see you soon."

They were planning to attend a special First Friday Maxfield Parrish exhibition at a Hartford museum and then go out to dinner. Kristen had read about the exhibit in the newspaper and picked up on it immediately because Maxfield Parrish was Chris's favorite artist. Without a second thought, she'd invited Eric to go.

I need to get my mind off everything, she'd told herself.

Both of us need a break.

Tapping her foot, Kristen organized the piles on her desk and saw a yellow sticky note from the day before that said "Call Louis."

Shit, she meant to do that too.

Louis had left her several voice mail messages the past couple days and he'd asked her to please call him back, it was important. Well, there were too many other things that were important, and she hadn't gotten back to him.

She picked up the phone and dialed his cell phone but only got voice mail. She was about to hang up before leaving a message and then thought better of it.

"Hey Louis," she said after the tone. "Got your messages but don't call me back tonight, I'm busy. I'll try to reach you again tomorrow."

Maybe he was calling to see if she'd heard any more news from the St. Maarten police. Paula's death had been ruled a drowning by the Dutch medical examiner and there was no evidence of a homicide, but there were enough loose ends dangling to keep the authorities interested. They still hadn't located anyone who'd sailed with Paula on a private yacht or found her luggage.

Even the exact day and time of her death wasn't certain. Kristen had learned more than she wanted to about drowning victims: Paula's body had been found beneath the surface of the water, which suggested she'd died less than a week before she'd been found. Otherwise, the medical examiner had explained, her body would have floated due to the gases accumulating in her tissues and cavities.

It was possible Paula had died just before, or even during, the time that she, Eric, and Louis had been in St. Maarten looking for her.

The recurring thought that her sister could have been saved made her eyes water again. Lately she was always close to tears. Maybe if she and Eric had spent more time searching they could have found her before it was too late. And who knew if Paula's mystery man was involved. Kristen envisioned Paula swimming by herself or maybe with this man at the remote beach where she was found. Maybe she had a cramp or got caught in a rip tide. Maybe the man she was with panicked and left her. In either case it was a horrible way to die.

She had no idea how long she sat at her desk staring at her computer screen, seeing nothing but images of her sister. Paula confiding her anguish about Louis's betrayal, her guilt about her divorce. Her restlessness and strangely desperate need to find someone else to fill the void. Her determination to get her life back on track.

A soft knock at the main door startled Kristen out of her reverie, and she checked her watch and rose from her chair. Almost six o'clock already and she hadn't accomplished a damn thing. It was just as well that she was going out tonight with Eric. He'd been such a support to her during this awful time.

She opened the door, expecting Eric, but the thin, unkempt man who pushed his way past her was someone she had never seen before.

"Where is she?" The man wheeled to face her, his face a bright red. "Where the hell did she go?"

He grabbed Kristen's shoulders, pressing her against the wall. He reeked of alcohol and the pupils of his eyes were tiny black dots.

"I don't know who you're looking for," Kristen said calmly, her mind whirling.

She didn't attempt to free herself from his claw-like grip.

"My wife," he spat. "I saw her come here. Tell me where she is."

"Sir, you have the wrong office," Kristen said, eyeing the door a few inches away, wondering if she could break his hold on her arms and run outside.

"I don't believe you."

The man's fingers dug hard into her flesh, but in the next second the door opened all the way and Eric stepped inside. He sized up the situation immediately and just as the man released Kristen, Eric grabbed him by the collar.

"What the hell do you think you're doing?" Eric hissed, jacking the man off his feet.

"Lookin' for my wife," the man sputtered. "Get off me."

He threw out a weak punch that Eric deflected easily. Kristen saw Eric tighten his grip and slam the man against the wall.

"Why'd you have your hands on her? Huh? We could have you arrested, you piece of shit."

"I'll call the police," Kristen whispered, her hands trembling.

"No. Let me go," the man whined, his eyes wide. "I'll leave right now."

Eric kept the man pinned to the wall as easily as if he were holding a child.

"What's your name?" Eric asked.

"Mel," the man muttered.

"Mel what?"

"Mel Blackstone. Let me go." His reedy voice quavered. "I'm sorry. I was lookin' for my wife. I saw her come in the building."

"What, you two have a fight or something?"

Eric's tone was almost friendly, conversational, but Kristen saw the tightness in his jaw and the way his gaze never wavered from the man's face.

"Yeah."

"Well, *Mel,* she isn't here. And if you ever step foot in this place again, I'll break your goddamn neck. Got it?"

Mel Blackstone nodded, silent. Eric slowly released his grip.

"Get your sorry drunk ass out of here."

The man did not need to be told twice. Eric shoved him out the door and he stumbled down the hallway. They heard him curse loudly as he tripped on the stairs. Eric watched him leave the building and then he closed the office door. He took Kristen in his arms.

"Are you all right?"

"Yes," she said, hugging him back.

When she drew away, he looked at her arms.

"Any bruises?"

"No."

"We can still call the police if you want," he said, straightening his tie and jacket as though the scuffle had rumpled his suit. "Although I doubt that clown will be back."

Kristen took a deep breath.

"I'd rather not wait around here all night for the police to come. I think you're right—he won't be back. He was so drunk he may not even remember this later."

"I noticed this isn't the greatest neighborhood," Eric said. "There were some bums hanging out on the corner when I got here."

Kristen shook her head, still rattled.

"Usually the door's locked. My staff must have forgotten. I didn't check it when Roshana left. A couple months ago a homeless woman came into the building and completely destroyed the ladies' room. She was mentally ill, I'm sure, but after that, we had to put locks on the restrooms too." Kristen realized she was rambling, her voice quivering. "I'm really glad you got here when you did."

"Me too," Eric said. "I don't know what would have happened otherwise. You could have been seriously hurt. Will you promise me you'll be more careful in the future?"

Kristen nodded, not quite liking his chiding tone.

"I usually am."

"All it takes is one time," he said.

Kristen felt tears sting her eyes. She blinked them away, feeling humiliated.

Did he think this was all her fault? Was it?

"Do you still want to go to the museum?" Eric asked. "I'm sorry, this really worried me."

He drew her again into his arms and she pressed her head against his warm chest. He smelled of mint and aftershave. She felt a fresh wave of tears threaten to erupt although she wasn't sure why.

"Yes, I want to go," she finally said, getting herself under control. She looked up at him and forced a smile. "I was looking forward to this all day."

They arrived shortly before the reception was to start. Eric circled the block twice before he located a parking spot.

"Must be a popular event," he said.

"Did you see the Caravaggio exhibit last year?" Kristen asked, trying to fill the silence.

They'd hardly spoken on the drive through the city.

"I haven't been to any art museums in a few years," he said. "I've been traveling a lot for work and haven't had the time." He hesitated. "Speaking of traveling, let's talk later about Montreal. I have a meeting there soon and it'd be great if you could come."

"I can't wait to go."

Eric took her hand as they walked down the sidewalk to the museum. They stood in line for tickets and finally made their way into the grand foyer where a string quartet played. Clusters of people mingled in the large ornate room with its high ceiling, deep auburn walls, and shiny marble floor. A bar was set up on one side with a table of hors d'oeuvres nearby. While Eric went to the bar, Kristen made her way to the table to get them a plate of appetizers

"Kristen?"

She turned her head, recognizing the familiar voice instantly. There he was, all six feet four inches of him, smiling down at her.

"Chris. How are you?" Kristen felt the blood rush to her face. She looked down at the floor and then back to his ocean blue eyes, crinkling at the edges. He wore an ivory silk poet's shirt, jeans, and alligator boots. With his long blonde-gray curls, he looked like a cross between a fourteenth century nobleman and a pirate. He looked exactly the same as the last time she'd seen him over a year ago.

"I'm doing well. Yourself? You still working in Hartford?"

"Yes." Kristen flushed. He was standing so close to her, she could smell him. Irish Spring soap. "And what about you? Still running the Iron Man every year?"

He chuckled.

"Not this year. I did a bike race in Iowa instead."

"Oh. Sounds like fun," she finally said, at an absolute loss for anything intelligent to say. Her heart was pounding. "So you're here to see the exhibit."

"You know I'm a big Maxfield Parrish fan," he said. "I still have that print you gave me. It's hanging over my fireplace."

"I remember."

"Can I get you a drink?"

"Oh no, no thanks," she said. "My, uh, my boyfriend is getting something for me."

She looked toward the bar and saw Eric approaching.

"Oh, so that means I can't take you out to dinner tonight," Chris said. "That's too bad."

Eric reached her side and handed her a glass of merlot.

"Cheers," he said, and Kristen saw a strange, hard expression in his eyes. She knew he'd heard Chris's remark about dinner.

"Eric, this is Chris, a friend of mine," Kristen said. "We bumped into each other in the appetizer line."

"Nice meeting you. Well, you two have fun in the museum," Chris said, turning away to fill up his plate.

"Yeah, bye," she said, and looked at Eric. She offered him the plate of snacks. Her hands were trembling. "Would you like some?"

"No thanks," he said. "I lost my appetite. What was that all about? Who was that guy?"

"An old friend," she stammered.

"Your face is beet red."

Kristen bit her lip. She felt like a sixteen-year-old in high school.

"Why did he say he couldn't take you out to dinner? Because

I'm here?"

"He was joking," Kristen said, although she wasn't sure of that at all. It would be just like Chris to sweep back into her life for one night if it suited him.

"No, he wasn't joking," Eric said.

She looked away, at a complete loss for words.

"So are you still seeing this guy or what?"

Kristen drew in a breath.

"Of course not. Why would you say that?"

Eric took a long sip of his wine, eyes not leaving hers.

"All day I was looking forward to a nice evening with you. A night where things could feel normal again."

"Me too," Kristen said, touching his arm.

He shook her off.

"Let's go to the exhibit since we're here," he said.

They both heard Kristen's cell phone ring inside her purse. She made no move to pick it up.

Eric's voice was sharp.

"Why don't you answer it?"

She reluctantly took the cell phone from her purse and saw Louis' name on the screen. She turned the ringer off. Why the hell did he have to call her now?

"Who was that?" Eric said. "Mr. Pirate of the Caribbean? Wanting to know when you can ditch me so you two can go out to dinner?"

Kristen stared at him.

Was he serious?

"What's wrong with you?"

"Who was it then?"

"Louis," she said. "He's called me a few times this week. I haven't gotten back to him yet."

Eric nodded.

"Oh, yeah, *Louis*. Another one."

He pulled his arm away from her.

"What do you mean?"

They edged to a less populated corner of the room. Kristen felt her face getting hot.

"Eric, what's the matter?"

"Haven't I been the one to stand by you? Haven't I tried to be supportive and show you how I feel about you? Especially these past few weeks?"

"I'm not seeing anyone else, Eric. I'm not interested in anyone else."

He looked up at the ceiling, avoiding her gaze.

"Sure. You know, I really don't care to see this exhibit anyway. I only agreed to go because you wanted to. And now I know why." He gestured in Chris' direction. "I'm behind at work because I took a lot of time off to be with you. That's what I should be doing tonight, catching up on work. Or spending more time with my father. No one else visits him."

She felt stung and fought back angry tears.

"Fine. Then why don't you bring me home."

They had never argued before, and she expected to call his bluff. She hoped he would realize he was acting childish and unreasonable. Surely he wouldn't ruin their night out.

"Let's go," he said grimly, and without looking to see if she was following him, he walked toward the exit.

Kristen couldn't believe her eyes. She hesitated but he did not turn around. He continued purposefully on his way and had there not been so many people present, she would have run after him and demanded that he stop. Stop this nonsense.

What the hell had she done to deserve this?

"Eric," she called, as he walked out the door. She caught up to him on the sidewalk and tugged at his sleeve like a child. "What are you doing? Why are you doing this?"

Was it because he was stressed about his father and taking it out on her?

She didn't dare ask.

He pried her hand off his arm. When he met her gaze, his eyes were cold and distant.

135

"I didn't do anything."

She followed him to the car. He drove her back to her office in silence, refusing to look at her and refusing to speak. The ten minutes felt to Kristen like an hour as she struggled to maintain some semblance of composure and think of what to say. This was so ridiculous. She wanted nothing more than to spend the evening with him, have dinner with him, make love to him later at her house and wake up next to him in the morning. Plan for Montreal. Instead she would go home alone.

He pulled up to her car in the parking lot.

"Eric. Is this what you really want to do tonight? I'm very sorry you're so upset." Now the tears spilled over in a flood. She couldn't help it. "Everything's gone wrong tonight. Why can't we start over? I want to go out to dinner with you. I want to spend the night with you."

He merely waited for her to get out of his car.

"Goodnight," he said, his tone clipped and impersonal.

"Why are you doing this?" she repeated, still bewildered.

He tapped his fingers on the steering wheel.

Kristen got out of the car and slammed the door shut. He was gone before she could get into her car. So much for his concern about the bad neighborhood and her welfare. Her cell phone beeped, and she looked at the screen. It was a text message from Louis.

Call me please. It's urgent.

CHAPTER TWELVE

FOR A LONG moment, Kristen sat in her car with the cell phone in her hand and the keys in the ignition. She wiped the tears from her eyes and wondered what to do. If she went home she knew she would be restless and unhappy, and replay the scene with Eric over and over in her mind. Or she would call him and make the mistake of asking for an explanation or apology when it was obvious she wasn't likely to get either.

Damn it, what was wrong with him? And why did Chris have to show up at the museum anyway?

Seeing Chris again had simultaneously been a guilty thrill and a punch in the gut. She had worked hard to get over that heartbreak.

She called Louis and he answered immediately.

"I've been trying to reach you for days," he said. "Are you okay? How are you holding up?"

"I've been busy. It's been a very tough week," she said. "I know you were trying to reach me. Sorry."

"Are you alone? Can you talk for a few minutes?"

Kristen scanned the parking lot, realizing that she didn't

quite care to sit there in her car for very long. It wasn't the best neighborhood, especially after dark. The lights were off in the office building and hers was the only car in the parking lot. What if the lunatic who attacked her earlier in the evening decided to come back?

"I'm at my office," she said. "Actually in my car. I was going to drive home."

"I'm at my office too," Louis said. "Do you want to stop by? I really need to talk with you."

Kristen hesitated.

"All right."

Truth be told, she was glad he asked. Glad she could postpone a long night alone at her house.

She pulled out of the parking lot and drove the quarter-mile down Prospect Street to Louis's office in the white house with black shutters. She parked behind the building, as close as possible to the back entrance. The lighting was poor and this neighborhood was sketchy too.

Louis was already on the stairway holding the door open for her. He looked worried.

"Come in," he said and she followed him without a word, the floorboards of the old house creaking as they walked down the carpeted hallway.

"This doesn't bring back good memories, you know," she said, inhaling the familiar mustiness, noting the frayed edges of the carpet in his office. A solitary lamp cast a soft glow. She hesitated and then sank into the too-soft beige couch across from his leather chair.

Just like old times.

Louis closed the door and sat down on the couch next to her, his fingers clasping and unclasping nervously. She thought he looked like he could use a therapy session himself.

"Are you doing all right?" he asked. "I haven't talked to you since—since the funeral."

"I'm hanging in there," she said. "It's complicated, dealing with Paula's estate. She had a will, thank God, but even so, it's going to take me awhile to get her house cleaned out and sell it."

"If there's anything I can help you with, tell me," he said.

"So what was so important?" she asked, studying his face more closely.

"Do you know who BD9908 is? Did Paula ever mention anyone she met online with that screen name?"

She looked into his narrowed gray-blue eyes. "No, she didn't. Why?"

"Paula was trying to meet other men when we broke up," Louis said. "She was emailing men from dating sites and there was one in particular that was playing her. He called himself BD9908. She told him she was going to St. Maarten and she even told him the name of the hotel where she was staying."

"I knew she was trying to meet someone new and that she was using some dating sites. What's the guy's real name?"

Louis shrugged. "I don't know."

"So how do you know about her emailing this BD guy?"

"Because I saw it," he said. "I read their emails to each other."

"How? You had her password?"

"I had her computer."

Kristen stared at him but before she could say anything, he picked up his phone and dialed the codes to access his voice mail.

"Listen to this," he said, and played Paula's last message to him on speaker.

Louis, just wanted to let you know I met someone here. I'm having fun. Maybe we'll talk when I get back next week. Beady nine.

"Her voice sounds odd, doesn't it? Took me until yesterday to make the connection," Louis said. "Beady nine…BD9908. If you listen carefully, it sounds like she's cut off before she has time to finish saying the rest of the screen name."

He played the message again, turning up the volume.

Beady nine. BD 9.

Kristen frowned.

"So what does this mean?"

"I think she was with someone who forced her to leave that message for me, and she tried to say who it was. She probably didn't know his real name either." Louis shifted in his chair. "I think it's this guy she was emailing. He knew where she was staying and he could have followed her to the island."

"But she texted me several times."

"Maybe it wasn't her doing the texting." Louis took a deep breath. "You never spoke to her once while you were there, did you? You never heard her voice. How easy would it be for someone else to text you from her phone? Was her phone ever recovered? Or her luggage? Did the police ever find the guy she was supposedly sailing with?"

"Not yet," Kristen said slowly, trying to absorb what he was saying. "But they said she drowned, probably accidentally. She had Xanax in her system. The police told me they were still investigating."

"Did they ask you about me?"

"Yes, yes, they did." She struggled to remember the details. Once they'd called with the news of Paula's death, things had gotten fuzzy. She'd been distraught. "They wanted to know why you were there and I told them you were looking for her. And yes, they did ask me about your relationship and I said you two weren't together anymore, but I didn't get into any details."

"I expect that at some point they'll question me," Louis said. "They could even contact the FBI and get them involved if they think I had something to do with Paula's death."

"That's crazy. You're kidding, right? Why would anyone think that?"

"The timing is such that Paula could have, *might have* died while we were there. I can't account for every minute of my time. I don't have witnesses to corroborate every place that I went on the island. You were with your boyfriend so you can't vouch for me if it comes to that."

"Oh my God," Kristen breathed. "You really think you're a suspect? What about the guy she was supposed to be sailing with? They'll find him, don't you think?"

"Who knows? I haven't heard anything other than what you've told me," he said. "But I think Paula was kidnapped and murdered. I think it was this BD guy who did it."

She looked at his grim face and then down at the frayed beige carpeting. Her lip trembled and she swallowed hard.

"Did you tell the police about these emails?"

"No. I took Paula's computer from her house when I got back from St. Maarten," Louis said, looking down at the floor. "I wanted to find out what she was doing. I know. It sounds bad."

"You went into her house?" she asked, unable to help the accusatory tone in her voice.

"Yes. I took her laptop."

"So give it to the police. They can trace who this guy is."

Louis shook his head.

"It's gone. Someone took it from my house the night you called me and told me they found Paula's body. But that's not all. Since then I've logged into her account from my own computer and all the emails have been deleted. There's nothing there from BD9908 anymore."

"I'm sure there are computer forensic people who can retrieve them," Kristen said, her mind whirling.

"I think someone's trying to set me up," Louis went on. "First the laptop was taken. Then an Avon cop paid me a visit because someone posted a sex ad on the Internet for his sister, and this ad was traced back to me. I didn't post it. I would never do something like that. But he did the Dutch uncle routine and made it very clear I better watch my step."

"That's weird. Who's his sister?"

"A woman named Victoria Rudemann," Louis said, looking away from her again. "You may have heard of her. It was all over the newspapers when she accused me of unethical conduct some time ago."

"I remember that," Kristen said. "But I don't understand how there's any connection between her and Paula."

"I don't know what the connection is exactly. But it seems pretty bizarre to me that both of these things happened in a short period of time." He told her about the fake blind date he'd set up with BD9908. "Maybe this guy knows I'm on to him. That's why I wanted to talk to you. I was hoping you might know who he is. Paula never said anything?"

"No. I'm sorry."

"I wish I could go back in time," he said. "I didn't cheat on Paula, and that's the truth. If she only knew that, maybe she wouldn't have gone to St. Maarten in the first place. I never had the chance to tell her."

She looked at him for a long moment and saw his eyes were watering.

"Is that really true?"

He nodded.

Kristen covered her face with her hands and there was no controlling the grief and guilt that welled up like lava.

"I miss her so much."

"Me too."

Her shoulders shook as she bowed her head and wept. Louis touched her arm and waited quietly until she settled down. He handed her a box of tissues.

"I'm sorry," she said. "It's been a terrible day." She wiped her eyes, suddenly feeling the same way she had when she'd seen him for therapy sessions: an uncomfortable mix of vulnerability, anger, and sorrow. Maybe nothing had changed for her after all. She'd lost her sister.

And now Eric too.

"No need to apologize."

Without thinking, she reached for his hand. "I want to help in whatever way I can. I'm sorry I was so awful to you. I was mad at you, really mad."

He patted her hand and drew away, rising to his feet. She

noticed in the dim light the dark circles under his eyes, his wrinkled khakis and scuffed shoes. He probably hadn't slept much lately. How could he, given what he'd told her? He looked past her as if he were studying something interesting on the wall.

"Are you going to be okay tonight?" he asked.

She took a deep breath.

"I'll be all right. Sometimes I can't stand being home but I'll be okay."

"I can't stand being home any night."

For a long moment neither one spoke. Then he turned toward the door.

"I'll walk you out to your car."

"If I hear any news from the police, I'll let you know," Kristen said. "Will you keep me posted too? Let me know if you find out anything?"

"Yes."

Kristen wondered how late he planned to stay in his office on this Friday night.

I can't stand being home any night.

She understood that. Understood it all too well.

They walked out into the warm night. A soft breeze stirred the leaves of the tall oak trees at the edge of the parking lot.

"That guy you with being supportive?" Louis asked. "Eric?"

She didn't answer. No need for more drama, she decided. Besides, the last thing she wanted to admit was that Chris was still rattling around in her heart somewhere, screwing things up in the present.

"Didn't mean to sound nosy," Louis finally said as they neared her car. "I wanted to make sure you'll be all right tonight."

"I'll be fine," she said.

"Take care of yourself."

"You too."

On impulse she leaned forward and gave him a hug. She felt

him recoil as though startled, but then he awkwardly hugged her back and released her. He stepped back as she unlocked her car door.

"Goodnight," he said.

She started her car and pulled out of the driveway onto Prospect Street. She was slowing down for the first red light when a car with its high beams on pulled out suddenly from a side road and tailgated her.

Kristen sped up when the light turned green and the other driver kept pace. She glanced in her rear view mirror but the bright light from the high beams made it impossible to see the driver behind her, inches away from her bumper. If she braked suddenly she'd get rear-ended.

Where were the cops when you needed them?

She was relieved when she finally reached the highway entrance ramp and the car behind her blew straight through the intersection.

CHAPTER THIRTEEN

Later That Night

VICTORIA RUDEMANN AND her friend Lindsey stumbled out of Lindsey's blue BMW, which Lindsey had parked haphazardly in Victoria's driveway. They were both giggling like raucous teenagers.

"You shouldn't be driving," Victoria said. "Lookit, you almost hit the fucking fence. Look how far up you parked."

"I didn't hit the fucking fence, I almost hit your fucking car," Lindsey slurred, pointing to Victoria's black Acura a few feet away.

She burst into a fresh fit of laughter.

Victoria stared up at her dark house.

"Shit, I shoulda left a light on. I thought we'd be back earlier."

She and Lindsey had spent the last several hours sampling Lindsey's new medical marijuana. That, coupled with a six-pack of summer ale, had made for a night of hilarity she thought was well-deserved after the shitty week she'd had.

"You sure you don't want to stay at my place tonight?" Lindsey asked. "Freddy's back at school, you can sleep in his room. He's got some fucking iguana in a tank but I'll cover it up with a sheet so you don't see it."

Victoria fumbled in her purse for her house keys.

"Nah, I gotta get up early tomorrow and meet with the security guys. They're gonna put in an alarm system. Thanks anyway."

"I'll go in with you," Lindsey said. "Make sure you're safe. I got pepper spray in my purse."

"Ooh, ooh, pepper spray, keep the guys with whips and chains away," Victoria sang.

"Send 'em over to my place," Lindsey said. "I'll take care of 'em. Forty shades of gray, here we come."

"It's fifty shades, isn't it? Whatever. Be my guest, you can have those sickos." Victoria peered at Lindsey and added "Your eyes are fifty shades of red. You should be the one who stays over. I got an extra room too."

Two extra rooms, as a matter of fact, since her two young boys lived with her ex-husband now. She wouldn't see them for another week or so, depending on whether the bastard allowed it. He had full custody and their arguments about visitation were constant, even with the court order. The thought of him, his arrogant fat face and his fat bitch new wife getting to spend time with her boys instead of her, made her teeth clench.

"Thanks for the invite, but I'll be fine getting home," Lindsey said. "I have to get up early for work. I'll take the back roads and anyway, if I get stopped I'll say I know your brother."

"Or you can flash your boobs," Victoria said. "That would work just as well."

They both laughed, and Victoria found her key and inserted it into the lock. The front door swung open and she flipped on the light switches for the hallway and the outside lights. The warm welcoming glow dispelled her momentary feelings of unease.

Ever since the stupid sex ad had appeared on the Internet, along with an assortment of smarmy men on her doorstep eager to tie her up, she'd been a little spooked living by herself in her big house. She was glad her older brother Ed, an Avon cop, had tracked down the asshole who'd posted the ad and put a stop to it.

Louis D'Maio. Dr. D'Maio.

She hated him as much as she hated her ex-husband, and boy, did the doctor make a mistake messing with her again.

"What's the matter?" Lindsey asked. "You look mad."

"It's nothing," Victoria said. The high was wearing off and she felt the start of a headache in her right temple. She thought about the stash of pills she had in the drawer of her nightstand. Hopefully she still had some Oxycodone left.

They walked into the large kitchen and Victoria chucked her purse on the granite center island. Lindsey opened the door to the pantry.

"All clear in here."

Victoria turned on every light downstairs while Lindsey stumbled merrily from room to room checking behind drapes and opening closet doors, holding her pepper spray out like a beacon. Victoria watched her, her annoyance growing with each painful pulse in her temple. All she wanted to do now was lie down and turn on the TV.

"Lindsey, I'm all set," she said, hoping her friend would take the hint and get the hell out.

"What about the basement? And the upstairs?"

"It's fine."

"I'll take a quick peek," Lindsey said and started up the carpeted stairs.

Victoria thought of the mess in her bedroom and wondered what personal things she may have left out on the bureaus. Probably nothing Lindsey couldn't see, but still.

"No, really, you don't have to do that," she said, hearing the sharpness in her tone. "The doors were all locked down here.

No one could have gotten in."

"You sure?" Lindsey hesitated and turned on the staircase. "Okay."

"Thanks. It was fun tonight," Victoria said.

"Anytime. Next time I fill my prescription, you can come right over."

Victoria headed upstairs to her bedroom as soon as Lindsey was gone. She slipped out of her tank top and shorts—everything reeked of marijuana—and tossed them in the laundry bin. She opened the door to her walk-in closet to fetch a robe.

The man who stood in the dark closet grabbed her arm.

"Oh Jesus!" she shrieked, and a hand clapped over her mouth just as he pulled her close to him and pressed something cold against her bare back.

"Don't you fucking move," he said in a low, calm voice. "Or I'll blow a hole right through your spine. Got it?"

She nodded and he propelled her out of the closet. She twisted her head around, trying to see his face.

"Don't move until I tell you," he said, jabbing the muzzle of the gun harder against her skin.

She relaxed in his grip, breathing heavily through her nose. His warm hand was still pressed firmly against her mouth.

"I'm gonna let you go. But if you scream or run, I'll shoot you. Understand?"

She nodded again and forced herself to stand still. He released her and the floor creaked as he took a step back. She licked her lips and swallowed hard, her heart hammering in her chest. She still hadn't gotten a good look at him.

"What do you want?" she asked in a tiny voice, facing the wall. "I didn't put that ad up myself, if that's what you're after."

She became aware that all she had on was her black lacy bra and panties.

"Turn around slowly."

She did as instructed. He had moved back some more and

now stood facing her, his expression dispassionate. She'd never seen him before and she took in his height, his athletic build. The revolver in his right hand was aimed at her chest. She closed her eyes for a moment, expecting his next move would be to make her strip naked.

"Get dressed," he said. She opened her eyes and he motioned to the dresser near her bed. "Open the drawer and take out a shirt and shorts."

She opened the drawer and took out the clothing, mind registering that he must have snooped around her room if he knew where to direct her. Her hands trembled as she pulled on her shorts and slipped a T-shirt over her head. She glanced toward her bedroom window but it was closed. Even if she did scream, the nearest neighbor was a quarter mile away. No one would hear her.

"Look, if you want money I'll give you whatever I have," she said, as calmly as she could manage. The fact that he hadn't bothered with any sort of disguise was a bad sign, she thought. She could identify him.

"I don't want your money," he said. "Shut up. We're going downstairs. I'm gonna follow you and like I said before, no sudden moves. You don't want a bullet in your spine, do you?"

Her mind raced.

If he didn't want money and he didn't want sex, what did he want?

She walked slowly down the stairs and he was right behind her, the gun to her back.

She decided that as soon as she reached the bottom of the landing, she'd bolt and run like hell. Maybe she could make it out the door and to the neighbors' or lose him in the woods. She was a fast runner and she knew the terrain.

Her body tensed on the bottom stairs. As if reading her thoughts, his left hand grabbed her shoulder and the gun nudged her spine.

"Don't even think about it," he said. "You wouldn't even make it to the door. I'll aim for your head instead of your spine, splatter your brains all over the wall."

"Who the fuck are you?" she asked as he led her to the couch in the living room.

She'd left one lamp on although Lindsey had closed the drapes.

"Francis," he said. "Now sit down."

She hadn't expected him to answer, and she searched her mental database. Francis? She didn't know anyone named Francis except for her dentist. She sat, arms crossed, covering her breasts although he did not seem interested in her body.

Try to engage him, she thought.

Make him see me as a human being.

He had moved slightly to her left, still standing. He sighed and she thought he looked distracted, maybe a little unsure of himself.

"Francis, I don't know what you want, but I can pay you a lot of money if you leave right now. And no one ever has to know," she said. "I have two little boys that rely on me."

His eyes narrowed and his mouth turned down in disgust.

"No, you don't. Your kids don't rely on you at all, you crack whore. They're with your ex-husband. You hardly ever see them."

She stared at him, shocked.

How did he know that?

"You're high as a kite right now, aren't you? You stink like weed," he went on. "You aren't a fit parent. You don't even deserve to have kids."

Tears stung her eyelids and she blinked.

"Get out of here."

Gun or no gun, she'd had enough of this creep.

"Too bad you're not my type," he said. "This is business, not pleasure."

"I don't know what you mean."

She fought back a wave of panic. She started to rise from the couch.

He pointed the revolver at her head and cocked the trigger. "I can't say I'm sorry I have to do this. It isn't fun, though." Her mouth dropped open, and she stared at his widening grin.

CHAPTER FOURTEEN

AFTER KRISTEN LEFT, Louis returned to his office. He'd
told her he couldn't stand being home at night and that was true,
but he could barely stand being at work either. He was
emotionally drained and grieving, and nothing seemed normal.

He opened the blinds and peered outside the dirty window.
The overgrown hedges in the front of the house partially
blocked his view of the street. One dim streetlight offered a
silvery glow that cut across the narrow front yard but there were
plenty of areas shrouded in darkness where someone could hide.
He checked to make sure the window was locked.

He was getting paranoid. He had no idea if the same person
who had gotten into his house and taken Paula's laptop was the
same person who used his name to set up the fake bondage ad
for Victoria Rudemann. If so, what was the connection?

Good ol' Victoria. Victoria Rudemann had been his patient
nearly two years earlier. She was a former model in her thirties
and in layman's terms, a sociopath. Hell-bent on destroying her
ex-husband. According to her, her husband Michael had the gall
to file for divorce when he'd caught her in bed with her yoga

teacher. He'd gone to court to gain sole custody of their two young sons after claiming she was a drug addict and emotionally unstable.

She came to Louis for a psychological evaluation that would prove to the court she was a fit parent. Except she wasn't. Not by a long shot, unless frequent drug use, emotional abuse of her two boys, and blatant infidelity were hallmarks of good parenting.

Louis's report enraged her. She'd demanded that he change it; she threatened to ruin his practice and his life if he didn't, and in the end she'd made good on her threat. She contacted the state Department of Public Health, the American Psychological Association, and the state ethics board and filed a complaint that Louis had made sexual advances toward her, she'd refused him, and because of that, he had retaliated and written an unfavorable report for the court.

For months afterward Louis endured a lengthy investigation and was in jeopardy of losing his clinical license.

Victoria had also approached the local newspaper and news stations, and he'd watched in sick fascination as she embellished her story with convincing details, appearing on the evening news with tears streaking her mascara, wringing her hands about the loss of her family and the public humiliation she'd suffered due to the abominable actions of her ethically-challenged therapist.

The press loved it. Her good looks and astonishing acting ability made her a staple in the newspaper as well. Publicly Louis could not defend himself due to the restrictions of privacy and confidentiality laws.

The investigation behind the scenes took months. His practice almost closed as new referrals dried up and current patients, especially women, were persuaded by their spouses or families to switch to other therapists. The financial consequences were devastating. He'd nearly lost his condo and his savings were wiped out.

In the end, the board cleared him of the ethics charges,

finding insufficient evidence. Plenty of evidence was uncovered during the course of the investigation that pretty Victoria Rudemann was a liar and an abusive parent to boot, but none of that mattered. By the time he was cleared and the press lost interest, the damage was done.

She had even sued him for malpractice and his insurance company had chosen to settle instead of fighting a costly battle. She'd ended up with a load of cash while Louis struggled to support himself and his daughter and rebuild his tattered business. He'd gotten seriously over-extended with credit cards and for a while had taken on consulting work with a local mental health clinic, but still barely made ends meet.

A year after the case had been settled he was still recovering from the financial toll. Victoria Rudemann. Just thinking about her made him hyperventilate. Her brother, the Avon cop, had warned she could sue him in civil court for slander, damage to her reputation and God knew what else related to the sex ad. He had no doubt she would be ruthless if she believed he was responsible.

He sat at his desk and stared at the neat stack of insurance forms he needed to submit for his patients. Paperwork was never his strong suit. But his bills were piling up, he couldn't afford an administrative assistant to help him, and he had to focus, get his mind off Paula, Kristen, and everything else.

He buckled down, got to work and in the next hour managed to make a small dent in the billing when there were two loud knocks on his office door. He glanced at the wall clock. Who would come to his office after 8 PM? The janitorial service had left long ago.

He walked to the door leading to the waiting area and called out, "Who is it?"

"It's me. Charlotte."

Louis unlocked the door and swung it open.

"Hi. This is a surprise."

He had not spoken to Charlotte since their ill-fated lunch

weeks earlier.

He took one look at her red-rimmed eyes and trembling lips, and put a hand on her shoulder.

"What's the matter?"

Instantly he thought of her daughter, Annie. Maybe she'd run away from the residential drug treatment program.

"I need to talk to you. Are you alone?"

She moved away from his touch.

"Yes. Come in."

For the second time that evening he perched on the edge of the couch but Charlotte remained standing. She clutched her purse close to her thin body and stared at him, blinking rapidly. She pushed a strand of brown hair away from her eyes.

"I can't wrap my head around this, Louis," she said. "I had to come see you in person and ask you myself."

"Ask me what?"

She bit her lip and held his gaze.

"Did you molest Annie when you lived with us?"

His jaw literally dropped.

"Of course not," he said, feeling as though he'd gotten sucker-punched. "Jesus."

"I got a phone call tonight from one of Annie's therapists at Silver Meadows. He said that Annie told him in a session today that you, that *you* molested her when she was thirteen. When you lived with us. She didn't want to tell me until now. The therapist said he was calling the state to report it. The Department of Children and Families."

Her eyes filled with tears.

"I never molested your daughter," Louis said, shaking his head. "Charlotte, it isn't true. Did you talk to Annie yourself?"

"The therapist said I couldn't speak to her tonight, but we'll have an emergency session tomorrow morning," she said. "I've known you for a long time, Louis. I didn't think you were capable of something like this."

"It isn't true," he repeated. "For God's sake, Charlotte. I

would never do something like that."

"The therapist seems to think so," she said. "He told me he's seen this a lot, it's very common. He thinks it's why she started using drugs in the first place, because she was repressing these memories. And he said I should expect you to deny it."

He took several deep breaths to calm himself.

"What exactly did Annie tell him? Do you know?"

She looked down at her sandals.

"That you fondled her, made her…do things to you when I wasn't around. Many times. The whole year you stayed with us."

"Who's the therapist?"

He wondered if he knew the man, not that it would matter. Therapists were mandated reporters and no practitioner could sit on a bombshell like this, even if there was no evidence to support such an allegation. The state had to investigate and make a determination.

"Someone I haven't talked to before, someone new working with Annie," Charlotte said. "Louis, I have a hard time believing you could be that kind of a monster, but why would Annie say something so awful? Why would she lie?"

"I don't know why she would."

Had there been any occasion, any possible reason, Annie could have thought his behavior was in any way inappropriate? He searched his memory and could not recall a single instance he had even touched her, other than the rare fatherly hug.

In his professional experience, sometimes false accusations were made by angry teens out of spite or in retribution for some perceived slight. Often the teen did not understand how devastating such a charge could be. He had worked before with families torn apart by sexual abuse allegations, and it wasn't pleasant. At the very least, the adult who was accused usually endured horrific consequences, whether guilty or innocent.

Given Annie's age, this was likely to turn quickly into a criminal investigation.

He realized that no matter what happened next, he needed to speak to a lawyer. Anything he said now could be misinterpreted by Charlotte, quoted in a police report, perhaps eventually heard by a jury. He felt sick.

"Louis, you need to know I have to stand by my daughter, no matter what," Charlotte said. "I'm grateful for everything you did to get her into treatment. She's making progress. I just don't know." She turned away, sobbing. "I don't know why I came here. I guess I thought I'd get some sort of resolution and know what to do next. But I don't."

"You know who I am, Charlotte. You know what kind of person I am. I'm not perfect and I regret some things that happened between you and me, but I'm not a pedophile."

She wiped her eyes.

"I truly wish I could believe that. I honestly loved and trusted you, Louis, even if things didn't work out with us. But if it comes down to believing you and calling my daughter a liar…"

"Have your session tomorrow," he said. "Listen carefully to everything she has to say, and everything the therapist says."

He was sorely tempted to explain to her how sometimes, bad and biased practitioners with an agenda could encourage false memories in vulnerable clients.

It was also possible that Annie was furious with him for getting her into treatment in the first place and was lashing out at him in the most destructive way possible. However, he knew that suggesting either of these possibilities to Charlotte right now would only make her feel more conflicted. She needed time to process everything and learn more about what was going on with Annie.

"That's my plan," she said, her mouth a grim line. "I wish I could see her right now. I don't know how I can possibly sleep tonight."

The sorrow in her face wrenched his heart.

"Goodbye, Louis," she said, and her tone suggested that this was a final farewell. She took a deep breath. "And by the way, I'm sorry about Paula. I read her obituary in the newspaper."

He nodded. There was nothing more to say.

If buckling down to work was difficult before, it was damn near impossible now. Louis paced back and forth from the waiting area to his office, thinking of the year he'd lived with Charlotte and his interactions with Annie. There was no way, no way in hell he'd done anything that was even remotely out of line. The very thought of molesting a thirteen-year-old was disgusting, abhorrent. But he understood Charlotte's dilemma and how difficult it was for her, for any parent, to be objective when faced with this kind of explosive revelation. If his ex-wife Carol lived with some guy and Heather accused the man of abuse, Louis was certain his own response would be primal.

Either Annie was outright making things up or she was being influenced by an incompetent, maybe unscrupulous, therapist whose name Charlotte had not revealed. When Louis did his networking to find Annie a program, he'd talked to several colleagues and taken plenty of notes. Maybe he'd written something about the key staff. As in any profession, there were bad apples to avoid. There were some psychologists, psychiatrists, clinical social workers and marriage therapists that Louis wouldn't refer his cat to. Not that it wasn't just a matter of time before the Department of Children and Families paid him a visit and he'd find out who Annie's therapist was.

He went to his desk and looked for the notepad he always kept in the top drawer, but there was nothing. He pulled the other desk drawers open but couldn't find his notes there either.

What the hell?

He opened the beige five-drawer file cabinet next to his desk and riffled through his administrative and client files. His practice was too small to warrant the investment of an electronic health record system, and this file cabinet held about three years' worth of patient records. Including Kristen's, it occurred to him, and for no particular reason he flipped through the "S's." Salinger, Sanders, Scanlin, Sells, Speller, Sutta, and then…Szjadaski. No Spencer. He went through the manila folders again, starting at the R's in case something had been misfiled, and then through the S's and the T's. Kristen's file was gone.

He stared at the manila folders in disbelief and then furiously paged through the records in the entire drawer. It had to be misfiled. When was the last time he looked at it? Quite some time ago…maybe over a year. He checked the "K's" in case for some absent-minded, stupid reason he had filed it under "Kristen."

Of course it wasn't there.

He went through the S's and the R's one more time, and something else nagged at him. He paused for a moment, trying to calm his racing thoughts. When it struck him, he thumbed through the R's and laughed out loud, but it came out as a strange and strangled noise that was nothing, really, like a laugh. Victoria Rudemann. Yeah. The Rudemann case. That was gone too.

What else was missing? He reviewed his list of current patients. Their folders should have all been in the top drawer of the file cabinet. He tabbed through the names and came up three short.

Three missing patient records. He spent the next quarter hour searching through every drawer, every piece of paper on his desk, until he finally gave up. Either he was losing his mind or someone had broken into his office too and taken some files. It didn't make sense.

He locked up the file cabinets and put the key in his pocket. He'd been a moron, leaving the key accessible in his desk drawer. He resolved to conduct a thorough search again in the morning, with fresh eyes and a calmer mind.

He was about to power off the laptop on his desk when he noticed a new email in his Inbox with the subject line of "Patient

Files."

He clicked on it.

What the hell?

An image of a naked pre-pubescent girl, spread-eagled on a bed winking at the camera, filled the entire screen.

CHAPTER FIFTEEN

KRISTEN'S BEDROOM WINDOWS were open wide and a mild breeze stirred the sheer white curtains. She tossed and turned in bed, vaguely aware of the distant rumble of thunder. She'd taken two sleeping pills in the hopes that she would fall asleep quickly and stop playing the movie reel in her head of the night's events. As she felt her body finally relax and her thoughts slip away, the wind picked up and the first raindrops pelted the townhouse.

For a moment she didn't know where she was when she half-awakened, hearing loud knocks downstairs over the sound of the rain. Groggy and disoriented, she tried to listen but soon fell back asleep. Her eyes fluttered open in the darkness again when she felt a warm pressure on her mouth.

A hand. She blinked and tried to focus on the dark shape that loomed above her.

"Kristen, don't scream," a low, stern voice ordered.

The sheets were pulled off her body and before she could react, the man was on top of her. Instinctively she drew up her knees but he was heavy, so heavy. His face pressed against her neck. In sheer panic she twisted beneath him and clawed at his back. She was unable to utter a sound.

"It's me, Kristen, it's me," he gasped and she recognized the voice but she couldn't see his face, could only feel the suffocating weight of his body on top of her.

His mouth was on her neck, licking and sucking, and then on her lips.

When he broke away and straddled her, she stared up at him in shock, her eyes finally adjusting to the dark. His face was an inscrutable mask. She sucked air into her lungs and felt her heart pounding, limbs like jelly from the sudden surge of adrenalin.

"Eric. What the hell are you doing?" she said, but her voice was weak, barely more than a whisper.

Her head felt heavy, her thoughts like distant pulses in her brain, and she remembered that she'd taken the Ambien.

In response he opened the top buttons of her nightshirt, exposing her breasts. Her back arched involuntarily as he caressed her and shifted his body farther down on the bed. He unbuttoned the remaining buttons and held her gaze, his brown eyes coal black in the pale sliver of light from the streetlight outdoors. The rain beat steadily on the roof.

"Do you want me to stop?"

She did not reply. She closed her eyes and felt his hands and then his mouth on her belly, trailing downward. His fingers and tongue circled softly between her legs and she squirmed. He stopped to strip off his clothes and when she opened her eyes again, he was positioning himself on top of her.

"Don't you know how I feel about you?"

His palms cupped her face and he stroked her cheek. He kissed her slowly, gently, and knelt above her. Eyes fixed on hers, he moved her knees apart and entered her.

"Oh," she sighed and her breath was hot against his ear.

"Don't ever do that to me again," he said, his voice so low she barely heard him.

Kristen dug her fingernails into his smooth bare back, moist with sweat. She pressed his head to her breast, her fingers entwined in his hair. She writhed beneath him as he made love to her in a slow and steady rhythm, the headboard banging against the wall.

Afterwards he lay next to her quietly, staring up at the ceiling. They listened to the rain.

Kristen's head was beginning to clear although she still felt foggy, her thoughts forming in slow motion.

"You scared the crap out of me," she said. "What were you thinking?"

"I tried to wake you up. I called your cell phone and I knocked on the door for a while," he said. "I got worried and it's raining out. I used the key you gave me to let myself in."

Was it the first time he'd used the house key she'd given him when they returned from St. Maarten?

She peered at her digital clock on the dresser.

"It's two in the morning."

"I'm sorry. I didn't mean to frighten you."

He turned on his side to face her, propping himself on one elbow.

She thought about his refusal to speak to her on the way back from the Wadsworth and dropping her off at her office hours earlier. She'd been miserable after she left Louis's office and gone home.

"I'm glad you're here," she said. "But what happened tonight? You wouldn't even speak to me in the car. You left me alone in the parking lot."

His face clouded.

"I saw how you looked at that guy, Kristen. It was so obvious. Whoever he is, he had a big impact on you."

She felt the heat rise in her cheeks and an irrational surge of panic. She pulled the thin sheet up to her waist and shook her head.

"It's all in the past, Eric. You're the person I want to be

with, not him."

"It didn't seem that way. I'm sorry."

"What have I done to make you distrust me?" she asked, her stomach cramping from anxiety. *This isn't normal*, the logical and sane part of her brain interjected, but she could not stop herself. "I didn't do anything wrong."

"I'm not saying you did." He sighed and took her hand in his, tracing slow circles on her wrist. "Kristen, I guess I come with baggage, and it's not fair to you. Maybe I should just leave."

He made a move to sit up and she grabbed his arm.

"No. What do you mean? What baggage?"

"I guess it's time we talk."

She hadn't known Eric for very long, but she suspected he was the type of man who would not find it easy to reveal things that troubled him. Kristen turned on the lamp on her nightstand and they sat up in bed, making themselves comfortable with extra pillows.

"I have a hard time trusting," he said. "I told you I was married for ten years before my wife passed away from lymphoma, right?"

Kristen nodded. He had told her on their second date that his wife, Elena, had died from cancer a few years earlier. He hadn't shared any details.

"She lived for almost four years after her diagnosis. All during that time I took care of her while she went through radiation and chemo. She had periods of remission, and we were so hopeful she would recover," Eric said. "At one point she was in a clinical trial for a new drug and it was working. She was feeling great and we were, well, cautiously optimistic. We even traveled to Italy."

He took a deep breath.

"And then I got the shock of my life. One night when she thought I was asleep, I overheard her talking on the phone to someone, and well…" He paused and squeezed Kristen' hand. "Let's just say I was totally blindsided when I discovered she'd been having an affair. Turned out it'd been going on for years, a guy she worked with, and I had no idea."

"I'm really sorry."

"Oh, it gets better," he said. "I confronted her and she admitted everything, because by then her cancer was back. She was terminal and there was nothing more the doctors could do for her. I guess she wanted to clear her conscience, a deathbed confession, shall we say."

His mouth turned up in a grim smile. "I'll spare you the nitty-gritty, but the kicker was that she'd gotten pregnant twice during our marriage, and she miscarried both times. And I wasn't the father. I never knew that, of course, but she just had to tell me. Do you think I would have stayed with her all of those years if I'd known?"

Kristen winced. She didn't know what to say.

"So even though it's been awhile—five years now—I still can't stand it when I think that…maybe I'm being lied to. When I met you, I thought I finally found a woman I could love and trust completely. I'm not so sure you feel the same way about me and that's okay, I just need to know. I'll move on. I'm too old to waste time."

"I do love you," Kristen said, feeling that irrational surge of panic again. "I don't want to see anyone else. I want things to work out with us, Eric, I really do."

Her stomach was roiling.

"Then let's make sure it's just us," he said.

She didn't know what he meant by that, but she nodded. He leaned forward to kiss her.

"Are you sure?" he asked. "Are you really over this guy?"

Her hand fluttered over her stomach. She felt like she was going to vomit.

"I'm over it, really. I mean it."

"Okay," he finally said. "But I also need to ask you

something else…and please tell me the truth. What about Louis?"

"What about him?" She frowned. "He was Paula's boyfriend."

"Yes, but why did he go to St. Maarten the same time you went? Don't you find that odd?"

Her mouth was dry and she licked her lips.

"He was worried about not hearing from Paula. I think he hoped they would get back together."

She debated whether she should come clean and tell him she'd seen Louis professionally, back in the day. But that would surely lead to more probing questions that she had no interest in answering tonight.

"Did you ever wonder if Louis had something to do with Paula's death?" he asked. "Think about it. The report said she probably died while we were there. He was there too."

"I don't think he had anything to do with her death."

"But could it be possible?" he persisted. "What if he got jealous—maybe went into a rage because he found her there with someone else? And then made it look like an accidental drowning?"

"He doesn't seem like the violent type."

"But he doesn't seem like a guy you could trust. He's got a pretty checkered past, if you ask me," Eric said. He looked at her. "When did you talk to him last?"

Kristen hesitated. What would he think if she admitted she'd stopped over at Louis's office a few hours ago? He would jump to the wrong conclusion, that's what. He'd walk out the door, and she would never see him again. She made her decision in a split second.

"I don't remember. Why?"

"I was just wondering."

There was a tension between them as thick as the humid night air and she didn't dare look away. *I shouldn't lie,* she thought but how could she explain herself at this point without upsetting him further? Now was not the time.

"I want to know you, Kristen. The things in your past, the good and the bad. How else can we have a real and honest relationship?" He paused. "Tonight I told you something that was hard for me to say. It was really hard, but I told you anyway so you can understand me better. Don't you want that too?"

"Of course," she said. "Of course I want that too."

Be careful, she thought.

Once words were spoken, there was no taking them back.

Eric moved closer and took her in his arms.

"Do you want me to stay with you tonight?"

"Yes," she said, holding him tighter.

She pushed the nagging, intrusive thought from her mind that in fact it would be better if she had time alone. That maybe this relationship was less than healthy, and what in hell was he thinking sneaking into her bedroom at two in the morning?

"Let's get some rest," he said. "I have to go to the hospital in the morning. My father's being discharged and I need to get him settled at the rehab center."

"Is he doing better?"

She had not met Eric's father yet, although she had offered to help in any way possible.

"He's still in some pain, but the hospital can't keep him forever," Eric said. "Thanks for asking. You tired?"

"Yes. I took an Ambien when I went to bed," Kristen said and yawned.

"Then you should sleep well," he said, stroking her hair. She fell asleep in his arms, feeling him rub her back as though she were a child.

A noise outside in the yard awakened her. Her eyes flew open and she heard the yowling sound again. The neighborhood cats in a love duel. The rain had stopped and the air was still. She reached across the empty bed in the darkness but Eric was gone.

She sat up, confused, and checked the time. It was 3:35 AM

and she remembered that he'd said he would stay with her. Why—and when—had he left?

A feeling of dread washed over her and she got out of bed and padded barefoot across the bedroom, noticing Eric's black shirt on the floor. She crossed the hallway and saw from the top of the stairs that the kitchen light was on. She stopped and listened, but heard nothing.

Finally she made her way down the stairs, slowly, carefully, not sure why she took such pains to be quiet. The kitchen was empty but the door to the basement was ajar and she could tell even before she peered down the stairs that the light was on in the cellar.

Eric stood near the washing machine, his back to her, head cocked up toward the ductwork. He wore his black jeans but was bare-chested. He clearly hadn't heard her come down to the kitchen, and she watched him for a moment in total silence, the blood pounding in her head.

What in God's name was he doing?

As if sensing he was being watched, he turned and she stepped away from the doorway.

"Kristen?" he called sharply. "Is that you?"

"Yes," she said, poking her head around the corner, letting him see her. "What are you doing down there?" She heard a tremor in her voice. "Is everything all right?"

He came up the stairs, frowning.

"Why are you up? Are you okay?"

"I heard a noise," she said, aware that he hadn't answered her question.

"I heard something too and it sounded like it came from the cellar."

"What did you hear?"

She was about to mention the cats yowling outside but changed her mind.

"A loud bang, like something fell. But I just went through the whole basement and nothing seemed out of the ordinary. No need for you to worry. Let's go back to bed."

"I never heard you get up," Kristen said.

"You were snoring, you know. Out like a light."

"Snoring?" She was mortified. "It must be from the sleeping pill."

"Maybe...or maybe you're tired from all that loving I gave you," he said, and this time his face relaxed and his smile seemed genuine. "Maybe you need some more of that to get back to sleep."

She stared at him, deliberately looking him up and down. Something in her wanted to take back control. She was tired of feeling afraid.

"Maybe you do too. Maybe you need a reminder of how I feel about you."

He raised his eyebrows.

"You think so, huh?"

"Yeah. I do."

She took his hand and led him upstairs, back to the rumpled sheets. The silver moon passed through clouds, casting pale light through the window. This time it was she who was on top of him, pressing his wrists against the cool white sheets, panting her hot breath against his neck and pretending she was in charge, doing what she pleased while he sighed beneath her and lay very, very still.

CHAPTER SIXTEEN

Saturday

FRANK ROTH AND LOUIS were sitting on the sun porch at Frank's house in West Hartford, a large beige Colonial on a quiet street lined with maple trees.

"I think it's gone," Frank said as he tapped on the laptop's keyboard.

They had been working for an hour that morning to rid Louis's computer of the disturbing images of child porn that had somehow been downloaded and were popping up randomly on the screen.

It was sickening. Children who looked like kindergartners posed nude, sometimes alone, and sometimes with other children or adults, whose faces were deliberately blurred.

"If it doesn't work, I swear to God I'm going to take the hard drive out, smash it to bits, and chuck it in the Connecticut River," Louis said.

Frank finished installing a software program intended to permanently wipe files from the hard drive.

"Don't rule that out. The last thing you need is the Feds coming to your door. They trace stuff like this all the time."

"I know. I read the newspaper. Seems every other week there's some shmoe who gets caught with a computer filled with child porn."

"Yeah, and they usually end up in jail," Frank said. "One can imagine how kindly they're treated by their fellow inmates."

"I really appreciate you doing this."

"Let me reboot and see if it worked," Frank said. "Lucky for you if it does. If not, I have a hammer in the garage."

Frank restarted the laptop, clicked on the control panel, tested some files, and finally pushed his chair away from his desk.

"Success. I think."

"How do I stop from getting hacked again?" Louis asked. "I have an anti-virus program that's up to date. Shouldn't it have caught something like this?"

Frank shrugged.

"I've worked in IT for many years and it's a constant battle to stay one step ahead of the bad guys. Ever hear of ransomware? That's particularly nasty malware that encrypts all your files and shuts them down until you pay a ransom to unlock them. Happened to a guy I know at work, and he has the same security suite you have."

"Never heard of that before. Is that something new?"

"Not really, but it's getting more sophisticated," Frank said. "I'm just hoping one day I won't wake up and find out all my bank accounts are gone."

"That already happened to me," Louis said. "When I got divorced."

Frank snorted.

"I hear ya. Thank God I have a wife who works her ass off and makes more money than I do. If she leaves me, I'll be the one demanding alimony. Hear that, honey?" he called out.

His wife, Lisa, was making coffee in the kitchen.

"You'll get alimony the day I get my own pool boy," she said. "You guys want more coffee? I made the strong stuff this time."

Louis was just about to reply when his cell phone rang. He looked at the screen and his mood deflated.

"It's Charlotte. Do you mind if I take this?"

Frank shook his head and Louis answered the call. He walked outside to the deck into the sunlight, his heart already hammering.

"Hey. How did the session go this morning?"

Charlotte's voice was low, subdued.

"There was no session."

"What do you mean?"

"I went to Silver Meadows and said I was there for the emergency session with Annie," Charlotte said. "But no one knew anything about it. There isn't even a therapist working there named Calvin. That was the name of the guy who called me yesterday."

"I don't understand."

Louis blinked and walked to the farthest corner of the deck. Frank and Lisa's gorgeous in-ground pool sparkled in the sunlight.

"That phone call I got? It was bogus," Charlotte said. "I even spoke to Annie and she had no clue as to what I was talking about. She said she never told anyone you molested her, Louis. And apparently she has no therapist at Silver Meadows named Calvin. Never had."

Relief washed through him like a wave. And then a surge of panic.

"So who the hell called you?"

"I have no idea," she said. "Who would do something like that? I can't tell you how awful last night was, thinking about all this. And what I thought about you...well, let's say I gave serious thought to some criminal acts." Her laugh was shaky and held no mirth. "I'm still so hyped up that I don't know what to think."

"Do you have a phone number you can call back?"

"It was a non-available number," she said. "When I tried to call it this morning, I got a recording that it was out of service. I don't understand what's going on."

Louis held the cell phone close to his ear.

"I don't either. I wish I did."

"I'm sorry about all of this, Louis," she said. "I accused you of something really terrible."

He said nothing. It hurt more than he wanted to admit that she had believed it might be true. He couldn't fault her for wanting to protect her daughter, but how could she think he was a child molester? They had been together for more than a year.

Annie's father had little contact with her and Louis had tried to be a positive male figure in her life, make up for the man's neglect. Of course that had made the break-up with Charlotte all the more painful when it happened.

"Well, I hope everything works out with Annie's treatment," he finally said, and they ended the call.

Louis returned to the sun porch and Frank handed him a mug of steaming coffee.

"Try this," he said. "It's called 'Wake the Fuck Up' Coffee. I got it in New Orleans a few months ago at a conference."

Louis took a tentative sip of the strong brew.

"Not bad. I was already awake though."

"So what did Charlotte have to say? Is her daughter still saying you're the Jerry Sandusky of therapists?"

"Turns out she never did," Louis said, and he told Frank about his conversation with Charlotte.

"That's pretty screwed up, dude. Whoever called Charlotte seems to know a lot about you. That you lived with them and such. The person even knows that Annie's in drug treatment. How many people know that? Most important, who would make a phone call like that to her mother?"

"The same person who would put an ad on the Internet in

my name to make Victoria Rudemann's life miserable?" Louis mused. "Same person who hacked my laptop? Or could it be some random prank caller trying to hurt Charlotte?"

Even as he said it, it seemed implausible.

Frank sat down at the kitchen table.

"I don't think it's a coincidence and it's not a simple prank. What's the common denominator in both cases? It's you. You were involved with both women. In very different ways, but you're the link. And think about it…the same night you're accused of molesting a kid, you get child porn on your computer? Whoever did it wants to scare you."

"The email I clicked on did say Patient Files," Louis said. "That's when the images came up. Guess whoever did it has a warped sense of humor."

"If that's what you want to call it," Frank said. "You get yourself lawyered up yet? Just in case the FBI comes calling about Paula's case?"

Louis rubbed his chin.

"I'm working on it."

He'd been playing phone tag for several days with an attorney who wanted a steep retainer, but it was less than the retainers quoted by two other firms he'd contacted. Between that, the trip to St. Maarten, and Heather's tuition to UConn, he was completely tapped out.

"Be prepared in case the shit hits the fan," Frank said. "Because I think someone's got it in for you. Does anyone else know what's going on?"

"I talked to Kristen last night," Louis said. "I wanted to find out if she knew who BD9908 was. I told her I read the emails."

"She knows you took Paula's computer?" Frank's expression was alarmed. "You told her about breaking into Paula's house?"

Louis shifted uncomfortably in his chair, sharp pains shooting down his sciatica.

"Yeah and I guess I shouldn't have."

"Next time pick up the phone and talk to me instead," Frank

said. "Or better yet, talk to your lawyer when you get one. You could be digging yourself a giant hole and not even know it. I won't go blabbing anything, but what about her? What if she tells the police or the FBI at some point that you took Paula's laptop? Who will believe it when you say it got stolen from your house?"

"I've been thinking a lot about this and what happened the night I went to Paula's," Louis said. "I think there was someone there and whoever it was wanted her computer too. I just happened to get to it first. The thing is, I used her laptop from my house and that can be traced, right? That there was a log-in to her email account and it originated from my Wi-Fi connection? I don't know how all of this works, but it might come back to me later and no matter what, it'll look like I got rid of her computer on purpose."

"Unless there's no investigation."

They both sipped their coffees.

"Well, now that you got this *one* problem solved thanks to my awesome technical skills, should I see if I can get a tee time for later this afternoon?" Frank asked. "Otherwise I'll have to vacuum the pool or mow the lawn. Besides, maybe I can kick your ass this time since your mind's not on the game."

"Yeah, later in the day should work. I need to go to my office after I leave here. Some patient files went missing and I hope I misfiled them somewhere."

"You don't sound too confident," Frank said. "You think they got stolen too?"

"Maybe," Louis said. "I hope not. It would be a reportable HIPAA breach and that's a whole other set of headaches."

"Get some security cameras for your house and your office. If I were you, I'd make sure I have a pistol handy too."

"I haven't been to the range in more than ten years," Louis said. He'd gotten his pistol permit in the late nineties and was never a good shot. "I'm probably safer with a can of wasp spray." He made a mental note to inspect the Smith & Wesson revolver he kept on the top shelf of his closet when he got home.

"Might be time to bone up on self-defense and personal protection in general. Who knows what kind of whack job you're dealing with?"

"Obviously one who's a few steps ahead of me."

"Yeah, well that's not raising the bar too high," Frank said. "Just kidding."

Louis drained the mug and brought it over to the kitchen sink.

"Thanks for the coffee. Call me when you get the tee time."

He called out a goodbye to Lisa and walked outside to his car.

Louis had just pulled into the driveway of his office when his cell phone rang. He looked at the Caller ID and frowned. Diane Wells? His patient. How had she gotten his personal cell phone number?

"Hello, this is Dr. D'Maio," he said.

"Dr. D'Maio? Where are you?" came the thin voice of the woman who'd been in therapy with him for six weeks. "I was a few minutes late but the maître d' said no one who looks like you was here yet, so I wasn't sure if maybe you were waiting outside?"

"Diane, what are you talking about?"

"I'm here right now at the Whitmore. Your message said to meet you here at eleven?"

He was perplexed. The Whitmore was a new and ritzy hotel that had recently opened in Hartford.

"What message?"

There was a pause.

"The voice mail you left for me yesterday," she said. "That you wanted to meet me outside the office today. I called your service back and said I would be here at eleven. But I was running late, so I didn't get here until ten after."

"I'm so sorry, Diane, I didn't leave you a message," he said.

"And I don't have an answering service." He felt his heart speed up. Diane's was one of the missing patient records.

"I don't understand," she said, and the letdown in her voice was unmistakable. "The message was from you, it was on my voice mail."

Louis sat in his car with the phone to his ear.

He winced at the image of her waiting for him at the hotel.

"Diane. I would never ask any of my patients to meet me outside of the office. And how did you get my personal cell phone number?"

"It's on the recording for your answering service," she said, and now she sounded angry. "It was a different number than the one for your office."

"Can you please tell me what number you called that was supposed to be my answering service?" Louis asked, trying hard to sound calm and professional while he searched for a pen and a piece of paper in the glove compartment. She told him the number and he wrote it down.

"So what does this mean?" she asked, her voice shrill. "It wasn't you?"

"I'm afraid not."

"Then who called? I'm going to go home and listen to that message again. It sounded like you," she said. "I know doctors don't usually meet their patients outside the office, but it sounded like you, and I thought—well, I thought—" she did not finish her sentence. "Oh, Jesus."

Louis closed his eyes.

Transference. When a patient falls in love with her doctor.

He was sure he had noted his impressions from their last few sessions and his plan to work with her through that stage. He was horrified at this violation of her privacy.

"Diane, I don't know what's going on here, but I'm going to check out this number that you gave me and make sure it's shut down immediately."

"I'm so embarrassed," she whined.

"It's not your fault. I promise you it isn't," he said, and he heard her begin to cry. "I'm very sorry this happened. I think it's some kind of mean prank."

"I feel so stupid."

"We'll get past it," Louis said, in the most reassuring tone he could muster.

"I can't come back," she sobbed. "I don't want to see you anymore."

And with that the call disconnected.

Louis didn't move for a moment, wondering if he should try to call her back. It was an excruciatingly awkward situation for both of them, he thought. She would certainly wonder who had set up the bogus meeting to stoke her secret hopes that her therapist was interested in her. Interested enough to break the rules and meet her at a hotel on a weekend, no less. The poor woman. She didn't deserve this.

Who was responsible?

He punched in the number she had given him for the so-called answering service. After one ring, a robotic female voice said: *Hello. You have reached the office of Dr. Louis D'Maio. The office is currently closed but please leave a message after the tone. Your call will be returned by Dr. D'Maio as soon as possible. If your call is urgent and you need to speak to Dr. D'Maio immediately, please dial....* It was his personal cell phone number.

"This is Louis," he said, after the beep. His teeth clenched. "I don't know who the hell you are or what your sick game is, but it has to stop. Now. I'll have this number traced. You have a problem with me, take it up with me. Leave innocent people out of it. Got it?"

He got out of the car and his phone buzzed. It was a text from the number he'd just called. Just an emoticon.

☺

CHAPTER SEVENTEEN

MICHAEL RUDEMANN EASED his Volvo into the driveway of his ex-wife's house and blew the horn to signal Victoria that he'd arrived to drop off their sons for the usual weekend visit. They avoided speaking to each other as much as possible, and she hadn't called him back to confirm today's drop-off time. But this behavior was typical and since her black Acura was parked in the driveway, he assumed she was home. The two boys in the back seat unbuckled their seat belts.

"When are you picking us up, Dad?" the oldest boy asked, gathering up his plastic toy soldiers scattered on the beige leather seat.

"Right after dinner," Michael told them. "About six-thirty."

"What if we don't eat by then?" the youngest asked. "Last time Mom didn't make us any supper."

"Then we'll go out to the Cheesecake Factory," his father said.

The two boys whooped and the youngest, Seth, said to his brother, "Let's tell Mom we're not hungry so we can go out later with Dad."

"Yeah."

They bounded out of the car and rushed to the front door of the big white Colonial with black shutters. Michael watched them pound on the door. They waited.

When Victoria didn't appear, he rolled down the driver's side window.

"I'll call her," he said to his sons, and picked up his cell phone from the console.

There was no answer.

"Come on, Vicky," he mumbled to himself.

Their last interaction on the phone a week ago had deteriorated as usual into a nasty argument. God knew about what, he couldn't remember now. She was always pissed about something.

The boys tried the door handle but the door was locked. They looked back at their father, their small tanned faces puzzled. They were seven and nine years old, towheaded and skinny as poles. They both wore khaki shorts and striped shirts.

"Maybe she's out back weeding the garden," he said.

Or gardening the weed, was his next thought, and it occurred to him that maybe she was sleeping off a hangover. It was only noon after all.

He sighed, turned off the radio and got out of the car. Much as he hated to talk to her in person, he decided he would get a good look at her before leaving the boys alone with her for the day.

Make sure she isn't drunk or high.

If she was still asleep, he would take his sons home. They deserved better than this. He was disgusted with her unreliability.

Seth and Luke ran to the back yard and Michael stepped up to the porch and rang the doorbell. A hornet flew by his head and he waved it away. There was probably another nest in the rhododendrons. When he used to live in this house he'd always battled bees. His wife, rather *ex-wife,* had been terrified of them.

In a moment the boys raced back to the driveway.

"She's not there," Seth announced. "So can we go home?"

"I want to see Mom," Luke whined. "Dad, where is she? Her car is here."

He looked at his watch and glared at the door. He was supposed to be at work in half an hour. His irritation rose another notch.

"I don't know," he said. Seth slipped past the shrubbery that lined the front porch and peered into the windows of the living room. "Dad, Mom's laying on the floor."

Michael rushed to the window, pushing aside the branches of an overgrown rhododendron. Inside the living room Victoria lay on her back next to a white blood-spattered couch. Her eyes and mouth were wide open and there was a round black hole in her forehead. A dark glossy pool extended from her head to her thin shoulders and her T-shirt was stained an ugly brownish-red. Her arms and legs were askew and pale gray.

"Don't look." Michael stopped Luke from pressing his face against the window and grabbed both boys' hands. "Get back in the car."

"Is Mom dead?" Seth screamed, and Michael opened the car door and pushed them both into the back seat.

He fumbled for his cell phone and considered breaking a window to get into the house. Except he already knew there was nothing he could do.

"What happened?" Luke wailed. "What did you see?"

Michael's hands trembled as he punched in 911.

This is war, Louis thought, although he didn't know who his enemy was.

Anyone could buy a non-traceable cell phone and set up a voice mail. But this went much further than the false answering service. He'd searched high and low for Kristen and Victoria Rudemann's files and the missing records of three current patients, but they were nowhere to be found in his office.

Given what had just happened with Diane, what was next? The thief had already demonstrated a total lack of decency. One of Louis' patients was suffering from severe depression and the other was struggling with post-traumatic stress. What if the bastard used the clinical notes to torment them?

The thought that his patients were vulnerable, on a psychological and maybe a physical level too, was appalling. He felt a new surge of anger. It was one thing to harass him, but quite another to target emotionally fragile people.

Coward.

By law he would be obligated to inform all five of his patients that there had been a breach in the privacy of their protected health information. The sooner he got a lawyer on board, the better. Victoria Rudemann was bound to flip out, particularly since she already thought he had placed the Internet ad. God only knew what trouble this would stir up.

He realized he should also notify the West Hartford police but decided he would talk to the lawyer first.

If the guy ever calls me back.

Louis had left two messages but it was the weekend, and he had no history with this attorney. Or any other attorney, for that matter, other than the one recommended by the insurance company for his malpractice case.

He phoned Frank and explained he needed to cancel golf. Instead he spent part of the afternoon at Home Depot looking at home security systems. Setting them up didn't look easy, and he thought he would do more research, maybe hire a security company instead of attempting the task himself.

And pay for it how? he wondered, but that was a question for another day.

In the meantime he bought new locks to replace the ones at his home and office. He made a note to contact his landlord on Monday and let him know what he'd done. It was worth it to do the work himself rather than to wait weeks for the landlord to get around to it. He drove back to Prospect Street and replaced the lock on his office door.

At home Louis swapped out the deadbolts to his front and back doors. It was odd that there'd been no evidence of a break-in either at his condo or at his office. He'd given Paula and Frank his house keys, but could not recall giving anyone else his office keys. There would be no reason to do so.

When he finished this task an hour later, Louis checked to make sure every window in his condo was secure. He'd have to keep the central air conditioning on instead of opening any windows to catch the late-summer breezes. It would be all too easy for an intruder to pop out a screen.

Finally he went to his bedroom closet and felt around the top shelf under a stack of folded jeans for the case in which he kept the Smith & Wesson .38 Special. He hadn't been to the range in years. He thought he might pay them a visit soon, brush up a bit and regain the small comfort level he'd once had with the revolver. Except the case wasn't there.

He felt the outline of a long smooth rectangle and pushed the clothes aside. It was a laptop. Stunned, he took it down from the shelf. *Paula's.* A large piece was missing from the bottom of the Dell, and he saw that the hard drive had been removed. Cursing out loud, he pulled down every item of clothing on the closet shelf. Nothing.

The revolver was gone.

When did this happen? He hadn't noticed other things missing the night Paula's laptop had disappeared from his kitchen table, but he hadn't done a top-to-bottom search of his whole house either. He didn't keep much cash around, just a couple of twenties on his dresser that hadn't been touched. It had never occurred to him to check on the gun.

A yellow sticky note drifted to the floor. Louis bent over to pick it up, his back muscles going into a spasm that made him grit his teeth.

TRADE YA it said, all caps in black magic marker.

Louis paced from his bedroom to the living room and back again. He opened dresser drawers and began a methodical search for anything out of the ordinary, his mind racing.

Trade ya?

Whoever had taken the Smith & Wesson had clearly spent some time in his condo. But when? It was conceivable that the same night he'd set up the false blind date with BD9908, the intruder had not only taken the laptop but removed the hard drive and stolen the gun. Or maybe it had happened later on, which meant his home had been entered more than once.

He went into the kitchen and looked around the countertops and through the mail on the table. The room had looked pretty much the same a few weeks earlier when the laptop had been stolen.

Anyone snooping through his personal effects would have learned a lot about his financial situation and his debts.

The UCONN tuition bill, he thought. *Heather.*

Did this lunatic know anything about his daughter?

He hadn't heard from her recently. She'd called him after Paula's funeral to say she was sorry to hear the news, but that was it. Louis felt a sudden stab of panic. He found his cell phone and called Heather's number. To his relief she answered right away.

"Hey, Dad," she said, voice bright and cheery. "What's up?"

He asked her how school was going, and they chatted for a few minutes about her classes.

When he sensed she was ready to make an excuse to hang up, he said, "Listen, sweetie, I've had some problems lately with someone who got hold of my personal cell phone number and some other personal information. You haven't had any strange phone calls or anything like that, have you?"

There was a pause.

"You mean from a patient of yours?"

"No, I don't think so," he said carefully. "I don't want you to worry. But let me know right away if—well, if anything seems odd or you get any unusual calls."

"You're creeping me out a little, Dad."

"I don't mean to scare you," he said. "I just want you to be careful."

"I'm not five."

"I know. But call me if anything, I mean anything, comes up that doesn't sound right or makes you nervous."

"Is it a man or a woman?" she asked. "Is it someone like the guy in that movie 'What about Bob' who stalks his doctor when he goes on vacation?"

Laughter.

Louis smiled. The two of them had watched that movie at least four times.

"Yeah, if you see Bill Murray, let me know. Seriously, Heather, call me anytime. Okay? And let me know the next time you're home. We'll go to dinner again."

"I'll be around next week," she said. "I'll see you then."

After his phone conversation with Heather, Louis left another voice mail message for the attorney. There was no question he should report the theft of his weapon to the police, but Paula's laptop presented a thorny dilemma. Should he disclose the whole story to the cops and come clean about removing Paula's laptop from her house, or would he risk arrest and a loss of credibility? The other option was to report the missing patient files, the stolen gun, and the strange things happening, but keep his mouth shut about the laptop.

The more he paced, envisioning each scenario, the more convinced he became that it would be a mistake to reveal everything to the police and trust that it would all get sorted out. His recent encounter with the Avon cop, Victoria Rudemann's brother, had been an unpleasant reminder of how things would go if he was perceived not as an innocent citizen needing help, but as a troublemaker.

And maybe even as a person of interest by the St. Maarten police.

Louis hadn't heard anything from anyone about how the investigation was progressing—or not. Chances were he wouldn't find out unless the FBI showed up at his door. He'd read enough recently about crimes on small Caribbean islands to know that most police forces were understaffed, overworked, and frequently inexperienced in dealing with homicides. And investigations spanning international boundaries had their own set of complicated legal procedures and protocols. Seldom did anything happen quickly even if the FBI was asked by a foreign government like St. Maarten to assist.

He thought every day about what might have happened to Paula, and his heart ached at the mental image of her drowning. It wasn't a painless way to die, and he was convinced it wasn't accidental. She was a strong swimmer. She wouldn't take foolish chances in the water.

Unless she'd been hurt or drugged, or—and his mind recoiled at the thought—*held under*. Her body had been found less than six miles from his hotel. Could he have saved her, had he only looked for her another hour? Another day?

He wondered if the questions would haunt him forever. If he'd told her right away about meeting up with Charlotte and his assistance with Annie, maybe she wouldn't have left. Maybe she wouldn't have gone to St. Maarten in the first place, or at least not without him. In hindsight there were a dozen things he should have said and done. If only he had, Paula would be with him tonight. It was hard to believe he would never see her again.

The dark thoughts were difficult to banish. Louis stopped pacing, sat on the couch and reached for the remote. Lately he'd used television as a distraction. Reading required too much concentration. Many nights when he couldn't sleep he'd turn on the TV and watch movie after movie until he finally drifted off into a fitful slumber that left him bleary-eyed and fatigued the next day. Sometimes he'd wake up in the middle of the night, stomach growling, and realize he'd forgotten to eat.

Physician, heal thyself.

He'd had enough training and experience, of course, to know that grief took different forms. Time was the one and only healer.

He thought about his patient, Diane, waiting for him at the hotel that morning. He hadn't called her again but he would the next day, and reassure her again that none of it was her fault. He planned to call his other two patients as well and tell them their records had been compromised. Hopefully the lawyer would contact him soon and offer some advice.

Louis turned on the TV, flipping from station to station. He settled on a golf channel and had begun to doze off when his phone rang. He saw it was Frank on the Caller ID.

"Don't tell me you got a hole in one this afternoon, because I won't believe it," Louis said as soon as he picked up.

"Two birdies," Frank said. "Too bad you missed it. Hey, did you see the news?"

"No." Louis sat up on the couch.

"Turn on NBC. I hate to sound insensitive, but the wicked witch is dead."

"What?" Louis changed the channel on the remote. "What are you talking about?"

"Victoria Rudemann. It's on the news. She was found dead in her home today. The story's coming up after the commercials."

"Dead from what?" Louis was fully awake now.

"I don't know. I don't think they said. Usually when someone's croaked in their house they committed suicide or overdosed or something. She was a drug addict, wasn't she?"

"You could say that."

Louis found the local news station, which still on a commercial break.

"I'll talk to you later. We're having dinner but I just wanted to let you know."

"Thanks."

Louis waited for the commercials to end, and finally the

news resumed.

"Avon police report that a woman was found dead in her home this morning," a perky news anchor announced. A picture of Victoria's large home filled the screen. The yard swarmed with uniformed officers and at least four cruisers were parked in the driveway. "The woman has been identified as former model Victoria Rudemann. Police have not commented on the cause of death at this time."

A photo of Victoria taken in her younger years appeared. She had wavy blonde hair and sea-green eyes. A beautiful woman, he thought. A beautiful, angry, malicious woman.

He couldn't help but feel a tiny bit of relief. Whatever happened next with regard to Victoria's stolen clinical record, he wouldn't have to endure her wrath.

The phone rang again and he answered it without looking at the Caller ID.

"Hello?"

Whoever was on the other end said nothing. Louis waited a few seconds and hung up. "Unavailable" was on the Caller ID screen. Then his cell phone buzzed, indicating he had a text. He picked it up from the coffee table.

Watch the news yet Dr D?

He texted back: *Who is this?*

Your friend BD.

CHAPTER EIGHTEEN

ON SUNDAY MORNING Kristen had just finished brushing her teeth when the front doorbell rang. She went downstairs, peered through the peephole, and saw her eighty-five-year-old neighbor, Maude, standing on the porch. She opened the door.

"Goodness, you *are* home," the elderly woman exclaimed. She wore long blue pants and a short-sleeved white cotton tunic that stretched across her ample chest. She held up a narrow green box. "This was just delivered for you. I was outside so I signed for it."

"Thank you so much, Maude," Kristen said. "I just got out of the shower a few minutes ago. I didn't hear anyone ring the bell."

"Looks like something special," she said. "From that nice beau of yours, I presume?"

Kristen smiled and took the box.

"Do you want to come in?"

"Sure, just for a minute. I want to see what you got."

Kristen held the door open wider and a mild breeze carried in the tempting smell of someone's lunchtime barbecue. Nearly as wide as she was tall, Maude stepped inside and made her way slowly into the living room and heaved herself into a recliner.

She smoothed back her curly white hair with one shaky hand and adjusted her glasses.

"I got my son and the grandkids coming this afternoon. Lordy, I hope they don't stay too long. I want to watch my TV shows without all them running around tearing up the house."

"But it will be good to see them, won't it?" Kristen asked.

Maude had often complained she rarely saw her son or her three young grandsons these days. She had won the state lottery years ago and had plenty of visitors then. When the money dried up, so had the visits.

"Yeah, but my son lets them act like a pack of wild dogs." She let out a deep sigh and stretched her short legs out. She wore brown sandals and her toenails were painted bright pink. "Plus they'll expect I'm gonna bake them cookies or some sort of granny thing like that. So I gotta make something quick and I don't got time to drive to the store. You got a box mix by any chance? Or maybe a package of cookie dough? The kind you just slice and bake?"

"I'll check." Kristen went into the kitchen and found a chocolate chip cookie mix in the pantry.

While she was at it, she fetched a pair of scissors.

"Whew," Maude said when Kristen returned and handed her the mix. "Saved by Duncan Hines. So let's see what you got there."

Kristen used the scissors to open the long green box. She peeled the top off to reveal a bouquet of red and white long-stemmed roses enclosed in shiny plastic wrap.

"Well, ain't that the bee's knees," Maude grinned as Kristen removed them carefully. "From your honey bunny?"

"I think so," Kristen said, and opened the small white card taped to the plastic. She read it quickly.

Dearest Kristen: These colors mean unity and harmony, a passion for the moment and hope for our future. With all my love, Eric.

Kristen cut an inch off the end of each stem and arranged the roses in the red vase that had been tucked into the bottom of the box. She leaned forward and inhaled their delicate scent, then brought the vase to the kitchen and filled it with cold water.

"You got yourself a good one, you know," Maude said. "Like my Clarence. He used to send me flowers for every occasion. My birthday, the holidays, Groundhog Day, you name it." Maude had been widowed for fifteen years.

"Groundhog Day? Really?"

"Well, maybe not," Maude said. "But you get the gist of it. Hey, did I tell you about the time me and my friend Shirley went to a flower show and she dared me to run naked through the hall? I won first prize for best dried arrangement." She chortled. "Did I already tell you that one?"

"First time," Kristen lied. "Can I get you a cup of coffee?"

"No thanks, my blood pressure is already through the roof thinking about those kids coming," Maude said. She rocked in the recliner and looked at Kristen, her face serious. "You holding up okay?"

She nodded.

Maude was one of the few neighbors who knew what had happened to Paula, and she'd been especially kind to Kristen in the days following the funeral. She'd brought over casseroles and store-bought desserts. She reminded Kristen of her buxom Irish grandmother, who had passed away when Kristen was in high school.

"Some days are better than others."

"How are things going with your sister's house?" Maude asked. "Ready to sell it yet?"

"I'm going over there today to box up more things," Kristen said. "If your church still wants household items and clothing, I'm sure I'll have quite a bit to bring over later in the week."

"They sure do," Maude said. "We're helping families in town that are in need. Lots of people unemployed these days."

Kristen nodded, suddenly feeling a lump in her throat. She

dreaded going to Paula's house but she'd been procrastinating for far too long. As the executrix of Paula's will, she needed to decide what to keep and what to donate and get the house ready to sell. Eric had accompanied her the first few times and helped her pack most of Paula's books for donation to the local library. Today she planned to sort through items in the kitchen and bedroom.

"Are you doing this by yourself?" Maude asked.

"Yes. Eric can't help me today," she said. "His dad just got out of the hospital and he's helping him get adjusted at a rehab center."

"He's a real nice man, that Eric," Maude said, pursing her lips. "A keeper. Did he tell you last week he helped me bring in my groceries?"

"No. He didn't mention it."

"Well, there I was, just got back from the Stop & Shop and I couldn't carry the bottled water in the house," the older woman said. "He brought all my bags in, every one of 'em, and insisted on putting the groceries away too. He even sat with me for a spell, had a cup of tea and we had a nice chat before he went over to your place." She smiled at Kristen with a gleam in her eye. "Ah, if I was thirty years younger, you'd have some serious competition. The man's a hottie if you don't mind my saying so."

Kristen grinned.

"A hottie? Yeah, he sure is."

"You can tell him I said so," Maude went on. "You can tell him he can stop by anytime. For tea, or…whatever."

She winked.

"Maude." Kristen pretended to be shocked.

"They don't call me Bawdy Maudie for nothing. But don't worry, I'll keep my mitts to myself," she sighed. "I don't wanna break his heart. You can tell he's the kind of man who's got a tender one." She wagged her finger at Kristen. "So don't you go breaking it either."

Kristen did not reply to the odd comment. She looked at Maude and thought the older woman was about to say something else, but then Maude pushed herself up and out of the recliner, groaning with the effort.

"Sucks to get old. Anyway, I gotta go and make those damn cookies."

"Have fun with your grandkids," Kristen said and offered her arm so Maude could steady herself.

Maude rolled her eyes.

"Guess I better enjoy them now. When they're older they might not come over at all."

"Sure they will." Kristen said.

Maude let go of her arm and made her way cautiously across the hardwood floor. She was too stubborn to use a walker or cane, but the day would come soon enough when she didn't have a choice.

"Summer's almost over," the older woman said wistfully as Kristen held the screen door open. "Sure went by fast, didn't it? I hope I live to see another."

After Maude left, Kristen threw some cardboard boxes into the back seat and trunk of her Altima and drove to Paula's house. She parked her car in the driveway and approached the front door of the gray Cape with a heavy heart. Every time she entered Paula's home, she felt a sense of deep sadness and regret.

I wish she hadn't gone to St. Maarten, Kristen thought for the hundredth time.

They hadn't been especially close growing up or later as adults. Plus Paula had never been the type of person to spill her guts, but during her divorce she'd confided in Kristen. She'd shared the troubles she'd gone through with Bill and then later, with Louis.

Kristen felt sorry for Bill, who clearly loved his wife and fought tooth and nail to stop her from leaving him.

No one ever felt that strongly for me, she thought. *Certainly not Chris. But maybe Eric?*

The flowers were nice, an apology in disguise. She was pleased he had sent them and she'd pondered at length everything he'd told her about the behavior of his ex-wife Elena.

Knowing what had happened to him made his actions at the Wadsworth more understandable. Not tolerable, she thought, but understandable, and she tried to put herself in his shoes. Could she really blame him for being upset with her? Deep down hadn't she known that Chris was likely to be there? How would she feel if the situation were reversed?

She unlocked the door and stepped inside the foyer. The air was humid and thick in the house, and she immediately opened the windows in the small dining room. The wind had picked up and she hoped the breeze coming in would freshen the air, make the house seem less oppressive. She turned on a small radio perched on a shelf in the kitchen. For starters she needed some music, some noise. She found an alternative rock station and turned up the volume as she opened the kitchen cabinets one by one.

It was daunting, this emptying of a house. She had vague memories of when she was ten years old and Paula was thirteen, the two of them helping their Aunt Norma and Uncle Pete empty their parents' home after their sudden deaths in a car crash. While driving home they'd been struck head-on by a drunk, who died days later as a result of the head injury he'd sustained. She remembered how angry she felt when their aunt and uncle sold or discarded items that carried sentimental value to their parents, as if doing so meant some kind of betrayal.

You can keep your mom's collection of crystal frogs and your dad's coins and stamps, Aunt Norma had said, *but that's it. We don't have any room for more.*

Kristin managed to squirrel away a number of photo albums that belonged to their parents, and Paula had taken small things too. Everything else had been given away or sold to strangers.

If there was an afterlife, maybe Paula was with Mom and Dad now. Maybe they were watching over her.

"Miss you guys," Kristen said out loud. And then she got to work.

By late afternoon Kristen had cleared out half the kitchen. She stacked the cardboard boxes of pots and pans, silverware and dishes in the corner of the dining room and surveyed the other cabinets she hadn't emptied yet. The cans of food could go to the town's food pantry. She left the microwave, toaster, and coffee maker on the kitchen counter, intending to pack them later to give to Maude's church.

Thank God Paula wasn't a hoarder. The only things in the living room were a couch, a recliner, flat screen television, and oak coffee table. There were a few knick-knacks on the mantel above the fireplace and a painting of a seascape, but that was it. This room would be easy, Kristen thought.

She was about to go upstairs but stopped. She had already seen Paula's bedroom and the next chore would be sorting through the large walk-in closet and Paula's two large bureaus, her clothing and shoes. All of Kristen's motivation drained away as she stood at the bottom of the carpeted stairs. She suddenly felt glued to the floor.

I can't do it. I just can't do it today.

There was something about rooting through Paula's clothes and personal effects that made her feel paralyzed. She didn't want to go upstairs to the bedroom. She didn't want to see or touch the clothes that Paula would never wear again. She didn't even want to be in the house anymore.

The radio in the kitchen blared a song by the Black Keys. She stood perfectly still and listened, trying to focus her attention on the music instead of the images of her dead sister, blonde hair swirling, her body drifting in a warm and gentle current.

Did she suffer? Did she know she was going to die?

Her heart was pounding and eyes closed, she put a hand on the stair railing. She thought if she opened her eyes at that moment she would see Paula standing in front of her. *What happened to you?* Kristen mouthed the words silently. She breathed in deeply in and out, in and out. When she finally opened her eyes there was nothing there but the staircase and the emptiness that even the music couldn't fill.

She thought she heard her cell phone ring. As if a spell had been broken, Kristen let go of the stair railing and walked back to the kitchen. Her iPhone was on the countertop. The screen indicated there was one missed call from Eric.

She turned the radio down and called him back.

"Hi."

"Hey, hon. You doing okay?"

She struggled to sound casual, normal.

"Yeah. How's your dad?"

"He's doing as well as can be expected," Eric said, and she heard him sigh. "Actually he's not doing so great. He's not happy with this rehab center and he wants me to take him home. That is, home to the nursing home, but he's not ready to go back yet. He's running a fever."

"I'm sorry to hear that."

"Where are you?"

"At Paula's house," she said. "I'm half-finished packing up the kitchen. I think I'm done for today." She waited for him to suggest that they get together that evening, and then realized she hadn't thanked him for the flowers yet.

"Eric, it was so sweet of you to send me those beautiful roses," she said. "I loved them."

"You're welcome. I really am sorry for the other night."

"Maude told me you helped her with her groceries the other day. That was nice of you."

"It was nothing," he said. "Kristen, are you all right? You sound funny."

She couldn't speak. Tears stung her eyelids and she gripped

the phone tightly.

"Kristen?"

"I'm okay," she said, and then she was crying soundlessly, her shoulders shaking.

"I'll be right over," he said. "Just stay right there."

"I'm sorry," Kristen said when Eric came in the front door fifteen minutes later. She'd had time to collect herself and wipe her eyes. "I just had a bad moment there. I'm fine now."

She offered him a weak smile. He hugged her and kissed the top of her head.

"Hon, it's better if you don't try to do this alone," he said. "Let me help you."

"I'm done for today."

"Did you eat already? How about if I take you to dinner?"

"Maybe something light," she said, although she had no appetite.

"Okay, something light. Let me just get that last box of books that I left in the cellar the other day. I'll drop them off at the library for you this week."

Kristen nodded and watched him go down to the basement. After a moment she heard him clear his throat.

"Well. That's strange."

"What's strange?" she asked, standing at the top of the stairs.

"Come here and look at this."

Kristen went down the basement stairs. Eric stood next to a box of books and pointed to a white wire dangling above his head near a floor joist.

"What am I looking at?"

"That's a phone wire," he said. "But it shouldn't be here. Do you have a flashlight?"

The lightbulb was on but this part of the basement was shrouded in darkness. Kristen went back upstairs and found a flashlight in the utility drawer. When she returned, Eric was standing several feet away underneath an air duct. She handed him the flashlight.

"What is it?"

His hand was behind the duct.

He shined the light on the other side of the duct. Kristen moved to his side to look.

"This is where the line comes into the house. I can feel tape here. I think the wires were spliced."

"What does that mean?"

"I don't know. Let's see where the wire goes."

They followed the white wire which was stapled to the wooden beams. It snaked behind another air duct and Eric patted his hand behind it.

"This is where it ends. Shine the light over here, I feel something."

She held the flashlight up while he searched behind the duct.

He pulled out a small black box attached to two wires.

"I'll be damned."

"What is that? A tape recorder?"

"Sure looks like it."

Eric took out the wires and they inspected the small device. There was a light film of dust on it that he wiped away with the side of his hand.

"Is there a tape in it?" Kristen pressed the power button and a small window opened to reveal a tiny cassette. She pressed "Play" and the machine clicked and stopped.

"The tape needs to be rewound," Eric said and examined the back of the recorder. "I think the way this works is that whenever there's a phone call, the recorder goes on automatically. It stops when the person hangs up the phone. A little old-fashioned but effective."

Kristen pressed the rewind button. The machine hissed.

"This is very odd. Paula lived by herself, didn't she?"

"Yes." Kristen looked again at the wire above her head and felt her stomach tighten. "So this would record every phone call made on her landline? Incoming and outgoing?"

"I think so."

She felt the hairs rise on the back of her neck.

"Is it possible Paula didn't know this was installed on the phone line?"

He shrugged.

"People who want to record their own phone calls don't usually hide recorders in their basement ductwork, do they?"

The machine clicked and stopped. They looked at each other.

Kristen nodded.

"Let's bring it upstairs and listen to what's on the tape."

CHAPTER NINETEEN

THIS HAD GONE far enough. Louis looked again at the texts on his cell phone.

Watch the news yet Dr D?

He typed.

Who is this?

Your friend BD.

What do you want? Did you break into my house?

No answer. Louis waited, sitting on his couch and staring at his phone while the newscasters on the television moved on to weather and sports.

Finally in frustration he typed *I'm reporting you to the police.*

Still no response. He decided there really wasn't a good reason to wait until tomorrow to notify the cops about his stolen Smith & Wesson. He Googled the non-emergency phone number of the Farmington police department and made the call.

He hadn't known exactly what to expect, but the person he spoke with at the police station told him they'd send an officer to his house. While he waited for the police to arrive, Louis tidied up the kitchen. He saw an opened can of cat food on the top shelf and realized he hadn't seen Bogie in a while, maybe not since yesterday. The cat often disappeared for hours, hiding somewhere in the house, although he usually showed up at night demanding food. Louis scraped what was left from the can onto a plate, set it on the floor and ran the electric can opener for a few seconds. The noise usually served as a dinner bell but Bogie did not appear.

Louis mentally rehearsed what he planned to say. Within a half hour the front door bell rang, and he opened the door to a uniformed cop who identified herself as Officer Santiago.

Her brown hair was pulled back into a tight ponytail and Louis thought she barely looked older than his daughter Heather. He invited her in and she followed him into the kitchen. They both sat at the table.

"So you're reporting a stolen firearm that was registered to you," she began. She opened her spiral-bound notebook. "Please describe the firearm and when you discovered it was gone."

Leaving out any mention of Paula's laptop, Louis chronicled the events of the past few days beginning with his discovery that the revolver and case were missing from his closet. He finished with a brief account of the stolen clinical records, the phone call Charlotte had received from someone implicating him as a child molester, the bogus answering service set up in his name, and the texts from BD.

When he mentioned the Internet sex ad that involved the posting of Victoria Rudemann's phone number, Officer Santiago's eyebrows raised but she listened without comment, writing in her notebook. When he finished, she tapped her pen on the table and fixed her attention on him.

"Seems like there's a lot going on, Mr. D'Maio. But first, let's go back to the revolver," she said. "You said you bought it from a licensed Connecticut gun dealer, you have a pistol permit, and you haven't fired it for at least five years or more. Is it possible you just misplaced it?"

"No, I always kept it in a case on the top shelf of my closet."

"When was the last time you saw it?"

Louis paused, thinking.

"Probably a few months ago. July maybe, when I did some cleaning."

"So you don't know when it was taken. It could have been any time since July?"

"I suppose so."

He took a deep breath in an attempt to quell his nervousness. Officer Santiago was young but clearly no pushover. He guessed most of the questions were routine but her manner was no-nonsense and a little intimidating.

"But you said there's been no sign of anyone breaking in and nothing else missing from your house?"

"That's correct," Louis said.

"Who else has access to your home?"

"My friend Frank has a key, and my girlfriend Paula did also. I don't know what happened to that key since she died. But I changed the locks in my house and office after I discovered the clinical records missing from my office in West Hartford."

"You'll need to file a report with the West Hartford police about that theft," Officer Santiago said. "Now let's get back to the harassing phone calls and the accounts that you say were set up in your name."

She went through a series of questions "for clarification" and he answered truthfully for the most part. No, he didn't know who might be targeting him or for what purpose. And no, he didn't think any of his patients were involved. The thought occurred to him that Bill, Paula's ex, had a grudge against him but he decided not to mention it. Bill was a piece of work but Louis seriously doubted he was a thief or that he'd go to these lengths to try to destroy his livelihood.

"And this all started after Paula Spencer's death?"

"Yes," Louis said. "But I can't pinpoint what the connection is, if there is any connection."

"Okay." Officer Santiago closed her notebook.

"So what happens next?"

"I'll be sending a copy of the report about your stolen revolver to the Commissioner of Emergency Services and Public Protection," the officer said. "It's required by the state. As you may be aware, many guns stolen from residences are used for criminal purposes. As far as the harassment goes, you haven't identified anyone we can question at this point. You said one of your patients was contacted by phone and harassed, but she would have to report the incident herself and it may or may not be considered harassment under the law."

Louis nodded. In order to protect Diane's privacy, he had given the officer a vague description of what had transpired the previous morning. He left out the child porn that had appeared on his computer.

"The same is true for that friend of yours who got the phone call from the supposed therapist about her daughter being molested. It's a terrible thing to do to a parent, make her think that that happened to her daughter. But unfortunately we can't arrest everyone who acts like a jerk."

Officer Santiago gave him a slight smile.

"Guess half the population would be in jail."

"It isn't clear if there's a link between your stolen revolver and these other incidents, whether the same person is responsible," she continued. "What's clear is that your identity has been compromised. If I were you, I'd keep close tabs on my credit report and set up account activity and fraud alerts."

"Can the police trace where I'm getting the text messages from?" Louis asked.

"It's possible, although so far you haven't received any threats. Those few text messages you've received aren't malicious. But keep a record of the texts and you can report them to your cell phone provider. They might put a trace on your line and if they get enough evidence, they'll instruct you to sign a form that gives us access to your telephone records. We need evidence to identify the person and prosecute." Officer Santiago considered. "Of course if you get a phone call or a text that's threatening your safety, call us right away."

"So I guess there isn't much else you can do at this point," Louis said. "But if anything else happens or if I find out who's responsible, should I notify you personally?"

"You can," she said, and handed him a business card. "Before I leave, do you mind if I take a look around?"

"Sure," Louis said, although immediately he thought about Paula's laptop in his room and felt a twinge of guilt. "Like I said, I changed the deadbolts on the doors. But if you notice anything else…"

Officer Santiago stood up. She did a quick survey of the kitchen and the sliding glass doors to the deck and inspected the locks on the windows.

"I notice you have a dowel in the lower track of the sliding glass doors. It's better than nothing but I'd recommend a Charley bar." She explained that this type of aluminum bar, locked in a bracket, was impossible to raise from the outside with wires or other devices. "Most burglaries are crimes of opportunity, so if you have enough deterrents, the burglar will go somewhere else. At least a third of the time, they get in through unlocked doors and windows. Some people get home security systems, so that's always an option too."

"I'm looking into that."

She walked through the dining room and the living room.

"Of course if someone wants to break in your particular house badly enough, they'll find a way to do it. You keep all the windows locked?"

"I do now."

"Is there an entrance in the basement?"

"No."

"Okay," she said. "I think we're done here. Like I said, call us if anything escalates to a threat."

Many guns stolen from residences are used for criminal purposes.

Louis thought about his conversation with Officer Santiago when another news report came on about Victoria Rudemann. There was still no information on how she had died. With a sickening feeling, Louis wondered if BD's message asking him if he'd seen the news yet was a simple taunt related to her stolen record, or if it meant something more.

BD had taken his gun. "Traded it" for Paula's computer.

Maybe BD wasn't planning another crime, he had already committed one.

With my revolver.

He didn't want to go there in his mind. Because if that were true, then reporting his stolen gun today was quite possibly the worst timing ever. He remembered the strange expression that had crossed the cop's face when he'd mentioned the Internet sex ad falsely linked to him. She hadn't said a word about Victoria's death splashed on the evening news and neither had he.

He turned off the TV and went upstairs to his bedroom. Paula's damaged laptop sat on his bureau. His thoughts raced.

I'm just being paranoid, he tried to tell himself.

But what if?

What if Victoria had been murdered, shot to death by his Smith & Wesson .38 Special? And what if his gun had been left in her house? It would be traced back to him in short order. He suddenly realized how thin his story sounded.

Nothing else was stolen from my house, just my revolver and I don't know when it happened. And oh yeah, I want to report that coincidentally there were clinical files stolen from my office, and someone is trying to set me up but I don't know who or why. And yeah, all of this happened after I got back from St. Maarten where my girlfriend was found dead.

It sounded suspicious even to him. He turned over the laptop and looked at the empty space where the hard drive had been, where Paula had saved all of those emails to and from her online admirers from the dating site, most notably BD9908.

With the hard drive gone, how much proof was left of BD's existence?

Officer Santiago was right, the few text messages he actually had on his cell phone from BD were benign. They didn't link BD to anything that had happened, not even the stolen gun.

And now I have Paula's laptop back, and who would believe it wasn't me that took out the hard drive?

His sense of dread felt like a weight in his chest. He didn't want the laptop in his house. Why had BD given it back to him? To mock him or incriminate him for something? God only knew.

I'll hide it somewhere. Just in case.

Hide it where? He needed to get rid of it. He knew he was panicking, but what if the police came back with a search warrant? What if BD had laid some other trap? Had Louis made things worse by reporting his stolen gun the very day Victoria's body was found?

Louis put the laptop in a plastic bag and left his house, checking twice to make sure the door was securely locked. Crickets hummed in the darkness and there was a chill in the air, a sure sign that summer was ending. He got into his car and headed toward the highway, feeling a sense of urgency he could barely control.

He thought about driving to the back of a store or restaurant and discarding the bag in a Dumpster. But these days surveillance cameras were everywhere. He thought about the crime shows he'd seen. People threw things they wanted to get rid of in bodies of water.

He remembered his remark at Frank's house about chucking his own computer in the Connecticut River. He hadn't committed any crimes but his heart was pounding. He glanced at the plastic bag on the passenger seat as though it contained the bloody knife from a murder.

The Connecticut River was deep and the current was fast. It

would be perfect, he decided, and he knew just the spot. He used to fish on the river in his younger years, and he'd lived close to one of the state piers accessible through a short path in the woods. At this time of night there weren't likely to be people around.

Twenty minutes later Louis was off the highway and on a winding back road. There were few houses here and no streetlights. He soon reached the empty parking lot for the small state park. A large sign warned that the area was closed at dusk, and he drove to the farthest end close to the wooded path. He turned off the ignition and headlights. It wouldn't take him long. If he remembered correctly, the path to the water was just a few yards away.

He smelled the river and the scent of damp earth as soon as he got out of the car. The night was alive with a chorus of peepers, crickets, and katydids. He slid the laptop out of the bag and retrieved the flashlight he always kept in the trunk. He tested it and was relieved the batteries still worked. The light was dim but sufficient to guide him to the edge of the woods, and he soon found the path.

He made his way carefully among the trees, pushing away stray branches from his face, keeping his flashlight low to the ground. He could tell he was close when the air became moist and cooler and the burble of water became louder.

When the path ended he stood on a sandy knoll above the inky blackness of the river. It stretched wide and long, and in the darkness he could barely make out the outline of trees on the opposite bank. As his eyes adjusted to the night he switched off the flashlight and turned left toward the pier that used to be his favorite fishing spot. It jutted haphazardly in the water and he saw broken posts and a prominent KEEP OUT sign warning people to stay away. Flood damage, he thought. He hadn't been here in years.

He weighed his options. If he threw the laptop from the edge of the bank it might not reach deep water. If he chucked it from the pier, it definitely would. He stepped gingerly across a boulder and onto the boards, testing his weight. A large crack ran through one of the beams and it creaked as he walked across slowly, avoiding rotting boards and a gaping hole where black water swirled beneath him.

He made it about ten feet when he heard a loud snap. A piece of broken beam splintered off and fell into the current.

Jesus.

Louis stopped. He didn't dare go further. He waved away the mosquitoes buzzing near his eyes and flung the laptop into the middle of the river. It landed with a faint splash and disappeared.

He made his way back to the shore, trying to ignore the ominous groans of the old wood beneath his feet. In spite of the evening chill he was sweating by the time he reached the safety of the bank. The moonlight cast a silvery glow on the water and he turned to take one last look before returning to the path.

"What the hell do you think you're doing?" came a loud voice behind him from the woods.

CHAPTER TWENTY

LOUIS WHIRLED AROUND and saw a shadowy figure move a few yards away in the gloom, half-hidden behind the trees. He tensed, instantly calculating the fastest way to get back to his car if he had to run off the path and make an escape through the woods.

"I said, what the hell ya doing you moron, the beer's the other way."

A young, bearded man, either very drunk or high or both, staggered into view, one finger pointing in the air like a pistol. When he caught sight of Louis he stopped and stared, his body swaying with the effort to remain upright.

"Sorry man, thought you were my buddy. You see a dude come out here?"

Even from a few feet away Louis smelled the liquor on his breath. He took a step forward.

"No, didn't see anyone."

"Hey, you got a smoke?" the man asked. He patted the pockets of his dirty jeans. "I'm all out."

"No. Sorry." Louis edged forward, looking down at the

ground, avoiding eye contact.

"The party's this way," the young man slurred and gestured to his left. "Few of us went fishing today and we're not ready to go home. You got beer, you're welcome to join us."

He grinned as though it were the most normal thing in the world to bump into a stranger in the woods at night.

"Thanks, but I gotta go."

"Wait a second," the man said, making no effort to move out of the way and let Louis pass. "You ain't a cop, are you?"

"Do I look like a cop?" Louis asked in a fake incredulous tone. Whatever was going on with the 'fishing party,' he doubted it was legal. "No. I'm not a cop."

The man squinted and looked at Louis with one eye closed.

"We don't want no trouble, that's all. Just a coupla guys having fun. You know?"

"No problem."

Louis took the opportunity to step around the man and continue on the path to the parking lot.

"Ya sure you didn't see anyone?"

"Nope."

Louis didn't hurry and he didn't look back, although he heard leaves rustling, a thump, and a flood of obscenities. He guessed the man had tripped and fallen or maybe bumped into a tree as he stumbled around in the dark.

The man called out in a hoarse voice, "Brian, where the fuck are ya?" And then, "Hey mister, come back here and help me find him."

Louis reached his Mazda and paused. The guy was drunk out of his mind and his missing buddy probably was too.

Dumb asses. Shouldn't be wandering around in the dark near a fast-running river.

It was their problem, he decided. He needed to get the hell out of there before anyone else showed up and started asking questions.

"Is your meal okay?" The nosy waiter hovered near Kristen's shoulder and she turned to look at him with an apologetic smile.

"Yes, everything's fine. Thanks for checking," she said, and speared a piece of swordfish with her fork solely for his benefit.

The carrots and mashed potatoes on her plate remained untouched. The waiter moved away.

"You've barely eaten," Eric said gently. "Are you all right? You've been really quiet."

He'd already polished off his own shrimp and scallop pasta dish. He leaned back in his chair.

"Yes." Kristen took a bite of the fish.

There was nothing wrong with it, she simply had no appetite. They were sitting in the back booth of a seafood restaurant not far from Paula's house and she was dawdling, trying to think of how to tell Eric she didn't want him to listen to the tape they'd found in the recorder.

The thing had died when they brought it upstairs from Paula's basement and while she checked around in the drawers for extra batteries, it occurred to her that maybe there were recorded conversations on that tape between her and Paula. She didn't know if there might be something they'd talked about that she didn't want Eric to hear.

What if she'd said something referencing Chris or someone else in her past? Or something private or embarrassing, or God knew what else?

So when she'd found a package of batteries underneath some tools in a utility drawer, she pretended she hadn't and suggested they grab a bite to eat first and stop at the store on the way back. She'd tucked the tape and recording device into her purse.

"No problem, we'll pick up some batteries and check it out later," he'd said, seemingly only mildly curious and she was relieved, at least for the moment.

But she'd spent most of the dinner thinking about past conversations with her sister and the things they'd discussed. Paula's divorce. Her problems with Louis. Men in general and what bastards they could be. Girl talk, she thought, but even so, Eric had never met Paula and what if he misinterpreted, took something out of context? Just when the two of them were getting back on track after the Friday night debacle at the Wadsworth.

Without asking her, Eric filled her empty wine glass with what was left of a bottle of pinot noir on their table.

"I presume you don't want any dessert?"

"No, I've had enough," she said and put the fork down. She wiped her lips with her napkin and smiled at him. "Thank you for taking me out for dinner. And for the roses too. It was very sweet of you."

His eyes were serious. "You're welcome, and you already thanked me. But you seem very bothered by something. What is it?"

Kristen shook her head and took a sip of the wine.

"Tell me. Is it the tape we found?"

Why do I feel so guilty? she wondered.

Something as simple as this and here she was, twisting herself into an emotional pretzel. She looked directly into his eyes, paused and then took the plunge.

"Well, yes. It is the tape. I don't know what's on it. I'm worried that maybe there's conversations between me and Paula." She shrugged. "Conversations that are private or embarrassing or whatever, because we used to talk a lot, especially when she got divorced and when she thought Louis was having an affair."

He nodded.

"I thought that might be it."

Kristen searched his face but his expression was neutral. She realized she was waiting for him to get upset, was expecting he would, and it was just as unnerving that he wasn't. She hastened to explain.

"It's not that I ever said anything bad about you, or about us. That isn't the case at all. But we might have—well, we might have commiserated about some things, maybe said things about men in general that weren't so nice, and well…"

She looked at him, suddenly tongue-tied, feeling the blood rush to her cheeks.

Eric reached across the table and took her hand.

"I can see why you'd be nervous about that and it's all my fault. I'm really sorry. I was out of line the other day. With everything going on, your sister, my father in the hospital…" His voice trailed off. "I overreacted. Big time."

She took a deep breath and squeezed his hand.

"The last few weeks have been really tough for both of us."

"I don't want you to be afraid to talk to me," he said. "What kind of relationship would that be? Not the kind either one of us would want, right?"

"Right." Kristen said.

Maybe it was the wine that had emboldened her, but whatever it was, she felt better she'd told him the truth.

And the world didn't end.

"So why don't we do this. You listen to the tape tonight after I leave, and if you decide you want me to hear it, then let me know. I promise I won't quiz you about it either."

"Fair enough," she said and looked at him. "But you can stay over tonight if you want."

"Thanks, but I need to go to New York tomorrow for a meeting at work. I have to be up early and catch the train from New Haven." He glanced at his watch. "Plus I have to do some prep for my meeting tonight. By the way, I'm postponing my trip to Montreal for a couple of weeks. I want to make sure my father's feeling better. You still want to come?"

"Sure. I just need a few days' notice so I can take care of things at work."

"Good," he said. "I think we'll have fun there. I usually have a lot of free time after I meet with my clients. I'll let you know when the plans are firmed up."

Eric paid their bill and they left the restaurant. He put his arm around her as they walked to his car.

"You look happier now than you've been all night."

"I do feel better," she said. "It wasn't easy, trying to decide what to keep and what to throw away at Paula's house. Being around all of her stuff got to me, I guess."

"Next time I'll go with you," he said, and pulled her closer to him. "I want to help you."

"Maude says you're a keeper," she said, smiling up at him. "She said something else about you too."

For a second he looked puzzled. "Your neighbor? The little old lady?"

"Yeah."

"So what did she say?"

"She thinks you're a hottie."

He laughed and opened the car door for her.

"Unfortunately for Maude, I'm already taken."

After Eric dropped her off at her condo, Kristen rummaged through her kitchen and found a pack of AA batteries. She popped them into the recorder and pressed Play.

"So what's up? What are you doing this weekend?" Kristen heard her own voice.

Paula: "Thinking of driving to Vermont to see an art show. You want to come? I'm not going with anyone."

It was so strange to hear Paula's voice. When had they had this conversation? Not too long ago.

Kristen: "I have to work on a grant that's due next week, sorry. Otherwise I would go. You still not talking to Louis?"

Paula: "I don't want to talk to him. Shithead. I figured something was up since he was acting so strange the past couple weeks. I just didn't think he'd go back to that woman he lived with...you know I told you about her before...Charlotte..."

Kristen: "The one with the kid? The girl?"

Paula: "Yeah. The one he lived with before he met me. I never had the impression he was really in love with her, so that was a shock."

Kristen: "Asshole men. That's just like Chris. Went back to some girl that he said was a bitch. But of course he never bothered to tell me, he just stopped calling me instead."

Kristen winced. Good thing she was listening to this by herself.

Paula: "Yeah well, forget him, he never deserved you anyway. How's that new guy you met online? What's his name again?"

Kristen: "Eric. He seems really nice. We've only been on a few dates so far, but I'm starting to like him a lot."

Paula: "When am I going to meet him? He has to pass my inspection."

Both of them laughed.

Kristen: "Pretty soon. He travels a lot for work."

Paula's tone was girlish.

"I'm trying the online thing too."

Kristen: "Really?"

Paula: "Yeah. I think Louis and I are through. Maybe it's for the best. It seems like we've been drifting apart for a while. I'm thinking it's time that I expand my horizons."

Kristen: "So—anyone interesting?"

Paula: "Sort of. I just started the online stuff so I'll have to see how it goes. What did you do, meet up for coffee first?"

Kristen: "Yeah. Obviously you don't want to give out too much information about yourself. And when you do meet in person, go to Starbucks or something. That way if you don't like the guy, you're only on the hook for an hour or so."

Paula: "I haven't decided if I want to meet any of them yet. We'll see."

Kristen: "Any of them? There's more than one?"

More laughter.

Paula: "Kristen, there's plenty of fish in the sea. Oh, I gotta go, I have a dentist appointment in twenty minutes. If you change your mind about Vermont, just let me know. I won't be leaving until tomorrow late morning."

Kristen: "Okay, I'll let you know."

There was a squeal and a click before the next conversation began. Kristen recognized the male voice as Bill's, Paula's ex-husband.

"Hey. Just wondering if you want to meet me for a drink tonight."

Paula: "What for?"

Bill: "Can you lend me a few hundred bucks? I'll pay you back in a couple weeks."

Paula: "You never paid me back the last time you borrowed a hundred. Or was it a couple hundred? I'm losing track. The answer's no."

"Thanks a lot." Bill's voice was sarcastic. "Thanks for helping me out. You're a real peach, you know that? It's not my fault you stuck me with this car payment. How am I supposed to pay for that and all my other bills too?"

Paula: "You wanted the car, remember? It was part of the settlement. We could have sold it but you didn't want to. Get rid of it if you can't afford it."

"Screw it then." Bill's voice, incensed. A click.

Kristen remembered Paula telling her that Bill still called her on occasion. She hadn't mentioned that Bill was asking her for cash. She guessed that the car in question was a Ford Explorer that she'd seen Bill driving. Apparently he could afford it after all.

There was another click, a quick burst of static and then Paula's voice, clear and angry.

"The thing is, you lied to me about this, so what else did you lie about? Where did you really go last week when you said you had a tournament? To Charlotte's then too?"

"No. That was the only time I saw her. I told you already, we're not having an affair." It was Louis. He sounded subdued, upset.

Paula: "Well if you aren't, then why did you lie? Obviously

because you have something to hide and you won't even admit it. That's the problem with you, Louis. You won't be honest and just tell me the truth. I saw her email, remember?"

Louis, his voice pained: "I'm not having an affair."

"Bullshit." Paula's voice cracked.

There was a murmur on the tape that sounded as though she was crying. Kristen closed her eyes, feeling like a voyeur.

Louis: "Don't go to St. Maarten by yourself. Please, Paula. I want to see you and talk with you in person about this."

Paula: "No. And stop calling me. Next time you call, I won't pick up the phone. Just leave me alone."

Louis: "Paula."

There was static on the tape and Kristen turned up the volume. She could barely make out the low voice over the crackling sound.

"You go and you're dead."

The tape clicked and stopped.

CHAPTER TWENTY-ONE

THE YOUNG MAN scratched his chin and the side of his face and glared at Louis.

"So you're saying my clinical record—with all of my private information and your notes from our sessions—is out there somewhere. It can be read by anyone," the young man said, eyes blazing. "I'm not happy to hear this. Not happy at all."

"I understand and I'm very sorry," Louis said. "I've reported the theft to the West Hartford police."

It was late Monday morning and since his first patient was one of the five whose records had been stolen, Louis had decided to tell him in person at the start of their session. Rick Sprague, a veteran who had served two tours of duty in Afghanistan, suffered from anxiety and post-traumatic stress disorder. He'd been treated by Louis for several months and was responding well to cognitive processing therapy.

Rick ran a hand through his beard and shifted back and forth on the couch.

"Doc, this is going to make me nuts, thinking about who's reading my record. What did you write about me, anyway?

What's in my file?"

"I'm not going to sugarcoat this, Rick, the stolen record has your personal information including your social security number, your diagnosis, and your insurance information," Louis said. "The clinical notes have information about your progress understanding your thoughts and emotions and the coping skills we've talked about to manage anxiety."

"Isn't that just great," Rick muttered.

"I'll be sending you a formal letter called a breach notification letter that details all of this and gives you information on how to place a fraud alert on your credit report."

Louis had researched the steps he needed to take and called his insurance carrier. He planned to run everything by the lawyer if and when the guy finally called him back, but the requirements for dealing with a HIPAA breach were pretty clear-cut, even for a solo practitioner. Besides the letters to his patients, he would have to email a report to the federal Department of Health and Human Services.

"Shit, that's all I need now. Identity theft too." Rick smacked his palms against his knees. "Is this something you can get sued for, Doc?"

Louis paused, considering what to say.

"In this country anyone can be sued for just about anything," he said. "I don't blame you for being upset. This kind of thing happens a lot these days usually by computer hacking, although this was a paper record that was stolen. I've changed the lock on my office door and I've asked the owner of this building to implement additional security measures."

The young man sighed.

"This sucks. My wallet got stolen a couple years ago and someone used my credit cards to run up a whole bunch of charges. It was a total pain in the ass to straighten out."

He launched into a tirade about identity thieves, banks, and creditor hassles, and by the time Louis managed to get a word in to redirect him, the session had gone totally off track.

Rick worked as a metal press operator at a large manufacturing firm in town, his first job after being honorably discharged from the Army.

"Let's get back to how you dealt with work stress this week," Louis said, relying on memory since his clinical notes were gone, stolen with Rick's file. "Last time I believe you said you were being more direct with your supervisor, is that right? You were planning to ask for more feedback on your recent performance review?"

"That's right," Rick said slowly. "And I did. I asked my supervisor for a meeting and that went over like a turd in a punch bowl, excuse the expression. The guy's afraid of me or something, like if he tells me something bad I'll freak out. So I let it go."

"Have you ever freaked out at work, Rick?"

"Hell no, Doc," he said. "I need this job. How else am I going to pay the bills when the little one comes?" He smiled, a proud craggy grin. "I didn't tell ya yet, but my wife found out last month she's pregnant. Looks like we'll finally start a family. I got you to thank for that," he said and then laughed hard. "Didn't mean it that way. What I meant is Carrie, my wife, is a lot happier than she used to be. With me that is. Things have been a whole lot better since I started coming here."

For the rest of the hour they talked about how life would change for Rick and his wife after the baby's birth. Although he tried to focus all of his attention on the young man, Louis found his thoughts drifting to the stolen records. He couldn't shake the nagging fear that whoever had Rick Sprague's patient file would use the information it contained to do something terrible.

And there was absolutely nothing he could do to prevent it.

After the session with Rick, Louis evaluated a new patient referred by a local physician and then it was noon. He checked his voice mails and was relieved that the attorney had finally called back with a suggested appointment time later that week.

He called back and left a message to confirm and then with some trepidation he called his patient, Diane, who answered on the first ring as though she had been waiting by the phone.

"I was going to call you, Dr. D'Maio," she said, sounding as if she were out of breath. "You said you would call me back."

"Yes. I wanted to let you know that my office was broken into over the weekend. There were files stolen, and yours was one of them. I think that's why you got that strange call on Saturday and I've reported the theft to the police. I'm really sorry, Diane, but it appears that someone used the information in your PHI—your protected health information—to play a nasty prank."

There was a silence. When she spoke, her voice was cold and hard.

"I had no idea until one of my friends told me today that you've had—shall we say—a problem before with one of your female patients. You know, with Victoria Rudemann, the woman who was shot just yesterday?"

For a moment Louis felt he couldn't breathe.

"What did you say?"

"That woman who was shot yesterday in her house. One of my friends told me that a couple years ago you tried to have a fling with her and she turned you down, and it was a big fiasco. It was in the newspapers and everything."

"Diane, your friend is mistaken. The whole incident did get publicity but it wasn't true about me trying to have a fling. I've never crossed any ethical boundaries with any of my patients," he said, forcing himself to stay calm. "And what is this about Victoria Rudemann getting shot?"

"It was in the news this morning," she said. "She was shot to death. I was talking about it with one of my friends at breakfast and I happened to tell her what happened with me, you know, about going to meet you at the hotel, and she said that woman Victoria Rudemann sued you for the same thing. For making a pass at her." Mixed with outrage was a note of excitement in her

2222222222222222222

voice that made his heart sink.

He recognized that she wanted to believe she had been next in line. Even though she might, subconsciously or not, cloak those feelings in righteous indignation.

"Hold on, Diane," Louis said, his mind whirling. "Please listen to me. I didn't ask you to meet me at the hotel. There was a theft of clinical records from my office, and one of those records was yours."

"So?" she challenged.

This wasn't the humiliated Diane he had spoken with two days earlier. He took a deep breath.

"I didn't call you on the weekend. I didn't ask you to meet me outside of the office. That would be wrong, it would be unethical, and I'm telling you it wasn't me."

She said nothing.

He waited and then continued, "Diane, I'll be sending you a letter. It will say what information in your clinical record was compromised and what I plan to do about preventing any further breaches. I'm so sorry this happened."

He heard her clear her throat.

"Dr. D'Maio?" she said in a shaky voice.

"Yes?"

"Go fuck yourself."

The line beeped twice as the call disconnected. For a few seconds he sat stupidly with the cell phone against his ear, then he placed it on his desk and put his head in his hands.

Victoria Rudemann shot to death. Not an overdose. Not a suicide.

Louis thought the day couldn't get much worse but he was mistaken. He left voice messages for Kristen and for a patient named Sarah informing them both of the records theft, advising them he would be in touch soon, and then his ex-wife Carol called.

"Lou, what the hell's going on?" Carol asked in a brittle voice when he answered his cell. "What did you do?"

"What are you talking about?"

"I just got a call from a reporter from the *Hartford Courant*," she said.

"About what?"

"He wanted to know whether I thought you might be linked to some shooting in Avon, some woman who used to be your patient. And whether this might be connected to your girlfriend dying in St. Maarten? And here's the kicker, the guy wanted to know if you abused me too when we were married. Ha."

He detected a mix of disgust and triumph in her voice.

"What do you want me to tell him, Lou?"

"Who is this guy?" he asked, his outrage growing.

"Like I said, some reporter."

"What was his name?"

She paused.

"I don't remember. I'm not sure if he said his name but he said he was calling from the newspaper."

"Carol, don't talk to him. It's probably an imposter. There's someone who's broken into my house and my office, causing all kinds of problems. It could be the same person pretending to be a reporter."

"Do you think I'm stupid? I didn't say anything," she said, but he heard the doubt in her tone.

"What *did* you say?"

"I said I didn't know anything about some woman getting killed and that's the truth. First I heard of it, as a matter of fact. And as far as your girlfriend who died on that island, I don't know and I don't care what happened there."

"What did he ask you specifically?"

"I told you. In a nutshell whether I think you're responsible for these women dying. And whether or not you abused me when we were married. Physically or emotionally."

He wondered how she had answered that question and decided not to ask. It didn't matter.

"Do you have the phone number on your Caller ID?"

"I didn't look. Why? What's going on?"

"I don't know," he said. "But I would appreciate it if you didn't talk to anyone claiming to be a reporter."

"You in some kind of trouble?"

"No," he said.

Not yet.

Maybe that depended on whose gun had been used to shoot Victoria Rudemann.

Watch the news yet Dr D?

"Then what's going on?"

"I told you," he said. "There's someone harassing me."

"A patient?"

"No."

"Oh." She sounded disappointed. "Well, I thought I should tell you."

"Thanks," he said. It was obvious she had enjoyed his discomfiture.

"Hey, did you finally get around to paying Heather's tuition for the fall semester?" Carol asked. "She was worried about whether she could get into all the classes she needs. I hope you took care of it."

"I already paid it," he said. "Has Heather been around lately?"

"No. But she's coming home this weekend," Carol said. "Why? Is someone bothering her too? Better not be."

Louis closed his eyes.

"I hope not."

"She would tell me," Carol bragged. "We're close, you know."

Another dig, he thought. Heather didn't share much about her life with him at all these days.

"Carol, I've talked to her already about being careful. Whoever this guy is, he seems to know a lot about me and now he's involved you. I'll remind Heather to be on the alert and to call me or the police if she sees or hears of anyone acting suspicious."

"Sounds like a lot of drama," his ex-wife said. "You sure you're not in some kind of trouble? Counseled the wrong person maybe? Gave some bad advice?"

She laughed.

Louis said nothing. He had no idea why the woman disliked him so much. It was hard to believe they'd once been married and lived in the same house. He couldn't imagine what life would be like if they'd stayed together. A living hell, no doubt.

"Thanks for letting me know," he finally said. "And be careful. I don't know who we're dealing with."

His last appointment for the day ended at six. After he ushered his patient out, Louis went online and looked for the latest news about Victoria Rudemann. Other than the new information that she had been shot and her death was considered a homicide, no other details had been released. No doubt the cops would question her ex-husband, any boyfriends, anyone with a grudge. He wondered when the cops would question him.

In the meantime he had work to do. He sat at his desk and completed and faxed paperwork for the insurance companies. When he was satisfied he was finally caught up, he shut down his laptop and locked the filing cabinets. He hid the key under the wooden zebra Paula had given him and drew the blinds, sending a swirl of dust particles in the air.

Louis double-checked the deadbolt when he left the office and made his way to his car in the near-empty parking lot. A warm breeze stirred his hair. This pleasant New England summer was waning and the days were getting shorter, but this was the kind of night he and Paula would have savored outdoors.

Sitting on the deck with a glass of wine...or listening to an outdoor concert at Elizabeth Park with a picnic dinner.

If only he had appreciated how precious those moments were. He doubted he could get through another endless night without obsessing about whether Victoria Rudemann had been killed by a bullet—or bullets—fired by his revolver. Or without checking the news online and on television continually, hoping not to hear that some drunk fisherman fell into the Connecticut River and drowned.

The party's this way...

Louis drove down Prospect Avenue in slow traffic and passed the beige brick building where Kristen worked. He spotted her blue Camry in the parking lot and wondered if she'd gotten his voice mail about her stolen record and if she would call him back. He briefly entertained the idea of turning around and dropping by at her office.

Too intrusive.

He suspected she had enough on her plate, what with clearing out Paula's house. He rolled down the windows of the Mazda, cranked up the radio, and tried to clear his mind as he zipped down the highway.

Louis was wary now when he entered his condo, first inspecting the door and the new lock for signs of tampering. He stepped inside slowly, looking around as though he expected an ambush and felt ridiculous.

I'm Inspector Clouseau waiting for Cato.

He dropped his briefcase on the floor in the living room and went to the kitchen, where he filled a glass with ice and water. The house was cool and quiet. So quiet.

He stood at the counter, caught sight of a small stack of cat food cans and frowned. Where the hell was Bogie? He hadn't made an appearance in the morning or yesterday all day, for that matter. Louis hadn't seen him since—when—maybe Saturday? He ought to be ravenous.

Louis called out the cat's name and listened, but there was no answering meow or the sound of Bogie jumping off the furniture somewhere to make his way to the kitchen. It was odd.

Quite possibly the cat had gotten himself trapped in a closet. On two previous occasions Louis hadn't noticed him slip past the closet door when he'd opened it and he'd discovered the cat hours later stuck inside, crouched in the corner and pissed as hell. One time the cat had been trapped for a full day and by the time Louis had found him, he'd pulled down most of Louis' shirts off the hangers and peed in his shoes.

Louis opened every closet door on the first floor and then went upstairs to his bedroom. Bogie was nowhere to be found. He changed into khakis and a polo shirt, saw that the laundry hamper was overflowing, and realized he hadn't been taking care of business. He picked up the hamper of dirty clothes and carried it the two flights down to the basement. If he did nothing else productive tonight, he could at least get his laundry done.

A fetid odor hit him as soon as he entered the cool basement. He put the hamper down on the floor and looked around for the source. It smelled like road kill after a day in the sun, he thought, grimacing. Besides the washer and dryer, he stored snow tires and other odds and ends in the cellar.

With some hesitation he moved these items aside but all he found were dust balls and spiders. He put his clothes into the washer and caught a stronger whiff of the foul smell. There was a tool box on the floor and he moved it aside and peered at the back of the washing machine.

His black and white cat was crammed beneath the black drain hose, small head facing up. Milky sightless eyes stared at him. A small sliver of pink tongue protruded from the cat's mouth.

"Jesus."

With both hands he struggled to drag the heavy machine farther away from the concrete wall. Flies buzzed around his head and a rancid smell of urine reached his nose. The washer scraped against the concrete floor and Bogie dropped with a soft wet thump.

CHAPTER TWENTY-TWO

KRISTEN OPENED THE main door of her office suite and greeted Paula's ex-husband Bill, who had just gotten out of work at his landscaping job. He wore dirty jeans and a sweat-soaked faded gray T-shirt, and his brown work boots were caked with dried mud. He smelled like cigarette smoke, earth and sweat.

He took off his cap. His damp brown hair was plastered to his skull.

"Sorry I didn't get a chance to go home and shower," Bill said. "I had to work late and I wanted to get here before you left."

"Come in," Kristen said and led him down the short hallway. All of her staff were gone for the day. "I have the stuff in my office."

She pointed to two medium-sized cardboard boxes in the corner. He stood awkwardly, shifting from one foot to the other.

"Thanks," Bill said. "How you are holding up?"

Kristen shrugged.

"Okay, I guess. Clearing out the house isn't much fun."

"I'll help you if you want," he said. "Just say the word."

"Thanks, but I have it under control," she said.

She had never been particularly close to Bill while he and Paula were married, but she'd gotten along with him well enough. But because she'd heard the tape recording of his conversation with Paula, she found herself feeling aloof. She had the fleeting thought that if he'd been the one to set up the tape recorder, maybe he wanted to help her at Paula's house so he could secretly retrieve it.

"Are you putting her house on the market soon?" he asked. "How is that whole probate thing going?"

"It's going. It takes time even when a person has a will. I have a probate lawyer who's helping me with the paperwork I need to file with the court," she said. "And I understand that you're the beneficiary of Paula's life insurance policy."

So now you can afford your car payments, huh? she thought.

"That's right, that was a real nice surprise," Bill said, grinning. "When the insurance agent called me I just about fell over. A hundred thousand dollars."

Kristen nodded. She'd been just as shocked as Bill to discover the policy and its designated beneficiary, but a possible explanation became clearer when she saw that Paula had taken out the insurance years ago while the two were still married. After their divorce, she'd probably forgotten to name another heir.

The probate lawyer had said this was a common mistake. Or maybe it wasn't a mistake, but regardless of the reason, for Bill it was like winning the lottery.

She added, "Plus you're the beneficiary of Paula's IRAs and the small amount she had in her 401K retirement plan from her previous employer."

Bill's grin grew wider.

"I gotta talk to an accountant about that. Don't want to get socked with a lot of taxes. I want to keep that money for my own retirement."

"That would be wise," Kristen said. "So anyway, these are the photo albums you wanted." She pulled out the first book from the box. It was filled with photos Paula had taken with a film camera years ago when she and Bill were first going out. "There are four in this box and two in the other. One of them is your wedding album, so I thought you would want that too."

"Sure," he said and took the album from her outstretched hands. He riffled through the pages, occasionally pausing and shaking his head. "Blast from the past, that's for sure." For a moment he looked hesitant as he stared at the boxes. "I didn't know there were this many. I'm not sure what I'll do with them all after I look at them…"

"You can do whatever you want," Kristen said. "I have a lot of photos already so I don't really want these books. If you don't want them either, just throw them out."

"Maybe I'll have them all converted to digital images, put them on disks," he said. "It wouldn't seem right to just—you know, toss them all in the trash."

"It's the memories up here that are important," Kristen said, tapping her forehead. "I'm coming to realize that as much as I don't want to get rid of Paula's things, I don't have the space to keep everything in my house."

"That's a good point." Bill placed the photo album back in the box and turned to look at her. "I was wondering if there was something else I could have?"

Kristen had been waiting for this. She'd doubted that Bill would take the trouble to arrange a meeting with her just to pick up some ancient photo albums. He didn't seem that sentimental.

"What is it?"

"Well, if you aren't planning to take these yourself, do you think I could have her TV and maybe her computer? It's going to take a little time before I get that insurance money and my TV went on the fritz last week. I could use a new computer too. Mine is so old it takes forever to open a program." He shrugged.

"Just thought I would ask in case you were going to give them away."

Kristen looked at him, thinking. It wasn't as if there were other relatives who wanted Paula's things. Besides the distant cousins she rarely saw and her elderly aunts, there was no one else in their family.

"I don't want her television. So I guess you can have it if you want. But I didn't find a computer. She didn't have a desktop computer."

"A laptop maybe? A tablet?"

"I didn't see either one of those in the house," she said.

That was true. There was no reason to tell him Louis had admitted to taking the laptop. That would really get him going and she didn't want to hear it.

He eyed her.

"Okay. Then I'll take the TV. When should I come over to get it?"

"Let's figure out a time on the weekend," she said, looking at the calendar on her phone. "I'll call you soon. Is that all right?"

She noticed that there was a missed call and a voice mail from Louis. She'd call him back later on.

"Fine," he said. He leaned down and stacked one box on top of the other. "I'll bring these out to my truck."

"I'll walk out with you," she said, and gathered her things.

Ever since the night the intoxicated man had entered her building looking for his wife, she hadn't felt comfortable being alone in the office after hours. She hadn't seen the guy again and apparently Eric had scared him away for good, but the neighborhood wasn't the safest.

"Any news on the investigation in St. Maarten?" Bill asked as they walked out to the parking lot. He unlocked his black Ford Explorer and shoved the boxes in the back seat. "Did they ever find that guy Paula was supposed to be sailing with?"

She saw empty coffee cups on the floor and caught a whiff of cigarette smoke and fried food.

"Haven't heard a word," she said. "As far as I know, her luggage is still missing too. They were supposed to do a trace on her cell phone, track all of her communications when she was on the island, but I haven't heard the results of that either. From what I understand, these investigations can take a lot of time, maybe months."

His face twisted into a mask of disgust.

"What did you think about that ass wipe going to St. Maarten the same time she went missing?"

"You mean Louis?"

His voice was hard.

"Yeah, that's the ass wipe I'm referring to. The one who ruined my marriage."

"I don't know. He went there to look for her."

"Or so he said." Bill snorted. "I still can't believe he had the balls to show up at the funeral. Lucky for him he didn't stick around. I would have cleaned his clock right there in the reception hall."

Kristen had heard this same refrain from Bill before, several times after Paula's funeral service in fact. He hadn't cared who heard him rant. She'd felt embarrassed for him then, for his immature and uncivilized comments, but had chalked it up to grief. Now it was just annoying. She looked at her watch.

"One of these days," Bill said, staring past her, his eyes narrowed. "One of these days that guy's gonna pay. And I plan to piss on his grave."

Kristen was just about to pull out from the parking lot behind Bill when her cell phone rang. She saw the caller was Eric, and she braked and picked up the phone.

"Hi, hon," he said in a low voice. "I've been thinking about you. I miss you already."

"Me too. How's it going in New York?" she asked.

"Better than I thought. Unfortunately I don't have a lot of time to talk to you right now, but I wanted to let you know I'll be here longer than I thought, maybe a few days. Turns out my client wants to introduce me to the CEO of another manufacturing business here, and it could lead to another contract for my company." He sounded excited. His company sold metal alloys to a variety of manufacturing firms. "I'm taking my client out for dinner in a few minutes. Can I call you tonight?"

"Sure," she said. "I'll be around."

They said their goodbyes but instead of going home, Kristen headed towards Paula's house. All day long she'd been thinking about the taped conversations. If the device started recording as soon as the call was answered, why did all the conversations sound incomplete, like snippets of calls?

Particularly the third conversation in which Paula lambasted Louis and his threat at the end: "You go and you're dead."

She'd listened to it a dozen times and even with all the static, she was pretty sure it wasn't Louis' voice. Not only that, had he actually said that to Paula, she would have responded. There was nothing on the tape after that. The whole thing was fishy.

Sometime during the afternoon the idea had come to her that Paula's home phone might have a record of calls in the handset's Caller ID list. Now that Eric wouldn't be back tonight...well, it seemed like a good time to play detective.

The first thing Kristen noticed when she got to Paula's house was that the motion sensor lights on the garage weren't working. She was sure that the lights had been on the last time she was here, when Eric had joined her. The driveway stayed dark as she edged her car in close to the garage door and cut the ignition. She found the key in her purse and made her way to the front door and into the small, quiet house.

The boxes she'd packed in the kitchen were stacked on the floor ready for delivery to Maude's church and the local food pantry. She opened the cabinet doors one by one, double checking she'd packed everything. She made a mental note to ask Eric for assistance in transporting the boxes when he got back from New York.

Kristen had called the phone company weeks earlier to disconnect Paula's landline but the white cordless phone was still in its cradle in the kitchen. It was a similar model to the one she had at home, and she pressed the menu button to access the Caller ID log. There were no calls listed.

Damn.

She wondered if Paula had erased the call log before she'd gone to St. Maarten, but what about calls that might have come in while she was away? Kristen paused for a moment and went upstairs to the master bedroom. She sat on Paula's neatly-made queen-sized bed and picked up the phone on the nightstand.

No record there either. Disappointed, she went back downstairs and then remembered seeing a phone in the spare room where Paula had a desk and bookcases.

The third time's the charm.

She accessed the phone's menu and scrolled down a list of a dozen phone numbers dating back to June. She remembered Paula mentioning the Vermont art show sometime in early June, and she looked for the sequence of the three calls on the tape recording: hers, Bill's and Louis' numbers. Interestingly, Bill's number didn't show up at all in June. Unless Paula had deleted it or had called him, she thought. The recorder would have captured the conversation but Bill's number would not have appeared on the handset's caller ID record.

But if the three calls on the tape were the last three Paula had ever received, the numbers didn't match the most recent three numbers on the handset's call record. Unless the batteries on the recorder had gone dead and it failed to capture additional calls that might have come afterwards? It still didn't explain why the conversations on the tape sounded—fake. Spliced.

Her head was beginning to hurt. She wrote down the numbers on the call list that she couldn't identify and put the handset back in the spare room. Something didn't make sense, starting from who recorded the calls in the first place, and why.

She had an uneasy feeling again that she was missing something important. And once again, the silence in the house was beginning to feel like a heavy weight, slowly descending like the ball on the end of a crane. She looked at the rows of books in Paula's bookcase that Eric had yet to pack up.

Time to go home.

Eric would be calling her soon.

Her elderly neighbor Maude was struggling to push her overloaded trash can out to the curb when Kristen arrived home.

She rolled down her car window when she pulled into the driveway and called out, "Maude, be careful. I can help you with that in a second."

"I got it, I ain't crippled," Maude answered cheerfully, but when Kristen came out of her garage, the older woman was waiting.

Under the sallow glow of the streetlight, her face looked wan and pale.

Kristen pushed the large gray barrel to the curb.

"Sheesh, this is heavy. You shouldn't be moving this yourself."

"Been doing a lot of cleaning this past week," Maude said. "Throwing a lot of junk out. I don't want to end up on one of them hoarder shows on TV." She rubbed her hands together in a gesture of finality. "Thought I'd save my son a lot of headaches the day he either puts me into a nursing home or into the ground. Whichever comes first."

"How did the visit go with your grandkids? Did they like your homemade cookies?"

She winked.

"They inhaled 'em like a pack of hyenas," Maude said. "I don't think they're allowed to have sweets at home. My son's a health nut. A vee-gan. Maybe that's why they came over, they're starving to death. Guess I'll have to keep some of those mixes on hand."

Kristen smiled.

"You need me to do anything else for you, Maude? I'm happy to help."

Maude took off her glasses and wiped them on the hem of her long cotton shirt.

"That's nice of you but I think I'm all set for now, dear. Oh, and I hope I didn't make your sweetie mad? When I waved at him today he kind of turned his back on me." She put her glasses back on and peered at Kristen with a worried look. "Hope he doesn't think I'm a busybody or something."

"Eric's in New York."

"Really? He must have a twin then. I saw him this afternoon at your house after lunch. I was out on my porch, taking a break from cleaning. I said hello and waved at him but maybe he didn't hear me?" She paused. "Well, maybe I was mistaken. I thought it was him in the driveway."

"Couldn't have been Eric," Kristen said, her thoughts racing. Who had been at her house? "Do you remember when this was?"

"No clue," Maude said. "I went back inside to watch TV. So that was around one o'clock in the afternoon. Am I telling tales out of school now?" She frowned. "Maybe it wasn't that early in the afternoon."

Kristen hesitated and decided to let it go. No use interrogating her elderly neighbor. "Well, I have to get going, Maude. You sure you don't need help with anything else?"

"Nah, I'm all set for now. It's bedtime for Bonzo. Have yourself a good night."

"You too."

Kristen stood outside and waited until Maude had shuffled safely back inside her house and turned off her front light.

Kristen was sipping a cup of green tea in her kitchen when Eric called her back. It was almost eleven o'clock and she was tired, ready to go to bed.

"Sorry I'm calling you so late," he said. "I just got back to my hotel."

"How was your dinner?"

"Great. I'm pretty sure I'll be getting another sizeable account. My boss will be very happy when he hears about it," Eric said. "I'll be introduced to the CEO tomorrow and it will be a matter of negotiating a contract that works for both sides. How was your night?"

"Nothing special," she said. "I saw my neighbor, Maude, when I got home after work. She said she saw you this afternoon. At my house."

Eric laughed.

"Hon, I'm in Manhattan. I've been in meetings all day."

Kristen felt foolish. All night she'd been wondering if he'd returned to Connecticut for some reason.

"Wasn't me," he said. "Maybe she got confused."

"I guess so."

"Oh, and by the way, when I was walking past Saks Fifth Avenue tonight I saw something in the window that I thought you'd really like. So I went in and got it. I can't wait to give it to you."

"What is it?"

"You'll have to wait and see. I hope it's the right size," he said. "I think it will look just perfect."

After they hung up Kristen stood at the kitchen counter and finished her tea. Maude hadn't seemed confused. In fact she seemed remarkably on the ball for a woman her age. But Eric was in New York.

How do you really know?

She detested that tiny voice of doubt in her head. There was either trust or there wasn't, and if in fact there wasn't, then the relationship was doomed. She'd learned that the hard way with men in her past.

Maude had to be mistaken.

Eric might be a little jealous, but he cared about her. She was sure he wanted things to work out as badly as she did.

She thought about the tape recorder hidden in Paula's cellar.

What a shock it would be to find something like that in your own house.

Particularly if it was set up by someone you loved or just as frightening, by someone you didn't. Talk about a breach of trust on so many levels, and illegal to boot.

She ought to notify the police and hand over the tape. Let them figure it out. Or would they just arrest Louis without delving further into the threat?

Kristen put her tea cup in the dishwasher, walked down the hallway, and opened the door to her cellar. It wouldn't hurt to check things out, make sure her own phone lines weren't tapped. After all, Eric had said he'd heard a noise down there that night he'd come over, the night of their fight. She turned on the light and made her way down the stairs.

She smelled a slight mustiness when she got to the bottom of the steps. She hadn't run the dehumidifier the past couple of weeks as she often forgot to empty it anyway. Nothing looked out of the ordinary as she scanned the large room. There were a dozen or so plastic bins with items from her parents' house as well as her own stuff.

Holiday decorations, a bicycle, old exercise equipment.

She looked up at the ductwork, thinking about Paula's house. She was too short to reach up that high, but she found a stepstool near the washing machine and dragged it over to the furnace. Starting there, she felt along the top of the ductwork, recoiling at times from the dusty, grimy feel of the metal. Hopefully there weren't spiders lurking there.

She hadn't gotten halfway across the room before she touched something solid and her fingers closed on a cold metal object on top of the duct. She knew instantly what it was.

Her heart began to pound and with trembling hands she took down a revolver.

CHAPTER TWENTY-THREE

KRISTEN HAD GONE shooting once in her life, at an indoor range with Chris a few years earlier. It had been his idea of an interesting date, but her aim was terrible and she ended up shooting holes in the ceiling. She knew very little about firearms but she knew enough to handle the revolver with care, pointing the barrel away while she pressed the thumb piece forward and pushed the cylinder to the left.

To her relief it was not loaded, and she snapped the cylinder back into place and examined it. It was a Smith & Wesson Air Lite .38 Special, a small revolver that could fit into her purse. She wondered if there was a box of bullets hidden anywhere else above the ducts, and she finished searching the basement but found nothing else.

Her mind whirled. Who did it belong to and who had placed it there? As far as she knew, the only person who had access to her house was Eric. She looked at the wall clock—it was close to midnight—and thought that maybe she should wait until the morning to call him.

Except I won't sleep all night wondering, she thought.

The hell with it. She deserved an answer.

His cell phone rang a few times before he answered it.

He sounded as if he'd been sleeping.

"Kristen? Are you okay?"

"Not really." She didn't bother with preliminaries. "I found a gun in my basement."

"It's mine" he said without hesitation. "I hid it in your cellar the other night. New York City has very restrictive gun laws and I didn't want to bring it with me. I was planning to tell you about it when I got back."

"What?"

"I have a pistol permit in Connecticut, don't worry. I just thought it would be a good idea for you to have a way to protect yourself. I didn't have time to talk with you about it before I left."

"I don't understand. You carry guns around and you left one at my house without telling me?"

"I do carry once in a while. Like I said, I have a permit and I own some firearms. I was going to discuss this with you when I got back," he repeated, and he sounded fully awake now and frustrated. "I'm sorry you're upset. It wasn't my intention, and that's why I hid it."

"I don't have a permit. So how would this help me?"

"You don't need a permit to have a firearm in your house. You need a permit to carry, that's all. Kristen, I'm just concerned about your welfare. The time I thought I heard something in your basement that night, it got me thinking you should have a way to defend yourself, especially when you're home alone. There's been so many terrible things happening in the news lately. I was going to talk with you about whether you might be interested in learning how to shoot, if you don't already know."

"So why didn't you just ask me? Why did you hide it instead?"

"It didn't seem like a good time to get into a discussion

about it, right after you being at your sister's house and pretty emotional," he said. "That's why I decided to wait. Bad judgment on my part, I guess. I didn't know you'd be searching your cellar tonight." He paused. "Was there some reason you did? Search your cellar, I mean?"

She was nonplussed.

"I don't know."

"What were you looking for?"

"I wasn't looking for anything in particular."

He was silent for a few seconds.

"Kristen, if there's something wrong, you need to tell me."

"I am telling you," she said. "It's very disturbing to find a gun in my house."

"And I just explained to you why it was there," he said, and she could tell his patience was wearing thin. "Do you want me to come back tonight so we can talk about it in person?"

She looked at the clock again.

"That would be silly, it's after midnight already. Don't you have an important meeting tomorrow?"

"Yes, but you're more important, and you're clearly unhappy," he said. "I can cancel. I'll tell them I have a family emergency."

"No, don't do that," she said. "We can talk more tomorrow. I have meetings tomorrow too, and I need to get some sleep."

"Kristen, please listen to me," he said evenly. "The last thing I want to do is cause any problems between us. I made a mistake. I'm sorry. The gun's not loaded, by the way."

"I saw that. Where are the bullets?"

"In a box. Under your bed."

She almost laughed.

"Under my bed. That's useful. If someone breaks in, I first have to find the ammo under my bed and then run down to the basement and get the gun."

"Why didn't you hide the gun under my bed? Why in the

cellar?"

"I don't know," he said. "Because I had it with me when I was downstairs. It was an impulsive decision. I said I was sorry. What else do you want me to say?"

She held the phone to her ear. What did she want him to do? She picked up the revolver and held it flat in her hand. Then she placed it back on the kitchen table.

"Kristen?"

She was tired and cranky, and it was obvious they weren't getting anywhere.

"I'm here. I guess we should call it a night."

"Okay," he said. "I'll give you a call tomorrow. I'm not sure what my schedule is yet, but I'll be in touch."

Later Kristen lay in bed tossing and turning, unable to sleep. She'd found the small box of .38 Special pistol cartridges under his side of the bed. She'd counted them: there were six bullets missing. She'd hidden the gun and the box of ammo inside one of the many shoeboxes in her closet.

If Eric hadn't wanted to bring his revolver on his business trip, why hadn't he left it at his own place? And for that matter, why didn't he ever invite her over? She'd never been to his house, not even once. Granted their relationship was still relatively new, but he always preferred to take her out and end their evenings at her house.

When he returned from New York she would confront him. She wasn't anti-gun but she was anti-secrecy and anti-bullshit, and this was over the top.

She'd been preoccupied and had forgotten to call Louis back also, she realized. His message on her cell phone had been cryptic, something about a stolen record. She had deleted it by mistake before listening to the whole thing.

Now she wondered—what stolen record? And what would he say when—if—she told him about the recording on the tape?

CHAPTER TWENTY-FOUR

The Next Day

FRANK WAS PUTTING for a greenie on the fifth hole, but his putt was two inches short. He looked at Louis and shook his head.

"Good thing you're playing worse than me today, buddy," he said. "Otherwise I'd pull a Happy Gilmore and start bashing my clubs into the ground."

"Yeah, you're lucky I'm distracted," Louis muttered.

His game was lousy today and his mood was glum. His two afternoon patients had cancelled and since it was a warm sunny day, one of the few left of the summer, he'd called Frank and asked if he wanted to play. They'd gotten a tee time at two in the afternoon.

At the next tee, Louis sliced his shot into the woods and the two of them walked into a thicket of oak trees to look for the ball.

"You upset about your cat?" Frank asked. "I meant to say I was sorry to hear he was gone to the Rainbow Bridge, even though I didn't like him much."

Louis had just filled him in about Bogie's demise and the theft of his revolver.

"I don't know if it was due to natural causes or what. He could have been trapped back there and died, or maybe he was poisoned. Who knows? I don't know how old he was, so maybe he had some disease."

"So what did you do with him?"

"I would have buried him in the backyard but I live in a condo, Frank. I'm sure there's some rule about pet cemeteries on the common grounds. So I put him in a heavy-duty garbage bag and I threw him in the Dumpster."

"No way."

"What else would I do with him?" Louis asked. "Cremate him in my oven? I didn't want to go back to the Connecticut River and send him off there either."

"When my son's rabbit died, we had to have a whole memorial service. Then I buried it in the backyard and a coyote or a raccoon dug it up," Frank commented. "There were little pieces of fur all over the yard. What if the Dumpster people find it? They'll think there's an animal killer on the loose."

Louis shrugged. "I don't know. If I could afford an autopsy—or rather, a necropsy—I might have brought the body over to the vet. But now's not a good time. I went to see the lawyer and his retainer is three grand. Pretty steep."

"For what?" Frank asked, bending over by some shrubbery. "Hey, is this your ball?" He held up a dirty Titleist.

"Yeah right," Louis said. "That one looks like it's been sitting in the mud for a year. I'll just drop a ball and play it from here since I really suck today."

"So what's with you and the lawyer?" Frank asked, shielding his eyes from the glare of the sun.

"I met with him yesterday. First there's the issue with the five stolen clinical records—and he's advising me to offer identity theft protection to those people," Louis said. "It'll cost me, but it might avoid other problems. I've heard back from all of them except for one, and they're not happy, as you can imagine."

The one person who hadn't called him back yet was Kristen. "And then there's Victoria Rudemann. I'm expecting the police will eventually want to question me because of that Internet sex ad that I didn't place. But thank God Charlotte found out the child molestation thing with Annie was a hoax. Otherwise I'd probably be sitting in jail right now. And did I tell you about the so-called *Hartford Courant* reporter?"

"Missed that one," Frank said, and Louis told him about Carol's phone call.

"I don't think for one second that the guy who called her was a real reporter," Louis finished. "I think it's the same person who broke into my office and my house and keeps causing trouble for me on so many levels."

"The million dollar question," Frank said. "Who? And why? Oh, sorry, that's two questions, so 500K each."

"If I can find out who BD9908 is, that's the guy. He seems pretty good at covering his tracks though."

"He also seems to target people that you know, people around you," Frank remarked. "Charlotte and Carol, for instance. Maybe I shouldn't hang around with you anymore. Maybe I'll go home one of these days and find a *live* cat left in my house. That would be terrible."

Louis laughed in spite of himself. "Maybe he'll do you a favor—he'll trade your clubs for a set of garden tools."

They were on the fifteenth hole when Louis' cell phone vibrated in his pocket. He looked at the number, saw it was his daughter Heather, and answered the call.

"Dad," she said, breathless. "I got into an accident. My brakes didn't work and I hit another car and went into a tree. I couldn't stop."

"Where are you? Are you hurt?" He heard a police siren in

the background.

"I hurt my neck," she said and started to cry. "I was just leaving school to come home."

"Okay," he said. "Where are you now?"

"Near campus. Hill Street. The cops are coming and I think an ambulance too. I called 911. I don't know if anyone in the other car is hurt. Dad, I couldn't stop, I tried to brake and I couldn't stop."

"I'm on my way," he said. "Heather, listen to me carefully. Let them take you to the hospital to get checked out. Okay? Will you do that? They'll probably bring you to Rockville General since that's closer to where you are. I'm leaving Farmington now and I'll meet you there. Call me or text me if they take you someplace else."

"Can you let Mom know?" she said in a trembling voice.

"Don't worry."

"The other people are getting out of their car," she said, and now he heard muted voices in the background. "Thank God, I think they're all right."

There was a pause and he heard a man's loud angry voice.

"What the fuck happened? What the hell's the matter with you?"

"My brakes didn't work."

Heather sounded near hysteria. Or shock, he thought. She might be more injured than she realized.

"Heather," he yelled, hoping she would hear him and put the phone back to her ear. "Heather. Don't say anything, wait for the cops to come." He motioned to Frank, who was walking toward him.

"Dad, the police are here now. I have to go." The call disconnected before he had a chance to reply.

"What happened?" Frank asked.

"I have to leave right now," Louis said. His stomach was churning with anxiety. "Heather's been in a car accident and she hurt her neck." He picked up his golf bag. "She's at UConn. She was on her way home. Her brakes failed."

Frank stared. "Holy shit. You don't think—"

Louis frowned and was about to say something when a sharp pain in his lower back jabbed him like a spear. He jerked and almost dropped the bag.

"You all right? You want me to drive?" Frank asked.

"Just a back spasm." He winced and straightened gingerly. "I'm okay. Let's go."

They walked quickly, cutting across the course past the Nineteenth Hole to the parking lot. A police cruiser was parked near Louis' Mazda, and two men emerged from each car as Frank and Louis approached. One was older, with short gray hair and a bit of a paunch and the other was a younger man who drew himself up to his full height as he walked over.

"Oh, no," Louis said. His first thought was that they were there to deliver the terrible news that Heather had been severely hurt. Or worse.

No, I just talked to her, she was okay.

"Dr. D'Maio," the younger one said, looking at Louis. "I'm Detective Anderson and this is Detective Loman."

"Is my daughter all right?"

The man looked puzzled and Frank spoke up.

"He just found out that his daughter was in a car accident. We need to get to the hospital. Can you escort us?"

"What's your name, sir?" the man asked. His eyes were dark and expressionless.

"Frank Roth."

"We need to go right now," Louis said. Then he saw "Avon Police Department" on the side of the cruiser and his mouth dropped. "You're not here because of my daughter, are you?"

"We'd like to talk to you about Victoria Rudemann," the older detective said. "We'd like you to come with us to the station and answer a few questions."

"He needs to get to the hospital," Frank said evenly.

"Please. Not now. My daughter's been in an accident," Louis

said, glancing back and forth at the two detectives. Their faces betrayed no emotion but their postures became more rigid. He sensed that things could go south at any second.

Then he remembered his conversation with the lawyer and said as politely as he could manage, "Am I being detained or am I free to go?"

The older man shrugged.

"You're free to go. But things will be easier if you cooperate with us. We just have a few questions to ask you, we won't take up much of your time. Then we'll make sure you get to the hospital to see your daughter. We'll call from the station and see how she's doing. Does that sound all right to you?"

"I have nothing to say to you until I speak with my attorney," Louis said, repeating verbatim what the lawyer had told him to say if he was approached by the police. Thank God he'd finally met with the guy or he wouldn't have known what to do.

By now there were several golfers edging closer to the parking lot, curious about what was going on. Louis stepped to his car and put his golf bag in the trunk.

"I'll drive you to the hospital, Louis," Frank said firmly.

The two officers backed off but didn't leave. They stood and watched silently as Frank walked past them, opened the trunk of his SUV and hefted his golf bag in the back.

Louis nodded.

"Let's get out of here."

They got into the Nissan Rogue and Frank started the vehicle, his lips set in a thin line.

"Watch if they don't follow me and try to pull me over for a traffic violation."

"I hope to hell not."

The cruiser didn't follow them. Louis alternated between looking in the side view mirror and his cell phone, hoping for a text or a call from Heather. In a few minutes a message popped up on his screen.

Dad, at Rockville Gen Hosp. Am OK.

He texted back: *Wait for me. Be there in 30 min.*

"Good thing you went to see the lawyer this week," Frank said. "You said the right things."

"I was just thinking that."

"You know what I was thinking?" Frank turned his head for a second and sighed. "What some people will do when they're losing a game. Shit, I was winning for the first time in weeks."

CHAPTER TWENTY-FIVE

THEY WERE OFF the highway and close to the hospital when Louis' cell phone rang. He answered but the caller wasn't Heather.

"Hey Louis," Kristen said. "Been trying to get hold of you. I got your voice mail the other day but I erased it by mistake so I'm not sure what you said about some record that was stolen?"

He hesitated. He couldn't speak to her about the theft of her clinical record with Frank driving and able to hear every word he said.

"I'm afraid you caught me at a bad time. I'm with a friend of mine and we're on our way to the hospital. My daughter Heather was in a car accident."

"Oh, I'm so sorry," she said. "Is she okay?"

"I hope so. I'll try to call you back tonight if I can."

"That's fine. I should be around. I hope everything's okay with Heather."

He put his phone back on the console and Frank glanced in his direction. "Everything all right?"

"Yeah, it was Paula's sister. Kristen."

"You guys are on speaking terms now? I thought she hated you."

"I don't think she does anymore," Louis said, wanting to change the subject. "Shit, do any of these lights ever turn green?"

They had stopped at yet another red light a block from the hospital. Frank drummed his fingers on the steering wheel.

"So you think you're going to be arrested?" Frank asked suddenly.

Up to this point he hadn't said anything else about the detectives that had met them at the golf course.

"I don't know. I guess it depends on what they think they have on me, which isn't anything or they would have arrested me already." He sighed. "The lawyer told me that when they want to talk to you, it's because they want you to incriminate yourself in some way, and it's practically impossible not to. So even if you're innocent, you should never talk to the police. Chances are they already think you're guilty."

"I didn't know that. I guess I'm going to learn a lot about the legal system," Frank said. "But just so you know? If I'm ever questioned about you, the only thing I think you *might* be guilty of is cheating on your golf score."

By the time Louis and Frank walked into the Emergency Department, Heather was in the reception area waiting for her discharge papers. She was shaken up and her neck was sore from whiplash, but she had no broken bones or other injuries. It was a slow night in the ED, and she'd been seen as soon as the ambulance brought her in.

"I don't think the other people went to the hospital," she said to Louis. Her hair was pulled back into a ponytail and her face was tear-streaked and pale. "The doctor told me I'll probably feel worse tomorrow morning and to take ibuprofen and put ice on my neck. I have to see my regular doctor in a week, or sooner if it really bothers me."

"No neck brace?" Louis asked.

"No. They said a brace or a collar can prolong the healing," she said. "Mom's on her way too. I texted her when I was in the ambulance."

As if on cue, Carol swept through the entrance like a human tornado and rushed toward them. She wore baggy black jeans and a long striped sweatshirt. Her face was sunburned and her light brown hair was a mess of curls.

"Are you okay?" she asked Heather and then turned to Louis. "Thanks for calling me."

He'd completely forgotten.

"Sorry."

She brushed past him, ignored Frank, and looked her daughter up and down.

"Tell me what happened, sweetie."

Heather explained to the three of them that as soon as she'd started driving, the brakes felt spongy and in seconds she had no control of the car's speed as it careened down a hill. She'd applied the emergency brake, which didn't work either, and rear-ended the other car. Then she'd spun and hit a tree after that. Her Kia was likely totaled.

"I'll get your car towed," Louis said. "It sounds to me like a catastrophic brake failure."

Frank rubbed his chin.

"Strange the emergency brake didn't work."

"It was pretty scary," Heather said. "I tried to downshift but I was going too fast. I couldn't avoid the other car."

"It's that shit box you're driving," Carol said, and glared at Louis. "I told you she needed a safer car. Something newer and more reliable."

"Mom, it's not his fault," Heather said miserably, looking back and forth at the two of them.

Of course it's all my fault, Louis thought. *I'm the one who bought her the 'shit box.'*

He turned away from Carol, unwilling to stoop to her level and get into an argument.

"Heather, I'll call the insurance company to report the accident and arrange for a rental car too. Did you leave anything in the Kia?"

"No, I took my purse," she said and pointed to a brown leather bag on the floor. "I don't think there's anything else valuable in there."

"Okay. Do you want to stay at my place?" he asked, already knowing the answer when he saw her glance at Carol.

"I have a couple days off from classes," she said. "I'll go home with Mom."

This was no surprise. He couldn't remember the last time she'd stayed with him.

Carol nodded.

"I'll take you home now. You need to rest." She gave Louis an icy look. "You'll take care of the hospital bill so we can leave? I'm sure there's a co-pay."

"Yes," he said, and resisted the urge to add a snarky comment. "Heather, I'll call you later tonight and see how you're doing."

She gave him a hug, and he caught a whiff of shampoo and perfume.

"Thanks, Dad. Let me know what happens with the car. I'll be surprised if they can fix it."

"Wow, I wouldn't want to meet Carol in a dark alley at night," Frank remarked as they drove back to the golf course. "She is one angry broad. No offense."

"Tell me about it," Louis said. "She's not just mad at me, she's mad at the world. Probably the most negative person I ever met. Hard to believe she teaches in elementary school."

"That's not so hard to believe," Frank said. "I had nuns in the Catholic school that were like her. They'd just as soon rap your knuckles to a pulp as look at you. Anyway, do you need help with Heather's car?"

"Thanks, I'll make some calls right now if you don't mind,"

Louis said. "I want to get her Kia towed to the garage I usually go to. I trust the guy who runs it and I've golfed with him before."

"Go ahead. Make your calls and ignore me."

Louis called the campus police at UConn. They confirmed the Kia was still there, gave him directions, and he told them he'd arrange for a tow. Then he called the mechanic, who agreed to send out a truck within the hour.

"I won't be able to take a look at it until tomorrow morning, though," the man said. "I'll get it into the bay tonight and you can check back with me before noon."

Louis agreed and thanked him.

"The fact that the emergency brake didn't work makes me think that if the brake lines were cut, so was the cable for the emergency brake," Frank commented. "If that's what happened."

"We'll see," Louis said. "If the brake lines were cut, it's a criminal matter and I'll hunt down who did it. There have to be surveillance cameras everywhere on campus. I'll get the police involved." He paused. "Reminds me I should call my lawyer too and tell him what happened with the Avon cops. I have a feeling I'm going to need this guy on speed dial."

"Looks like the coast is clear," Frank said when they pulled into the near-empty parking lot of the golf course. He parked next to Louis' red Mazda. "You're safe from the hoosegow tonight."

"I've had enough of the law for one day," Louis said.

He was relieved there wasn't another contingent of cops waiting for him, and then realized if they could wait for him at the golf course, they could wait for him at his home or office. Anytime, anywhere. It was nerve-racking.

"I'd say let's go have a drink—on you, of course—and celebrate that I *would* have won our last game, but I have to get home and chase off the pool boy, stuff like that," Frank said.

"Keep me posted. Let me know what happens with

Heather."

"Thanks. I appreciate it. The ride to the hospital and all."

Frank shrugged.

"No big deal. Just try to stay out of trouble, will ya? Who else am I gonna golf with if you end up in the slammer?"

"You're right, nobody else would putt up with you."

Frank groaned.

"That was so bad. I'll see you later."

Louis got into his car and called his attorney. He left a voice mail message with a brief summary of his encounter with the Avon police, and then he dialed Kristen.

"That really stinks," Kristen said after he told her about the theft of her record from his office. "What can I do about it?"

"I'll be setting up identity theft services," Louis said. "But what I didn't tell the others is that whoever took the records made a crank call to one of my patients already. Basically she was set up to think that I wanted to see her outside the office, if you know what I mean. I'm afraid that it isn't just identity theft we have to worry about."

"You're kidding."

"Unfortunately not. Since I last saw you, some pretty disturbing things have happened to me and to other people I know, and it all seems to be connected. Possibly to that BD guy I told you about. I'm letting you know in case you get any strange calls."

"Speaking of disturbing, there's a tape I want you to listen to," she said. She told him about the tape recorder Eric found in Paula's basement. "There were three recorded conversations, and one in particular you should hear."

"Okay," he said. "Can you play it right now on the phone?"

"No," she said. "There's too much static on the tape and I want you to listen to it very carefully."

He had the sense she had an ulterior motive and he glanced at his watch.

"When? Tonight?"

"That would be good because I'm really busy tomorrow. I'm free now if you are. It won't take long."

He hesitated.

"All right."

He wasn't that eager to go home anyway. His condo was even quieter and lonelier without Bogie around.

"Should I come to your office?" she asked.

"That would work. I'm in Farmington so I'll be there in about fifteen minutes."

A few minutes after Louis got to his office, he saw Kristen's blue Camry pull into the driveway. He met her out back in the parking lot. The sun was setting and the warmth of the day was vanishing quickly. He felt cold in his short sleeve polo shirt.

"I feel like a spy in a movie," she said, holding a small black tape recorder. "How's your daughter doing? Is she okay?"

"She has whiplash," Louis said. "She'll be hurting for a few days, I think. Thanks for asking."

He led her into the building to his office.

Kristen sat on the worn couch and set the recorder on the coffee table.

"So Eric found this hidden in Paula's basement. It was attached to the landline phone wire. It automatically records calls when the phone is picked up."

Louis inspected the device.

"This is really old school. Any idea of who set it up?"

She studied him and he became aware that she had wanted to see his facial expressions in person.

"What, you think I recorded her calls?" he asked crossly. "Is that what you think? I'm getting pretty sick of people accusing me of things I didn't do."

He knew he was tired and upset from the events of the day, but couldn't help himself.

"I didn't accuse you," she said. "It could have been Bill." She cleared her throat. "You won't want to hear this, but he was the beneficiary of Paula's life insurance policy. She probably forgot to change it when they got divorced."

"I didn't know she had a life insurance policy. Too bad you weren't the heir instead of him."

"Whatever," she said.

Then she pressed the Play button and he listened to the voice of the woman he loved and her conversations with Kristen, Bill, and himself. He listened to Paula refer to him as a 'shithead' to her sister and say she was through with him and ready to expand her horizons. He listened to the conversation he'd had with Paula before she left for St. Maarten, when he'd told her he hadn't had an affair with Charlotte. He relived her vehement reaction. He remembered it all very, very clearly.

"Louis?"

He swallowed hard, staring off into space. He looked at the wooden zebra on his desk, at the dingy wall, the worn couch he was sitting on, and finally at Kristen.

"I didn't say to Paula 'you go and you're dead.' It doesn't even sound like me. You know what I said when she told me to stop calling her? I told her I loved her. I told her I wanted things to work out between us. Those were the last words I got to say to her before she was killed. Do you understand?" His voice rose. "That tape is not accurate. That part was left out. I distinctly remember what I said."

Kristen turned off the recorder and Louis stood up, so agitated he could barely breathe.

"Every time I turn around something else happens. Since I saw you last, I've been accused of child molestation, my office and my house were broken into, Paula's laptop was taken, and that's just for starters. Oh, and my gun was stolen at the same time Victoria Rudemann was shot. Did you hear about that? That Rudemann got shot and killed?"

"Yes," Kristen said softly. She fiddled with the buttons on her cardigan. "I heard it on the news."

"Yeah. And the Avon police want to question me, probably because of the sex ad for her that went up on the Internet. Which was supposedly traced to me. What else do you think might be traced to me? Maybe my revolver? And what if this lunatic cut the brake lines on my daughter's car tonight? She could have been seriously hurt or killed."

He saw a look cross her face.

Fear? Was she afraid of him?

He realized he was standing too close to her and he backed away and sat down in the chair at his desk.

"I'm sorry."

She looked at him and blinked. "What kind of gun did you have?"

"A Smith & Wesson revolver. Why?"

He saw her hesitate, weigh something in her mind.

"No reason. I was just wondering."

"I don't know what to say about that tape you have," he went on. "To me it's just another example of someone trying to frame me. I have no idea what to expect next and it's making me nuts. Even my cat is dead and I don't know why, whether it was from natural causes or because this person—BD or whatever his real name is—did it when he broke into my house.

"I can't relax anywhere and now I'm worried about whether I'll be arrested or whether my patients are going to be contacted with their information used against them somehow. Some of them are emotionally fragile and it's the last thing they need. Not to mention I can't afford another professional disaster like that. I can't afford what's already happened."

He stopped talking and started breathing again, deep shuddering inhalations. He looked away from her and struggled to regain his composure, surprised at himself, how easily he lost control. He realized he'd reached his limit.

"Whether or not you believe me, I'm telling the truth. I've told the truth all along."

Kristen was silent but her eyes flickered back and forth from him to the office door. His heart sank even further. Was she so afraid of him that she wondered if she had an escape route? Did she think he was going off the deep end? Maybe he was.

"I believe you," she finally said. "I wish I knew how to help you."

"I appreciate that." He sat quietly as his breathing returned to normal. "Sorry if it seems like I'm losing it. There've been too many things going on, especially today."

His cell phone buzzed, indicating a text message. "I have to check this, it might be Heather."

The message was from an "unavailable" number. He read it and sat as still as a statue until Kristen said in a worried voice "What is it?"

He handed her the phone.

Hi Dr D, How's your daughter? She and I have a lot in common, we're both 'braking bad.'

☺

CHAPTER TWENTY-SIX

KRISTEN HANDED THE cell phone back to Louis.

"Can the police trace this?" she asked.

"I already asked about that when I filed a police report," he said, staring at the screen. "One of the problems is, there are no direct threats. And he hasn't sent very many texts either, so it's not really harassment."

He typed furiously: *Show yourself, you coward.*

Kristen watched silently. He waited for a response and then added another text: *Come on, asshole. Be a man.*

"He's skulking around in the shadows somewhere, watching what's going on," Louis said.

"Maybe you shouldn't provoke him," she said when he showed her the messages. "You'll make matters worse."

He snorted.

"It can't get much worse. I would love to flush him out like the weasel he is. Weak bastard finds it easy to pick on teenage girls and people with emotional problems and play a lot of mind games, but he won't confront me directly."

"Which is maybe a good thing. He's dangerous. And he's the

one who stole my clinical record?" She frowned.

"If he's the one who broke into my office—and I think it's the same person responsible for all of this—then yes, he has your record and he might try to use that information."

"Like how? What was in it? Session notes?"

"Yes, progress notes, diagnosis, et cetera," Louis said. "You saw me what, about two years ago?"

"About a year and a half ago."

He watched her face cloud.

"Sorry to bring up bad memories."

"What did you write about me?" she asked, and she looked at him so intently he averted his eyes.

"I couldn't tell you verbatim. You came to see me because you were unhappy in your relationship with Chris. You wanted to figure out how to make it work. If you recall, you saw me once a week for a few months and then you stopped coming." He decided it was more diplomatic to word it that way.

"I stopped coming because I was angry," she said. "Nothing was changing. No matter what I did, I couldn't make him— different."

You couldn't make him love you, Louis thought.

"Kristen, now that time has gone by, do you have a different perspective on how that all turned out?"

"Do you mean, did I think it was all for the best that he finally broke up with me?"

He was surprised by the bitterness in her voice.

"Yes," he said. "In retrospect, do you think there was really any future with that guy?"

He didn't know why he was even asking her these questions. He saw her start to fidget on the couch.

"I thought we got along fine. When we were together we did exciting things, and it was like a whirlwind." She looked up at the ceiling, a faraway expression in her eyes. "He was unlike anyone I'd ever met before. He had no—obligations, no commitments, he did whatever he wanted, whenever he wanted. He had no fear of trying anything, whether it was climbing a mountain or riding a camel in the desert, or swimming the English Channel. Of course, that lack of commitment also extended to relationships. He didn't want to be tied down." She smiled sadly. "You know what the funny thing is, Louis? I ran into Chris at the Wadsworth a couple weeks ago. He acted like nothing happened. He could have taken me to dinner and slept with me that night and it would have made perfect sense to him. But I wouldn't have heard from him afterwards. I would have felt destroyed all over again."

"Was it difficult for you to see him?"

"I was with Eric and he got upset. I guess he could tell I still had some feelings."

"Is Eric a jealous guy?" Louis asked gently, already knowing the answer.

She hesitated.

"Sometimes. But he had a tough time when he was married, so I think it can be hard for him to trust. His wife cheated on him."

Louis said nothing.

"He's very good to me," she said, and he could tell she was getting defensive. "He really cares about me. I want it to work out. I'm tired of being single, of being alone, you know? Before I met Eric all I did was work, work, work, and maybe once in a while hang out with Paula." She shrugged. "I don't have many friends, Louis. The ones I had in college are married with kids, and we don't have much in common anymore. I'd love to get married and have children but the clock is ticking. I'm already thirty-three."

"Oh, so old," he smiled. "You have time. Don't settle."

She brushed a strand of hair away from her face.

"No relationship is perfect, right? Look at you and Paula. She thought you were cheating on her, but you know what? I think she was already looking for something—or someone— else and was searching for an excuse, a reason to move on. I

263

don't think she knew what she wanted. Or maybe she just didn't appreciate what she had."

It hit home. Louis felt a familiar stab of pain, the same twist in the gut he'd felt when he read Paula's emails to the men on the dating sites.

"Unfortunately I didn't appreciate what I had either. Until it was too late."

Maybe they'd all been chasing something they weren't meant to have.

They were both silent.

He watched her rock back and forth slightly, her small freckled hands clasped between her knees. He smelled the mustiness of the rug and the curtains, and the light floral scent of her perfume.

Kristen cleared her throat.

"We really got off track, didn't we?"

"Yes. Where were we?"

"You were warning me that BD—or whoever this guy is—could use my clinical record against me. He did that with someone else already?"

"Yes. He set up a fake answering service and made a female patient think that I wanted to see her at a hotel."

"That's terrible."

Louis nodded.

"If anything strange happens and you feel threatened, just call the police."

"What if this guy causes trouble between me and Eric?" she said. "That would really suck, because I never told Eric that I was in therapy with you and I don't plan to. So I can't warn him my record was stolen."

"What would happen if Eric knew you were in therapy with me?" Louis asked, watching her closely.

"He would want to know why, and that would lead to a lot of questions about my past and it would upset him," she said. "There, that's the honest answer. I told you, Louis, I want this to work out. He doesn't need to know everything about me."

"Sounds like you have to do a lot of self-censoring," he said, aware he was crossing a line. "He can't know too much about you because he'll be jealous of your past? We all have a past. He has one too and I doubt he's a perfect human being, even if he wants you to think he is. Be careful, Kristen. Don't mistake love with a need to control someone's life." He saw her eyes flash and knew he'd gone too far. "Okay, I'll just shut up now."

"Good idea." Her tone was frosty. She picked up the tape recorder. "What should I do with this?"

"What is there to do?" he asked. "No one's going to step up and admit putting it in Paula's house."

"You think it was Bill?"

"It wasn't me. So if it wasn't Bill, then it was our old friend BD, unless there was someone else stalking Paula that we don't know about."

"Can I leave it here?" she asked. "I don't want to take it home."

"Why not?" he asked and she squirmed.

Then he understood.

"Remember what I said, Kristen. You shouldn't have to walk on eggshells."

"I thought therapists weren't supposed to be so directive."

"I'm not talking to you as a therapist. I'm talking to you as a friend."

She got up quickly, avoiding eye contact.

"Goodnight, Louis. I think I'm all set with the lectures tonight. Okay? It's time for me to go home."

"I'll walk you out." He locked the doors and they went outside to the parking lot.

"You've lost weight, haven't you?" she said.

"I've brought my belt in a few notches, but it wasn't intentional. It's called the Worry Yourself Thin diet. I wouldn't recommend it though." He thought he might have dropped ten pounds or so since Paula's funeral. Many times when he was feeling stressed he had no appetite.

He waited while she searched in her purse for her car keys. She was a grown woman but in the moonlight she looked so young and vulnerable, he thought.

Thirty-three and she thinks the clock is ticking. What I would give to be thirty-three again.

The next morning Louis cancelled his appointments up to noon and made phone calls to Heather, the insurance company, the UConn campus police at Storrs, and to his own attorney, who had left a voice mail message earlier informing Louis that he'd contacted the Avon police department and had requested that any further communications be relayed through him.

To his relief Heather reported feeling slightly better, although still a little sore. She intended to stay at her mother's for the next two days and he cautioned her to take it easy.

"No parties, no skydiving" he joked.

"Shoot, I wanted to start bungee jumping today."

"Seriously though, call me right away if you see anyone suspicious hanging around or you get any strange phone calls."

"*Yes,* Dad."

Later he heard on the news that police had arrested no suspects in the Rudemann shooting nor had a murder weapon been found at the scene. He found himself pacing in his living room and glancing out the window, half-expecting a squadron of cruisers to pull up in the parking lot. Would he ever feel at peace again? How could he not worry every second of every day if his daughter was at risk? Later in the morning he drove to the garage where Heather's Kia had been towed.

"The brake lines were cut, including the cable for the emergency brake," Kip Lange, the mechanic, said to Louis. He was in his fifties with longer silver hair tied back in a ponytail. They stood in the garage bay near the wrecked Kia on the lift. Its golden hood was buckled and bent, and there was a large dent on the passenger side door. It looked to Louis like it was destined for the junkyard.

"Your daughter would have noticed a problem right away," Kip added.

"She did," Louis said. "Unfortunately her apartment's at the top of a hill so she lost control as soon as she started driving."

Kip frowned.

"Whoever did it knew a little something about older cars that have cables. Newer cars have electronic emergency brake systems and it's not so easy to cut the cord, so to speak, because it's actually a solenoid that presses against the brake pad."

"Thanks, Kip," Louis said. "Can you keep the car in the lot until the insurance claims adjuster looks at it? I expect it will be within a day or two."

"Sure," the man said. "I'll take some photos and when you need me to put something in writing about the brakes, or sign some form, just let me know. These insurance companies are pricks. This car is probably totaled. If they think your daughter was driving recklessly, they'll raise your rates to the moon."

On his way to the office in the afternoon, Louis got a response to his text messages the previous night. His phone buzzed and he pulled into the nearest parking lot and idled while he found his reading glasses.

Dr D—how rude of u.

Call me, he typed back. *Leave my daughter alone.*

We'll talk soon came the response.

NOW he wrote. He sat and waited in his car for a few minutes, but there was no reply.

CHAPTER TWENTY-SEVEN

KRISTEN HAD JUST gotten out of a meeting at work in the afternoon and was back at her desk when Eric called.

"I'm coming home tonight, hon," he said, his voice cheerful. "I'm on the train already. I should be back in New Haven by five and I was going to stop at the nursing home and visit with my dad for a few minutes. I can head over to your house after that if you're free?"

"Sure. Do you want me to make dinner?"

"I can pick up some steaks on my way over," he said. "We'll cook them on the grill. Can't wait to see you."

She felt relieved that he sounded so happy. Since her meeting with Louis the previous night, she'd had anxious moments imagining Eric getting wind of the details of her therapy sessions. Or even worse, the thief contacting Chris. Then she wondered why someone would go to all that effort to hurt her, anyway.

And why was Louis a target?

"Hey, looks like we finally got a check from the state," Roshana, her administrative assistant, announced when the mail came. "Do you want me to open it?"

They'd been waiting months for reimbursement for a large grant-funded program. Kristen worried the agency would have to take out a short-term loan to meet expenses if payment didn't come soon.

"Go ahead," she said and walked over to the reception area. Roshana made a production out of opening the letter and pulled out a check.

"Woo hoo," she cheered, her round face beaming. "At last."

Kristen smiled. Payroll would be met for at least another two months. Something to celebrate.

Kristen wasn't sure when Eric would arrive at her house, and she found herself fussing before the mirror, checking her hair and makeup. She wore the white blouse, black slacks, and high heels she'd had on at work, but dressed up her outfit with a pastel oblong scarf and gold earrings. She put a dab of perfume on her wrists and paced around her house, feeling that same jittery sense of anticipation she'd felt before their first date. When she heard the Lincoln pull into her driveway, she brushed her hair one more time and met him at the front door.

He wore a gray suit and a baby blue tie, and he looked like he'd just stepped out of GQ.

"Hi, hon."

He held a plastic grocery bag and a bottle of wine.

"Don't you look nice," she said. He put the bag and the bottle on the ground and swooped her up in his arms. She breathed in the smell of expensive designer cologne and kissed him. His mouth tasted like mint candies and she prolonged the kiss, closing her eyes and savoring him, her arms around his neck. When she let him go and stepped back, he smiled.

"That's a very sweet welcome." He held her at arm's length. "I missed you."

"Me too."

"I have some things to bring in, but let's put this salad in the fridge first and have a glass of wine," he said, picking up the bag of groceries.

"How's your father doing?" she asked as he followed her into the house.

"He's feeling much better. He was awake and alert and didn't complain of any pain. He's in good spirits."

"Glad to hear that," she said, and found two crystal glasses in the dining room hutch. When she returned to the kitchen, he was at the counter mixing spices and brown sugar in a small bowl.

"A dry rub for the steaks," he explained.

She watched him prepare the two thick ribeyes.

"I didn't know you could cook."

"A few dishes here and there. Steaks and ribs mostly." He turned to her with a sly look. "I'm better at other things though."

"Like what?" she teased.

"I know what you're thinking, but I wasn't going there...yet," he said.

He popped the cork and poured the wine, a cabernet the color of rubies, and filled their glasses halfway.

"Let's sit out on the deck," she said. "It's a beautiful night."

"It might be too cold for you."

"I'll put on a sweater if I need to. Do you want to change?" she asked him.

"I'm fine for now. I have a change of clothes in my suitcase but I'm in no hurry...seems you like me in a suit. So maybe I'll keep it on all night." He raised his eyebrows. "Or not?"

"We'll see about that," she said and felt her heart speed up.

He looked so polished, so elegant.

So damn sexy.

They went out to her deck and he moved two chairs close together.

"Cheers," he said, holding up his glass. "To you, and to the last lingering days of summer."

"Cheers." They clinked their glasses together and she sipped the wine. It tasted like a silky blend of black cherries and licorice and warmed her throat. "So tell me about your trip to New York."

"Well, as I told you on the phone, it was very successful," he said. "I brought in two sizeable accounts, more than what my boss expected. Both are die casting companies and they'll bring us a lot of business. It does mean I might be traveling a little more though, and I need to make that trip to Montreal soon."

"I'd love to go," she said.

"I'll take you to the Notre Dame Basilica," he said. "And the botanical gardens, and of course, we'll walk around Old Montreal. I think you'll enjoy it." He reached over and his fingers traced slow circles on her hand. "By the way, you look fantastic tonight. You always do, but especially today."

"Thank you."

"Let's look at our calendars later tonight and figure out when we can go," he said. "Now that my father's feeling better, we have a window of opportunity before something else happens." He sighed. "I don't mean to complain. He's an old man. He's not getting any younger. You think about your folks a lot, Kristen?"

She nodded.

"Even though I was just ten years old when they died."

She had told him about the auto accident that killed her parents, but not about the aftermath.

"And you lived with your aunt and uncle?"

"Yes. My Aunt Norma and Uncle Pete took us in. Norma was a doll. Her husband, not so much." She stared off into space, those days a blur of memories best tucked away and forgotten. "Once in a while I think about it."

"What happened?"

Her lips pressed together in a thin line.

"He didn't overtly abuse or molest us. But we'd catch him looking, spying on us when we got dressed, things like that. It was creepy as hell. I think Paula got the brunt of it…since she was older than me."

Eric frowned.

"You ever tell your aunt?"

"No. We were afraid of what would happen. She didn't work and if she left him, what would become of us then? We were worried for her and afraid we'd end up in foster care. I'm not sure that would have turned out any better," she said. "But—it's all water under the bridge. They both passed away years ago."

"I'm sorry you went through a difficult childhood."

"What about yours? All rainbows and unicorns?" she asked in a light tone.

He shook his head.

"Far from it, I'm afraid. I was an only child, as you know. My mother was mentally ill and never stayed on her meds for long. Bipolar disorder."

"Oh."

"I left home as soon as I possibly could and joined the Army right after high school." He paused. "She committed suicide on my nineteenth birthday when I was home on leave. Hanged herself in the basement. I was the one who found her."

"Oh, Eric," she said. "I'm so sorry. That must have been terrible."

"Like you said, it's all water under the bridge. I'm not even sure why I mentioned it. The only other person who knew about this was my wife." He looked away, his posture rigid. "I'd just as soon not think about it and focus on the future instead."

They were silent for a moment and sipped their wine. Kristen reached over and took his hand, thinking about what he'd just said. She imagined him as a teenager, as a young man. She imagined what it must have been like to find his mother dead and to remember that every year on his birthday.

"So what were we saying before we got sidetracked about our shitty childhoods?" He relaxed in the chair. "I think I was saying how nice you look tonight. And did I say how much I enjoyed that welcome back kiss you gave me before?"

She smiled.

"Encore."

He leaned forward and kissed her, one hand rubbing her knee. She closed her eyes and tasted the wine on his tongue. She thought about the last time they'd made love, how she'd stroked his back while he was on top of her, his weight. The silky heat of his skin. His hot breath on her neck.

"We should get this out of the way now, so we don't have to talk about it later," he said when he let her go. "The pistol. I'll take it back tonight. Where is it?"

"In my closet," she said, snapping back to reality and feeling a surge of anger she didn't want to acknowledge. "You know, I'm not averse to guns in general. I wouldn't mind learning how to shoot if you want to teach me sometime."

"Sure, I can do that," he said. "And I'm sorry I left it at your house. I realized when we talked on the phone that it was very poor judgment on my part. The last thing I wanted to do was alarm you." He squeezed her hand. "Especially after we found that tape recorder at Paula's house. No wonder you were checking out your own cellar."

She looked away, feeling her face flush.

"Hon, I told you I wouldn't ask you what's on the tape. Don't worry. It doesn't matter. If it was important you would tell me. Otherwise it's none of my business. Right?"

She smiled but said nothing. She drank more wine.

"I promise you I won't bother you anymore about things that happened in the past," he continued. He took her hand and pressed it to his lips. "None of that matters. I just want to have a happy life with you. No drama, no lies."

She nodded, feeling a sudden guilty twinge at the thought of meeting with Louis the night before.

You shouldn't have to walk on eggshells.

"That's what I want too, Eric. We're not kids anymore and

we're not perfect people. I've made mistakes and I'm sure you have also. At least I know what I want now."

"Tell me," he said. "Tell me what it is that you want."

His voice was low and hypnotic. He brushed back a strand of hair from her forehead. Their knees touched.

"Someone who cares about me," she said. "Someone who's loyal and reliable. A real friend. Someone I can laugh with and cry with, and at the end of the day, I know he has my back no matter what." She put her wine glass on the table and grinned. "Oh, and he has to be a good lover, very passionate, makes me see stars..."

"And cook a decent ribeye?"

"Yeah, that too," she said.

She turned her face to him and they kissed again.

"I want to give you the present I bought," he said. "Can I get it for you now?"

She took a deep breath. Her nerves were sizzling. She didn't want to stop.

"If you want to."

"Don't go anywhere," he said. "I'll be right back."

He opened the sliding screen door to the kitchen and while his back was turned, she studied his long, lean form. He was right. She did like to see him dressed up.

While she waited, she settled back in the chair and looked out at the woods beyond the narrow patch of grass that extended past the deck. Someone was starting a barbecue in a charcoal grill a few doors down. Kristen barely knew her neighbors, besides Maude. She presumed they were all busy professionals like herself.

She inhaled the tantalizing smells of roasting meat that drifted on a faint plume of smoke. The crickets took up their chorus in the deepening twilight and the trees at the edge of the yard cast long shadows on the grass. Their leaves and branches rustled with birds ready to roost for the night.

Eric returned in a few minutes carrying a black and white

shopping bag. "I hope you don't mind, I brought my suitcase inside. I left it in your bedroom so I can change later." He handed her the bag. "This is for you. I hope you like it."

She reached inside and took out a rectangular packet wrapped in white tissue paper. She peeled it open to reveal a neatly folded emerald green satin sheath.

"Oh my God. It's beautiful."

She stood up and held the dress against herself, glancing at the tag on the neckline.

How did he know her size?

"Do you think it will fit?" he asked. "I took a guess."

"I'll try it on right now," she said. "Wow. Thank you." She leaned toward him and kissed him. "You didn't have to do that."

"Kristen," he said. "You deserve it. A beautiful woman should wear beautiful clothes. This dress was in the window display and the second I saw it, I thought it was made for you. I can't wait to see you in it."

The green dress with its low-cut V-neck and V-back was stunning, showing off her creamy shoulders and toned arms. Alone in her bedroom, Kristen reached around and pulled up the zipper. The sheath hugged her slim hips and the back slit was just high enough to be sexy, not slutty. A classic strand of pearls she found in her jewelry box completed the outfit.

He will love this.

She inspected herself from all angles in the full-length mirror. Smiling at her reflection, she reached under the dress, hooked her thumbs on both sides of her silk panties, and shimmied out of them. Wait till he found out she was commando. He'd love that too.

She sat on her bed and was just about to put on her strappy black high heels when she heard a faint buzzing sound.

At first she thought it was a bee but when it repeated, she realized the sound was coming from Eric's black suitcase propped against the wall. She got off the bed. A cell phone on vibrate? She hesitated, then unzipped the outside pocket of the suitcase and sure enough, there was a cell phone inside.

It buzzed once more and stopped, and she picked it up and read a message from Louis D'Maio.

You bastard. I'm still waiting.

Puzzled, she tapped on the screen and accessed the recent message thread:

Dr D—how rude of u

Louis: *Call me. Leave my daughter alone.*

We'll talk soon

Louis: *NOW*

For a moment she felt she couldn't breathe. She scrolled to the top of the screen, to the beginning.

☺

Watch the news yet Dr D?

Louis: *Who is this?*

Your friend BD

Louis: *What do you want? Did you break into my house?*

Louis: *I'm reporting you to the police.*

Louis: *Show yourself, you coward. Come on, asshole. Be a man.*

Hi Dr D - How's your daughter? She and I have a lot in common, we're both 'braking bad.'

☺

She heard the stairs creak. He was sprinting up the steps. Would he hear her zip the suitcase? Heart hammering, she shoved the phone under the bed.

"Hey hon, did the dress fit?"

She whirled, pasting a smile on her face while she tried to catch her breath.

Eric stood in the doorway.

"You look gorgeous. I knew it would be perfect."

"I love it," she gasped, straightening up. "I was just putting on my heels."

She glanced at her shoes still on the carpet.

He came closer and she forced herself not to move.

"You are beautiful," he said, and cupped her face. "Now where did we leave off?"

He kissed her gently and then with more ardor, his tongue exploring hers, his breath a soft sigh. His hands trailed along her back and bottom and slid across the satin fabric.

"I love you," he murmured in her ear. She felt his fingers search for the zipper on the back of the dress.

"Sweetheart, let's save this for later," she whispered. "We have all night."

Oh, God, what if the phone buzzed again? He would hear it under the bed.

"You sure?" he said, kissing the side of her neck.

His fingers brushed against her erect nipples, sliding across her breasts. Ten minutes earlier she would have been in heaven. Now it was all she could do to remain calm, stay focused.

Act normal, she thought, but her thoughts were racing, connecting dots, putting pieces together of a puzzle she didn't want to see.

He took her hand and guided it past his belt buckle and between his legs. He took a deep breath as he pressed her hand against the wool fabric of his pants. He was already hard.

"Look what you did. You're going to leave me like this?"

She gently pulled away and he released her hand.

"Patience," she said. "I want to make it last."

He smiled.

"You're teasing me."

"I think you like that."

"Well, I do have patience and I'm hungry, so maybe it's a good idea you feed me first. Plus I want to look at you in that dress while we eat."

"I'll be down in a minute. I'm going to put on my shoes."

"You all right?" he asked.

She looked at him, at the doorway.

"Of course."

"You look flushed."

"It's the wine," she said and turned away so he wouldn't see her trembling hands. "I'm a lightweight, remember? Especially on an empty stomach."

What do I do now?

Her mind searched wildly for an answer.

"I'll go start the grill."

She realized she had a few minutes at best before he would wonder where she was.

Get out. Just get out. Now.

For one disorienting second she thought it was Paula's voice she heard in her own head. As soon as she heard him open the sliding screen door to the deck, she edged down the stairs, still barefoot, her heart pounding. Thank God, her purse was on the kitchen counter just out of his line of sight. He stood outside in front of the Weber fiddling with the knobs.

She grabbed the purse, opened it and saw that her cell phone was inside, but where were the car keys?

Shit.

Had she tossed them on the table?

"Won't take long for the steaks," he called out.

Kristin edged over to the kitchen table. Thank God, there they were, her car keys next to the day's mail. She snatched them, went back to the hallway and opened the door from the house to the garage. If he turned at that second he would see her.

"Hon? Are you coming?"

She heard him say her name just as she stepped into the garage. She pressed the button on the wall unit and the garage door rose with its usual loud clunking whine. Surely he could hear it.

She bolted to her Camry, her hands shaking so badly that once she was inside, she could barely get the key into the ignition. She started the car and put it in reverse.

Thank God he hadn't blocked her in. His Lincoln was parked at the bottom of the driveway and there was just enough room to maneuver around it. She was close to the road when he came out the front door.

"Kristen? Where are you going?"

She half-expected he would rush to her car and try to drag her out, but he simply stood on the porch and stared.

"What are you doing? What's the matter?"

He looked perplexed and concerned, not angry, not raging. Not evil.

Go, said that inner voice that was Paula's, but not Paula's. *Go.*

He took a step down the driveway, hands outstretched, palms up.

"Hon, where on earth are you going?"

She rolled up the windows, locked the doors, and backed out into the street. She narrowly missed an oncoming car. The driver slammed on his brakes and blared his horn.

"Kristen," Eric called out.

He ran towards her car and she floored it.

CHAPTER TWENTY-EIGHT

KRISTEN TRIED TO steer, keep an eye on the highway, and press the security code to unlock her cell phone.

Oh Jesus, what the hell.

The numbers looked blurry and she was dizzy and disoriented. She checked the rear view mirror and wondered what she'd do if Eric's green Lincoln appeared behind her. She had no plan, no idea where she was going. She didn't even have shoes.

Her cell phone rang and she snatched it up and saw that it was Eric. She threw the phone back on the seat and took the next exit to the mall. She could park in a sea of cars, get her bearings, call the cops, call Louis, call someone for help. Her head throbbed and she felt woozy, as though she were standing on the edge of a tall building looking down. She realized she shouldn't be driving.

Your friend BD.

Eric was the one texting Louis? He was the one who cut Heather's brakes? BD. He'd been emailing Paula before she went to St. Maarten?

She pulled into a parking spot in a crowded lot behind one of the anchor stores of the mall and picked up her cell phone. Her hands trembled and she tried several times before she got the code right.

Eric had left a voice mail and she listened to that first.

His tone was urgent but not angry.

"I think I know why you're upset. But the cell phone that was in my suitcase isn't mine. I found it at Paula's house the same night I found the tape recorder, but I didn't want to tell you right away. Kristen, please call me back. You need to know something about Louis. It's very important you call me, okay? Please."

Her phone rang again and this time she picked up.

"Kristen," Eric said. "What the hell's going on? Did you get my voice mail?"

"Yes."

"Where are you? Why did you leave?"

She didn't answer.

"I should have known you would snoop in my suitcase," he said. "Listen, I have nothing to hide. That cell phone's not mine. I found it at Paula's house and I brought it to a friend I know who works for AT&T. It's a prepaid phone, but my friend helped me track down who registered it. It was Louis. And he's got more than one of these phones."

Her voice sounded shaky and far away to her.

"Why would Louis send text messages to himself?"

Her vision seemed to telescope in and out as she sat in the driver's seat and felt her face and neck flush and droplets of sweat trickle down her back.

"He wants everyone to think he's being stalked and harassed. He's covering his tracks, he's up to something," Eric said. "I'm worried for your safety. Kristen, please. I can't believe you left your house like that. I can't believe you didn't even talk to me first. What were you thinking?" His voice rose. "I'm still having trouble wrapping my head around this, your behavior is so bizarre."

She felt a glimmer of doubt. She looked down at the green dress hiked up on her thighs, her bare feet. She licked her dry lips and wished she had a bottle of water in the car.

"Are you coming back?" he asked. "Or should I just leave?"

"I think you should leave," she said, feeling suddenly nauseous. "I need…some time."

There was a long silence. She held the phone away from her ear and looked at the screen to see if the call had disconnected. Her vision was blurry.

There's something wrong with me.

Then he spoke.

"Take all the time in the world. But don't call me, okay? I don't need this craziness in my life, I have enough on my plate to deal with," he said, his voice breaking. "I'll never understand why you did this, Kristen. Goodbye."

The call failed and in seconds her phone rang again. It was Louis.

"What's up? I saw you called me. I'm in my car."

What?

She didn't remember calling him. Did she? Did she call the cops too? She pressed the phone against her ear. She thought she might pass out.

"I have to see you right away," she said, and couldn't hold back her tears.

"This is the worst possible time," Louis said. "I'm on my way to see my attorney and we're going from his office to the police department. I'm going to be questioned. Maybe arrested."

She took a few deep breaths in an effort to collect herself.

"Why?"

"One of my patients filed a complaint. She's claiming I made obscene and harassing phone calls. I didn't. Supposedly there's some sort of evidence that points to me." He sounded as if he were on the verge of a breakdown himself. "What's the matter?"

In a halting, barely coherent voice she told him about what she saw on the cell phone in Eric's suitcase, and what had transpired. Then she remembered and told him about finding the Smith & Wesson revolver in her cellar.

"Jesus Christ," he said. "Where are you?"

"The mall," she managed.

"Call the cops. Never mind, I'll call them."

"And say what? That I found a cell phone with text messages from you? He didn't threaten me. He said he would leave."

"Stay where you are and I'll come get you. I'll go with you to your house and we'll see if that gun you found is mine. Jesus Christ Almighty. My lawyer's going to have a heart attack when I tell him I can't meet him right away."

She had no idea what he was talking about and could hardly follow her own train of thought.

"Maybe they already have a warrant." He was clearly agitated. "I'll tell him what's happening so he can tell the cops. Where are you parked?"

She peered out the window at the store signs and told him she was at JC Penney. Not sure where. Toward the back entrance maybe? She couldn't remember what exit she had taken.

"All right," he said. "I'll find you. I'll be there in ten minutes."

It was the longest ten minutes she'd ever spent. Every time a car drove by she hunkered down in the seat and watched people pass, her senses on high alert and yet so fuzzy she could barely focus.

She thought about what Eric had said, that maybe the phone wasn't his. Part of her mind believed him.

You're acting crazy. He didn't do anything wrong. He loves you.

A random memory surfaced of when she was a child. Catching her uncle pushing the bathroom door ajar, peering inside while Paula was taking a shower. The steam escaping through the crack in the door.

What are you doing? she'd asked. *"Why are you looking in there?"*

"You're crazy. I'm not doing anything wrong. I was just walking by. What the hell's the matter with you?"

She thought about Louis's suspicion that BD had stolen the clinical records and another unwanted piece of the puzzle snapped into place.

And you lived with your aunt and uncle?

Eric had said tonight. Had she mentioned that to him before? She didn't think so. But she had told Louis in their sessions, and it was another reason she'd stopped going to therapy. She had no desire to explore *that* link between her past and her present.

She slumped lower in the seat, feeling so tired that even taking a deep breath required effort. Was it the adrenalin beginning to wear off? Or was it the wine on an empty stomach? She hadn't had more than a glass and a half, she thought. It had to be something else.

Did he drug her?

She closed her eyes for a moment and when she opened them again, she saw headlights and Louis's Mazda pulled in beside her. She stumbled out of her car, nearly falling on the pavement.

"Are you all right?" He sprung out and opened the passenger door for her. "Where are your shoes?"

She slid in the seat, shivering. "At my house. I left in a hurry. Do you have a sweatshirt? Or a jacket?"

"Hold on a second."

Louis opened the trunk and after a moment he got back in the car and handed her a wrinkled gray zip-up golf jacket. She put it on and the sleeves were baggy and frayed, but she was grateful for the warmth.

"Start from the beginning and tell me exactly what happened with Eric," he said as they left the mall parking lot and drove to the highway.

"What should we do if he's still there?" Kristen asked as they approached her street.

"I'm going to kick his ass, that's what," Louis said. "The only reason he would have a cell phone with my texts on it is that he's BD and he's made my life a living hell. Not to mention what he did to my daughter and what he might have done to Paula."

"You're very worked up. But what's the plan?" she asked. She still felt woozy and disoriented. "Are the cops coming?"

"Yes. I always knew he was an asshole, Kristen, but why did he target me? What's he got against me?"

"What if the gun's not yours?"

"Then he still has a lot of explaining to do, and maybe that cell phone's enough proof that he's connected to all these other things." He glanced at her. "I know this must be hard for you. You had feelings for the guy. I just want to fucking kill him."

The Lincoln was gone when they reached her condo.

Louis parked in the driveway and Kristen fumbled in her purse for the house key. Her fingers closed around the small can of pepper spray she always carried and without thinking, she slipped it in the pocket of the oversized jacket.

With Louis at her side, Kristen unlocked the front door and turned on the hallway light.

"Wait. I should make sure the grill's not on," she said, remembering.

He brought steaks. He was cooking the steaks.

Louis followed her to the kitchen and out through the sliding door to the deck.

The Weber was off and she noticed when they came back inside that the two crystal wine glasses were in the sink. Something nagged at her, a thought that seemed about to break to the surface, but she couldn't grasp it.

"Let's get the gun."

"Upstairs," she said, and he followed her up the stairs and

down the hallway to her bedroom.

"Shit."

She stared at the open closet door.

Her clothes were pushed to one side and the shoe boxes formerly stacked neatly on shelves and on the floor were overturned and scattered all over the carpet, her pumps and sandals thrown in a pile. She knelt down and found the box where she had hidden the revolver. The lid was off and there was nothing inside.

Louis stood and stared at her.

"Where is it?"

She shook her head, still on her knees. The room was beginning to spin.

"He found it. Shit. He asked me tonight where I put it. I told him, I did, I told him, uh, it was in my closet. Shit."

Her tongue felt like a wooden block in her mouth and when she looked up, Louis was standing over her. He was saying something but she couldn't make out the words. She swayed, fell to her side, and everything went dark.

CHAPTER TWENTY-NINE

LOUIS WAS ON his knees, still holding Kristen's limp wrist after checking her pulse. It was slow but even.

"Looking for this?"

Louis turned. Eric stood in the doorway and pointed the revolver at Louis' head.

"What did you do to her?" Louis demanded, ignoring the gun and turning back to Kristen, rolling her on her back.

He opened her eyelids with his thumbs. Her pupils were dilated and her breathing was shallow.

"She'll be fine," Eric smirked. "She had some Xanax with her wine. Just enough to make her sleepy."

"You bastard."

Louis made a move to get up.

"Whoa, cowboy. You just stay right there on your knees and face the wall."

Without warning he delivered a sudden, swift kick to the base of Louis' spine. Louis felt an explosion of pain and fell forward, cursing. Then Eric kicked him hard in the ribs.

"On your knees," Eric said calmly. "Hands on your head.

Stand up or scream and you're a dead man. I'll blow a hole in your goddamn spine."

Louis struggled to his knees, trying to catch his breath and not groan out loud. He looked up and saw that the bedroom window was closed. If he called for help, would anyone hear him?

I'm too old for this, came the sudden random thought.

I can't bounce back.

He put his hands on his head, leaning to one side. The right side of his chest was on fire.

"Why me? What did I ever do to you?"

"What did you ever do to me," Eric repeated sarcastically. "Where should I start? From when I was a teenager and you fucking ruined my life?"

Louis breathed hard, the pain in his ribs like a flaming spear.

"What?"

"Think back, you asshole. Does the name Susanna Lake ring a bell?"

Louis lay still.

Susanna Lake.

The name was familiar. He tried to ignore the pain in his ribs and think.

"Means so little you can't recall?" Eric's voice was scornful. "Figures. You don't remember me either, do you? Guess that shouldn't be too much of a shocker. You were still wet behind the ears. You didn't know shit. You still don't know shit."

Louis searched his memory.

Susanna Lake. Susanna Lake.

Then it came to him.

"She was…she was someone I saw in my first job at a state hospital."

Had to be almost twenty years ago. But he hadn't really forgotten, just buried the memory.

"You're making progress, Louis," Eric said. "Excellent start. Now tell me why she was in the hospital. The nuthouse, that is.

Tell me why you discharged her when she was clearly unstable. Suicidal, as a matter of fact. Does that refresh your memory?"

Louis said nothing. Eric kicked him again.

This time he cried out before he fell on his face, and he stayed on the floor, moaning. He was hardly exaggerating, but realized it was better if the man thought he was incapacitated.

"Yes! Christ. Stop it."

"Good. I'm glad it's all coming back to you," Eric said. "Maybe you'll remember the family session we had. You were fresh out of grad school, weren't you? I was eighteen so you were what—early twenties? Dumb as a bag of rocks. Couldn't see what was right in front of your eyes."

Louis was sweating and every breath was an effort. The woman, Susanna Lake. She had killed herself. Hanged herself, he remembered. After he had discharged her.

"She was your mother?"

Keep him talking, Louis thought. *Where the hell were the cops?*

"Yeah she was my mother," Eric said tightly. "She was bipolar. In and out of the hospital the whole time I was growing up. Her sister—my aunt Patty—came to live with us to *help out*." He snorted. "She helped out all right. Pranced around the house half-naked when my mother was gone. Came on to my father. Came on to me when I was only ten years old. Crazy bitch. And you and your *therapy team* didn't see it, didn't believe my mother when she thought something bad was going on."

He was quiet for a moment, and Louis struggled to remember. A family session. He'd had hundreds of them in the past twenty years. He vaguely recalled meeting with Susanna Lake, her husband and her son.

A young Eric.

The details escaped him but he'd not forgotten Susanna Lake taking her life.

"No one would have discharged your mother if they knew what she planned to do," Louis said in as calm a voice as he could muster. "She wasn't suicidal when she was released. I do remember that."

He braced himself for another kick. He sensed that Eric had stepped closer.

"Bullshit," Eric snapped. "All you had to do was ask a few questions, I would have said what was going on in that house. It wrecked up my life."

"What wrecked up your life?" Louis asked quietly. "Being molested by your aunt?"

Eric ignored the question.

"Then you pop up again all these years later. Imagine my surprise to see it was you who screwed up my whole fucking trip to St. Maarten. But you know what? I think I managed to make your life a mess too. And I've had a lot of fun doing it. It was better than I expected."

He laughed.

"I enjoyed it," he went on. "You should have heard your fuck buddy Charlotte when I told her you molested her precious little Annie. She believed me, Louis, she thought you were a pervert. How does that make you feel?

"Oh, and dear old dejected, rejected Diane, loser in love. You could have met her at the hotel and fucked her, Louis. That was a freebie for you, buddy-boy. You blew your chance on that one."

Louis wanted to turn around and look the evil bastard in the eye but thought better of it. Instead he spoke to the wall.

"You made your point, Eric. Or should I say BD?"

"Francis. Eric. BD. Whatever you want to call me. Doesn't really matter."

"What does BD stand for?"

"It's Benevolent Dictator. Ask Paula. Oh, sorry, you can't," Eric said in a mocking tone. "She's dead as a doornail. You're lucky your daughter's still alive. So far, anyway."

Louis stayed quiet. His stomach contracted and he thought he might throw up from the pain, a kaleidoscope of agony at his side and at the base of his spine.

Focus. Focus.

From his vantage point on the carpet, he saw the dust bunnies under Kristen's bed. No sharp objects anywhere he could use as a weapon. Out of the corner of his eye, he saw Kristen's still form. She had rolled into a fetal position.

"You're lucky, Dr. D, I'm going to make this short and sweet. You won't have to spend the rest of your life in prison. Which is what would happen, you know, if the cops get hold of your gun. The same one they'll think you used to kill the Rudemann bitch. You should thank me for that, by the way. I did the world a favor."

"Tell me about it," Louis said, turning his head to the side. "So how about we call it even. You destroyed my life, so now you can go. Crawl back to whatever hole you came out of. It's less risky for you if you just disappear."

"Wouldn't that be convenient for you," Eric said. "Sorry, it's not part of the plan."

"What's your plan?" Louis asked.

Just try to keep him talking. Even if it pisses him off.

"You've been pretty clever so far. You've managed to hurt a whole bunch of people who don't know you're responsible."

"Shut up. I'm getting tired of your big mouth."

"So what's next? You going to pick on some little old ladies?"

Louis tensed, expecting another kick, but this time he was going to go for it, roll over and try to grab the bastard's foot. He had nothing to lose.

Kristen mumbled something and moaned.

"Don't fucking move, Louis," Eric warned.

Louis stayed still, listening. Out of the corner of his eye he saw Kristen's hand move at her side and Eric bend over her. Louis scrambled upright just as he heard a faint hiss.

Eric yelled and Louis whirled around and saw Kristen twisting away from him, a small canister dropping out of her hand. Pepper spray.

"You bitch."

Eric backed away. He clawed at his eyes and stumbled backwards.

With a grunt, Louis lunged at him, swinging. His fist connected with a satisfying crack against Eric's jaw. The man went down and Louis landed another punch to Eric's face.

Blood spurted from his nose but just as Louis drew back to hit him again, Eric's hand snapped up with the gun. He waved it in the air, his other hand rubbing his eyes. Before Louis could grab the barrel and twist it away, Eric made contact with Louis' shoulder, driving the muzzle into his flesh.

Then he squeezed the trigger.

CHAPTER THIRTY

WHAT IN SAM Hill was going on over there? Maude peered out the screen of her second-floor bedroom window, straining to see in the dark. First there'd been that curious incident of Kristen backing out of her garage and taking off like a bat out of hell while that hottie of a boyfriend—all dressed up in a suit— ran after her in the driveway. Then the boyfriend had driven away in his Lincoln. Ten minutes later he'd come back on foot. Why?

Then of all the strange things, another car had soon pulled in. Kristen and some tall, older gray-haired guy, someone Maude had never seen before, got out of the car. Kristen was barefoot and wearing a man's jacket over a dress. She was stumbling as the man led her into the house.

How odd. Another boyfriend? Maude had wondered. A love triangle?

And just now, was that a gunshot she'd heard? Or a firecracker set off by a kid? Lord knew the kids loved to set them off in the woods surrounding the complex.

Suddenly the front door of Kristen's condo opened and the

hottie came out, his face a bloody mess. He carried Kristen over his shoulder like a fireman, her body bent so that her head and arms were dangling. From what Maude could tell, he was struggling to keep hold of her legs.

"Hey. Eric. What's going on over there?" Maude called out to him through the screen. "What's the matter with Kristen?"

He turned and looked up. He was squinting, rubbing his eyes with one hand. Blood was dripping from his nose, staining the front of his shirt. Maude saw Kristen's face in the glow of the streetlight, some kind of tape across her mouth. Looked like her hands were taped together too. He was laboring under her squirming weight.

"Maude, I need to borrow your car," he said. "We were attacked and Kristen's hurt. I have to get her to the hospital. Right now."

"I'll call 911," Maude said, staring at the spectacle and wondering why he didn't want to take the vehicle that was sitting right there in the driveway. The one that the older guy drove. The attacker's?

"Let me in," he called out. "I need your keys."

Maude hurried downstairs as fast as she could manage. She remembered she'd left her cell phone charging on the kitchen counter. By the time she got to the kitchen he was pounding on the door.

"I'm coming, I'm coming. Lordy." She was breathing hard from the excitement and exertion. She grabbed her cell phone and looked around for her glasses, finally spotting them on the table.

"Maude." The voice outside the door was frantic now.

"Okay, okay." With shaky hands she unlocked the deadbolt.

Louis came to and at first didn't know where he was. The pain in his chest and right shoulder was intense and he saw that the front of his shirt was soaked with blood. He tried to get up and a wave of dizziness and nausea forced him back onto the bloody carpet.

Kristen.

The room was dark, quiet. She wasn't there.

He rolled over to his knees and held onto the bedpost with his left hand. Groaning, he finally managed to stand upright. His right arm dangled uselessly. The effort caused a fresh flood of warm blood to seep from his wound and drip down his chest.

The pain was like hot knives jabbing him over and over, and for a moment he thought he might pass out again. He swayed on his feet and held onto the post until his vision cleared. Then he staggered out of the bedroom and made his way carefully down the hall.

Maude gasped when Eric burst through the door. His eyes were red and swollen and his nose was crooked, broken maybe? He immediately set Kristen down in the foyer where she thrashed like a hooked fish. Her green dress rode upward, exposing her thighs.

"For Chrissake, get that tape off her," Maude yelled.

She started to press 911 on her cell phone. Her jaw dropped when Eric knocked it out of her hand and kicked it down the tiled hallway.

"Give me your keys."

Maude backed away, looking at him, his bloodstained clothes, and then Kristen, curled up on the floor.

"Give me your fucking keys. Where are they?"

He pulled out a revolver from his waistband and pointed it at Maude's head.

"You're not going to no hospital, are you?"

Reflexively she looked past him into the kitchen, not sure exactly where she'd put the damn keys anyway. He saw her looking and he backed into the kitchen, scanning the countertops and pulling open the drawers with one hand. He trained the gun on her with the other.

"I don't have time for this, you old bag." He stepped over to her and grabbed her arm. "Where are they?"

"Get your hands off me." She shook him off in a wave of indignation. The nerve. "I don't know where I put 'em."

He swore and shoved her backwards. She landed hard on the couch—thank God he hadn't pushed her into the glass bookcase—and saw him grab the keys from a candy dish where she kept spare change. God Almighty.

What had happened to the nice man who'd helped her with her groceries and sat down with her for a cup of tea?

"Shut up and stay right where you are," he ordered.

He put the gun back in his waistband and bent to pick up Kristen, who had rolled onto her back, her knees up against her chest.

Maude hoped that Kristen would be able to kick him right in the balls, but he flipped her over easily and hoisted her over his shoulder.

"Leave her here," Maude shrieked. "Just take the car and go."

He ignored her and opened the door with his free hand.

Maude's eyes opened wide as the tall, gray-haired man burst inside.

"I'll kill her, Louis," Eric said, backing into the living room. "Get away from me."

Maude saw him slide Kristen off his shoulder and prop her upright. He held his forearm against her throat.

"I'll snap her fucking neck right now."

Eric's back was to her and Maude heaved herself off the couch. She saw that the older man had a large steak knife in one hand. His shirt was stained with blood and his right arm hung at an awkward angle. His face was pale white and he was staggering a little. He was clearly in bad shape.

"Let her go."

"Get out of my way, Louis. You want her dead?"

In a split second Eric dropped Kristen and fell into a crouch. Maude edged closer as the two men circled each other. Eric lunged forward and tackled the older man to the floor. He landed with a thud and a groan. Maude saw him roll away but Eric leaped on top of him and straddled him, jabbing his knee into the man's damaged shoulder. The man grunted and struggled to get free.

"Christ on a crutch."

Maude winced and watched as Eric rained blow after blow to the man's head, ribs, and bloody shoulder. She was sure it wouldn't be long before he passed out from the beating. Then it'd be all over, and what would happen to Kristen then? She looked around frantically and grabbed a heavy brass paperweight from the coffee table.

Eric stopped for a moment and pulled the revolver from the waistband of his pants. The man's face was a swollen bloody pulp, but Maude saw he still clutched the knife in one hand. His arm shook as he raised it.

Eric cocked the trigger.

"This time I'll be sure to finish—"

Maude moved forward just as the older man stabbed Eric in the thigh.

"Fuck!" Eric screamed.

He dropped the revolver and Maude closed the last few inches between them.

"Surprise."

She slammed the paperweight directly onto his skull.

There wasn't much she could do for the gray-haired guy who looked like he lost a battle with a semi. His eyes were swollen shut and he was covered in blood, but at least he was breathing.

"Just hang in there, mister," she said.

Eric lay silent and still next to him on the floor. Blood poured from the wound in his thigh and the nasty gash on his head. A lot of blood from the looks of it. She stepped past him, taking care to avoid the crimson puddle. Was he dead? Maude wasn't sure. She poked him with her foot but he didn't move. Good.

Someone rang the doorbell and she heard loud voices outside.

"Are you okay?" a male voice called out. "We called the cops."

One of the neighbors?

Sounded like it.

So she wasn't the only one who'd noticed all the commotion tonight. She opened the door and to her relief, it was the nice young couple next door. They stood with their mouths open, staring past her at the two men on the floor.

"I know, looks bad," she said. "You wouldn't believe what happened. We need the EMTs."

"My God," the young man said, his mouth still hanging open.

His wife clutched his arm.

Sirens suddenly pierced the air, getting louder and louder. Maude felt another surge of relief and turned toward Kristen, who had rolled to her side.

"We're gonna get you free."

Maude was about to retreat to the kitchen and get a pair of scissors when Eric moaned and opened his eyes.

"Well. Butter my buns and call me a biscuit," she said. "This bastard is still alive."

CHAPTER THIRTY-ONE

Three Months Later

FRANK AND HIS wife Lisa had invited Louis and Kristen over for Thanksgiving dinner. The four had just finished a meal that could have fed half the town and the table was filled with platters of leftover roasted turkey slices, stuffing, mashed potatoes, creamed onions, turnips, homemade rolls and cranberry sauce.

"I seriously don't want to look at a piece of turkey again for a year," Frank groaned, settling back in his chair and patting his stomach. He looked at his wife. "So when are we having dessert? Do we have to save some for the kids?"

Their two sons and older daughter had already left to visit friends.

Lisa raised her eyebrows.

"How about if we take this party outside on the deck while it's still light out and enjoy the seventy degrees. It's unusual to have such a nice day this late in the year."

"That sounds great."

Kristen rose to her feet and began gathering the plates.

"We could have gone golfing," Frank said to Louis, who had just put his fork down.

"Could have," Louis said, and unconsciously touched the area of his right shoulder where he'd been shot. He'd been lucky. The bullet had made a clean exit, missing his brachial and subclavian arteries. The wound had healed well although his shoulder often ached.

"You're going to use that as an excuse for the next ten years, aren't you?" Frank said, watching him.

"What?"

"I can hear it now. Every time you hook one into the woods or three putt, you're going to say, 'it's because I've got shrapnel in my shoulder.'"

Louis laughed.

"There's no shrapnel there, you moron. But of course I'll use it as an excuse to get more strokes from you."

He hadn't played since the injury, and they might not be on the course again until spring, but who knew? Maybe they'd go to Florida in the winter and play.

"Speaking of that, what's the latest on Bastardly Dick?" Frank asked, his nickname for BD9908, A.K.A Francis Lake, A.K.A. Eric Welch. "Haven't seen you in a while for an update."

They both knew why. After Louis was discharged from the hospital, he'd taken some time off to heal. For weeks he'd looked like an extra in a horror flick. And then there'd been the calls from the media when the story hit the news. He wouldn't—couldn't—deal with any of it. Thank God Frank had a friend who offered Louis his empty condo on a quiet beach at Cape Cod. He'd relaxed, read books, and taken long walks along the shoreline. Heather had stayed with Louis a few weekends there too.

"Good old Francis is sitting in jail, and I'm sure he's not enjoying a meal like this today," Louis said. He saw Kristen's lips purse and she turned away to help Lisa stack the dirty plates in the dishwasher. "Seems we find out something new every day. Thank God for forensic science and DNA. They've got trace evidence in the Rudemann case, and he's been linked to an open case in Virginia Beach, a nurse who was strangled in a hotel room.

"They're doing DNA analysis and getting evidence on another murder in New York and one in Montreal. His sales job took him up and down the east coast and parts of Canada, and it seems he left a trail of—" He was about to say "—dead women in his wake," when the wine glass in Kristen's hand slipped through her fingers and shattered on the tile floor.

"I'm so sorry," Kristen said, and Louis saw her face turn red. She bent down and picked up the larger pieces of glass.

"Don't worry about it, Kristen," Lisa said softly.

She opened a cabinet under the sink and took out a dust pan, looking over her shoulder at Louis. She shook her head, and Louis got the message.

They were silent for a moment as Lisa swept up the smaller glass pieces and patted Kristen on the arm. Kristen had lost weight the past few months and was on the verge of being gaunt. The black slacks she wore seemed a size too large, hanging off her thin frame. Louis had been happy today to see her chow down like the rest of them.

"Let's go outside on the deck. Do you want a coffee?" Lisa asked.

"No thanks, I'm fine," Kristen said, and she followed Lisa out of the kitchen.

"How is she doing?" Frank asked as soon as the two women were out of earshot.

Louis took a deep breath.

"It will take a long time before she feels safe or can trust anyone again. It's hard for her to accept that she had feelings for a man who was such a monster…and that BD—Francis— planned to murder her too. The suitcase he had in her house had duct tape and rope, along with his passport and a hotel reservation in Montreal. He drugged her and as small as she is, it's a damn miracle she managed to zap him with the pepper spray." Louis looked around to make sure they were still alone. "She saved my life. So did the old lady next door." He had told this story to Frank before but he wanted to tell it again. He *needed* to tell it again, and each time he did, the memories loosened their grip on his mind and the nightmares weren't as frequent.

"I think it's the lies that bother her too," Louis continued. "Just about everything he told her was a lie and she believed him. He lied about his ex-wife, who divorced him years ago because he cheated on her, he lied about his past except maybe one thing...his family."

Louis paused. Over the past few months he'd spent a lot of time thinking about that. Eric's dysfunctional family, his abusive aunt and mentally ill mother who'd killed herself after her discharge from the state hospital where Louis worked.

She was my patient.

The records were likely shredded years ago and the details lost forever. He'd tried to find Susanna Lake's obituary online without success.

Maybe none of this would have happened had he known what was going on in young Eric's life back then, had he asked the right questions. If he'd been able to stop the disease before it took root in the boy and festered in the man. Whatever the sickness was that drove him to kill.

"But why did he target Paula? Or you?" Frank sat back and looked at him. "I've been wondering that."

Louis thought about how he'd sidestep the question. Confidentiality was confidentiality, no matter how many years ago he'd seen the Lake family.

"He trolled for women on the Internet and unfortunately he and Paula met that way...and she made it so easy for him to stalk her, follow her to the Caribbean. By that time he was already dating Kristen too, and I think he got a charge out of stringing them both along. The FBI investigator said he had a ton of online profiles, all with different names. And half a dozen prepaid cell phones with false names. Including one he set up in *my* name."

"And he was the one who cut Heather's brakes?"

"Yeah. He told Kristen he was in New York. I've been piecing things together because the cops aren't sharing everything with me."

"Christ, he was busy," Frank said. "And what's the latest with the St. Maarten investigation?"

Louis sighed. "It's going slowly, at a snail's pace, but at least the FBI is involved now. They found the villa he rented on the French side of the island, the place he took Paula before he drowned her. They found Paula's luggage there."

He looked down at the floor. He didn't like thinking about what Paula had endured. It made him crazy to think of the bastard abducting her, holding her hostage. Forcing her to leave voice mails saying she was having fun.

She'd tried to tell him.

Beady-nine.

If only he'd been able to figure it out and save her.

He collected his thoughts and continued.

"When we were on the island and he suddenly showed up, he told Kristen he'd flown in from Miami to surprise her but the cops can prove he was there before Paula arrived. Waiting for her."

"And those texts that Paula supposedly sent to me and to Kristen? He had her cell phone. He sent the texts himself."

"What a shithead," Frank said, and let Louis keep talking.

"He broke into Paula's house and put the tape recorder in her basement so he could monitor her conversations, and he knew what her plans were. Of course when he pretended to find the recorder and gave it to Kristen, it had a tape on it that he spliced from a few conversations so I would look like the bad guy."

"Tried to set you up for Victoria Rudemann's murder too," Frank said.

"Yes, and he came damn close to succeeding."

"I forgot to ask you—how did he get into your house to steal Paula's laptop and your gun? And what about your office? You said there was no evidence of a break-in at either place?"

"That was easy; he got the key to my house from Paula's place. She had a key to my house and she never gave it back when she broke up with me. As far as my office...well, the old lock I used to have could have been opened with a credit card, so I doubt that was much of a challenge." Louis said. "All that shit he put my patients through...I'm still cleaning that mess up and it's been months. I'm just lucky that most people were understanding."

Diane had withdrawn her complaint with the police and he hadn't been arrested, but with her, the damage had been done. Ironically the publicity and unwanted attention he received from the media about the murders had recently increased the number of referrals to his practice.

"I wish I'd killed him," Louis said, running out of energy. "It would be so much easier, especially on Kristen. He'll go to trial and all we'll hear is his name on the news. It'll go on for years..."

And suddenly he felt weary, bone-tired of it all.

"Yeah, it would have been a public service if that old lady had hit him on the head just a little bit harder," Frank said. "You ever wonder why he did all this though? Went through all of this effort to be such a dick?"

Louis shook his head.

"Mind games? Control? I think he hated women, and there could be all kinds of reasons for that."

Many, indeed.

"He liked manipulating people like puppets. He enjoyed playing God with people's lives. It's hard to understand, and I'm in the mental health field."

"So how would you diagnose someone like that? What would you call him?"

Louis considered.

Narcissistic, sociopathic?

"In layman's terms? A monster."

After they all had coffee and pumpkin pie on the deck, Louis wished he could lie down on the couch and take a nap. He looked over at Kristen and she glanced at her watch and nodded. It was their pre-arranged signal.

"So I guess we'll be on our way," he said to his friends. "Thanks so much for the dinner. It was fantastic. I gained at least ten pounds in two hours."

"Me too," said Frank. "I'm bulking up for the winter."

Lisa gave Louis and Kristen a hug and handed them each a huge plate of leftovers.

"You take care now," she said, and they walked out to Louis's car parked in the road.

"I feel so stupid," Kristen said when they were inside his Mazda. "Breaking a glass the first time I meet your friends. They're very nice, by the way. Both of them. Frank is funny and Lisa is sweet."

"Don't worry about the glass. It's nothing."

He saw her stare out the window and he turned on the radio and found a rock station. He turned the volume on low.

"I don't want to go home right away, Louis," she said.

He hesitated.

"What would you like to do? Do you want to go to my place for a while? Heather's stopping by later on, after she has dinner at her mother's house, but you're welcome to hang out."

"I don't want to impose."

"You're not imposing. I can drive you home later on. Okay?"

She did not respond.

"Heather's bringing a kitten over that she's fostering," Louis said. "She's convinced I'll fall in love with it and want to keep it. Crazy, huh? Like I need a little loveable kitten running around the house."

His lame attempt at conversation fell flat. She turned her face to the window again.

"What if he gets out of jail?"

This wasn't the first time she had said this in the past three months.

"He won't get out of jail," Louis said. "There are so many charges against him now in so many states, he might end up getting the death penalty."

"What if he escapes from jail?"

"Are you having nightmares often?" he asked quietly.

"Every night."

"Kristen, you've been through trauma that few people experience. Call that woman, Dr. Hansen, and make an appointment. You'll be glad that you did."

He had given her a referral to a colleague he trusted who specialized in post-traumatic stress. So far she had resisted the idea.

"I'll probably see someone too," he added. "It helps to talk things over"

"Whatever," she said. "I can talk to you. You understand what I went through. You know what he was."

"I'm not your therapist. Don't take that the wrong way, but I'm not in that role anymore. You should call her."

"Maybe I will."

They were quiet for a time and listened to the radio.

Then she said, "It's complicated, isn't it? You and me. We're friends but we're not friends. It's too awkward. You know too much about me and I don't know enough about you. It's unequal. That barrier will always, always be there."

He said nothing, but she was right. And he realized how it pained him.

"You can take me home, Louis," she said. "I'll go over to

Maude's and give her the leftovers. She'll be happy to visit with me."

"Tell her I said hello too," he said, and turned off the next exit to go to her house. "You're going to be okay, you know. You're very strong and you're smart. You'll get through this. It will just take some time."

They didn't speak until he pulled into her driveway. He walked with her to her front door and waited until she turned the lights on in every room and checked that all the doors and windows were locked. He wondered who would do this with her in the days to come.

"Thank you," she said. "Good night."

She hugged him, tilted her face toward his and kissed him.

And then he let her go.